WHEN THE
RAVEN SINGS

WHEN THE RAVEN SINGS

From the Beginning She Knew Only Hatred and Pain, an Experience She Was Desperate to Share

A G Nuttall

First paperback edition 2023

978-1-80227-975-7 (paperback)
978-1-80227-976-4 (ebook)

www.angiebooks.com

I dedicate this book to the honour of my dad,
the memory of my wonderful mum and
with grateful thanks to my children and family
for their continued love, help and support.

CONTENTS

CHAPTER 1

The journey had been long with hours of tedious driving, but Meg was eager to reach her destination before nightfall.

Dusk was sweeping across the land and the light was fading quickly.

A full moon guided her transition from motorway to country lanes. Meg was grateful for its generosity as she drove the labyrinth of lanes searching for a familiar one.

There in the distance, a glint of something red; an unused letter box standing like a small bright soldier in the moonlight, signalled the entrance to her turn.

It was with a sense of deep relief that she passed the little road marking - missing it could have left her lost for hours in the maze of country lanes. From here, the road was familiar, though it appeared somewhat narrower than she remembered, and the hedgerows seemed somewhat taller.

Meg smiled to herself. It had been many years since she had driven this way, and nature had a way of changing the landscape, just as time had changed Meg herself.

Moments later, she slowed to a stop outside Pebble Cottage, her new home.

She stood in silence with only the sound of her heart dancing excitedly in her chest. Never had she felt so alive as she did in this moment. A Prima Donna, basking in the glory of her work and the appreciation it would afford her. Tonight, she had played judge, jury and executioner, literally.

The room was dimly lit with only the dying embers of a once roaring fire gasping for life in the shadow of a stone hearth.

The moon flashed a beam of light across the room, just long enough to highlight her accomplishment. She surveyed her work, and a morbid sense of achievement swept over her. It had been easier than she imagined. They hadn't seen her coming, hadn't expected her after all these years.

She had afforded them the dignity of a quick, though not painless, death. It was the terror in their eyes that satisfied her most - their death mask, her reward.

She glanced around the old familiar kitchen with its gingham tablecloth and faded lace curtains, fireside rocking chairs and empty cocoa mugs, the symbols of a cosy family home, perhaps.

She retched with indignation.

She had stripped away the pretentious facade, and drawn back the veil of horror secreted within these stone walls.

She felt the warmth of the dagger in her hand, a jagged steel blade coated with blood; their blood. It had cut and thrust its way through their ageing bodies, ripping and tearing with ease, claiming their lives with its sharpness. She cleaned the knife with care and tucked it out of sight. This was the beginning of a dangerous partnership, and there was much more work to do.

She was pleased with its performance tonight - she had chosen a worthy assistant.

She should leave now, but the sight was intoxicating; the need to bask in the glory of her work was overpowering. She would remember this moment forever; the smell, the feel, the whole scene and she brushed a solitary tear from her cheek. The tear was not for them, but for the moment it represented - her rebirth, her resurrection.

She forced herself to leave, turning back just once. 'I am an artist after all,' she thought.

Outside, the moon had taken up residence above the farmhouse, glowing like a giant light bulb. It lit the way for her escape as she vanished into the woods and disappeared.

CHAPTER 2
New Beginnings

The morning light poked through the bedroom window waking Meg from dream-filled slumber. She hadn't unpacked the previous night; sleep had dragged her through the cottage door and up the stairs to bed. Clothes were cast spontaneously across the floor, as she had collapsed with exhaustion and sleep had devoured her immediately.

Pebble Cottage was a sweet, white picket fence, roses around the door kind of place, with scenic views across the village green to the front, and uninterrupted views of the vast and bleak Manston Moor to the rear.

Meg had been lucky to buy it, as cottages seldom became available in Brightmarsh. She had Aunty June's insatiable thirst for gossip to thank for the cottage sale. It needed a little in the way of TLC, but its structure was sound and it had a good family history.

Aunty June had thankfully stocked the fridge and cupboards with essentials and left a jam jar of meadow flowers on the table with a 'welcome to your new home' card beside them.

Coffee was the first thing on Meg's mind. She stood by the back door, mug in hand, surveying the moor beyond, breathing in the fresh air and listening to a chorus of birdsong in the distance. How different life was going to be she thought. Different because this was as far removed from London as she could be and different because here, she was alone, Michael no longer by her side.

Momentarily, his face appeared in front of her, wide-eyed and beautiful, smiling his approval at her change of lifestyle. He faded slowly from her thoughts and she was back in the moment, coffee still warm, admiring the view.

That day, Meg busied herself unpacking boxes and cleaning out cupboards. She organised her pantry, mopped the floors, hoovered and dusted, sprayed and polished. She embraced the wood-burning stove, and by evening, the cottage was warm, bathed in candlelight and smelling of lemons and patchouli. It already felt like home.

Meg had invited Aunty June for supper, a thank you for her inside knowledge of the cottage sale. They sipped wine and dined. They reminisced about the old days and laughed and cried as Meg spoke of Michael.

Meg retired to bed that night with a sense of contentment. Tomorrow she would visit some old haunts and catch up with friends she hadn't seen in years. The rest of her stuff was arriving at the weekend so she was free for a couple of days to explore.

Morning came too soon. It was a fine and breezy day with just enough of a nip in the air to warrant a bobble hat. Fuelled by coffee and croissants, Meg left the house. The village was much the same as she remembered; nothing had really changed in the last twenty years.

The same curtains twitched as she passed the cottages in her row, the same old tattered sign still swinging above the door of the Snooty Fox public house. Meg could have sworn there were even the same old ducks swimming in the puddle of water that mimicked a village pond.

There was one thing Meg knew for certain. She was a different person now from the little girl who had grown up here.

Meg's parents had been killed in a fatal car crash when she was five years old, so her memories of them were faint. The only mother she had known was Aunty June, her father's oldest sister, who had stepped in to raise Meg as her own.

Aunty June had done a relatively good job as a single parent and Meg's life in the village had been a happy one.

Meg's father had been a sergeant with the Metropolitan Police in London, and the young Meg aspired to follow in his footsteps. She worked hard at school and college, and her drive and enthusiasm soon saw her achieve constable status. Then, a couple of years later, she joined the Firearms Unit.

It was here that she met Michael, her wonderful Michael. Brave, romantic and just as ambitious as she. He was tall and handsome with a mop of dark, wavy hair and eyes the colour of the ocean.

He had risen through the ranks and became the firearms

unit commanding officer. They'd hit it off immediately. Same cheeky sense of humour, same sarcastic wit, same dreams for the future. A couple of dinner dates later and they had moved into a small apartment within walking distance of the police headquarters.

Meg became a domestic goddess, throwing together dinner menus, worrying about what colour cushions to match with the sofa and becoming obsessed with kitchen gadgets and appliances. She loved him and she loved her life with him.

A year later, on Christmas Eve, Michael proposed and the following November they flew to Barbados and sealed the deal with a romantic wedding on the beach.

Life with Michael was great, and then ... disaster struck.

His unit was deployed to an armed robbery with hostages. Michael had taken charge of the operation and Meg was part of the back-up team.

Shots were heard, a lot of shouting and a scrambled message on the radio. Everything went quiet. The first phase of officers came running back, their eyes wide and sympathetic as they passed her. Panic shuddered through her body, engulfing her. She waited, and waited, but Michael never came back.

He had been killed that day in the line of duty.

Following his death, Meg lost interest in the job and London no longer felt like home. There were too many reminders of what she had lost. Michael's toothbrush still lay in the bathroom, his robe still hung behind the door, his scent still lingered on the bed sheets, and memories of him were everywhere.

Meg couldn't live with what should have been, haunted by unrealistic possibilities. Life would never be the same, so it was time to start afresh; a new beginning.

She sold the London apartment, said goodbye to her old life, and travelled back to the village she knew so well, where remnants of her family and childhood friends still lived.

CHAPTER 3
Old Haunts

Meg strolled across the village green admiring a collection of pretty coloured flowers, sprinkled around the edge of the pond, still fighting for survival in the autumn chill. A lonely duck waddled past and a heavily laden hiker in red wellington boots muttered "good morning" as he walked by. Down the lane and across a wooden bridge to the west of the village lay a cluster of log cabins. They hugged the side of a man-made lake, each with its own pontoon. The lake was a favourite haunt of village children, where, during the summer months, swimming and water sports were particularly popular.

First stop was the Manor House.

Its driveway, almost a mile long, was lined by ageing gnarled and twisted oak trees. Years before, Meg had climbed those trees, scraping her knees and tearing her clothing in the process. She sighed with contentment. It was good to be back.

There in the distance stood the Manor House, silhouetted against the bright morning sky, a monumental structure amidst a sea of manicured lawns and topiary.

Finally, she stood before the large oak doors of the place she had once dubbed her second home.

CHAPTER 4
Childhood Friends

In a village as small as Brightmarsh, friends were hard to find, but Meg, Abby Attwood and Joby Cross were an inseparable trio.

They met at primary school and became the best of friends immediately.

Abby lived at the Manor House. Her family, Sir Henry and Lady Isobel Attwood, were rich and influential, but Abby was just a regular girl with a privileged lifestyle.

Joby was the youngest son of the local farmer and lived at Molecatcher Farm with his parents and older brother Gully.

Joby was a smart kid, but his tattered attire and messy hair made him the butt of cruel jokes and a punching bag for the school bullies.

His brother, Gulliver Cross, was a mute who had learning difficulties, but what he lacked in intelligence he more than made up for in brute strength and stature. His giant silhouette was intimidating, but he was a gentle soul who viewed the world through a child's eyes.

He rarely left the comfort of Molecatcher Farm and its one hundred acres of land.

CHAPTER 5
Abby

The door of the Manor House opened slowly and there stood Darrow, the long-time family butler. His once-black hair was peppered with grey. His face and body were weathered by age, but his eyes danced to life as he recognised Meg's face.

"So lovely to see you again, Miss Meg. I do hope you're well," he enquired stepping aside for Meg to enter.

"And you, Darrow," replied Meg.

It had been such a long time since Meg had visited The Manor House, but nothing had changed. Once inside the mighty wooden doors, she was propelled into a bygone era. Tudor decor echoed through the rooms and hallways, and antiquities and fine art adorned the walls and fireplaces.

It was the perfect setting for a period drama, although the Manor House had seen more than its fair share of real drama over the years.

Sir Henry and Lady Isobel had divorced, citing irreconcilable differences, but everyone, including the Attwood children, knew that it was Sir Henry's many public dalliances that were the real reason.

Isobel had left the family home on the arm of her new love interest. She hadn't glanced back as the children sobbed and called after her. She drove off into the distance and was never seen or heard from again.

There had been several potential Lady Attwoods since Isobel, each one younger and prettier than the last.

Unlike Abby, Meg's memories were of happier days, playing hide and seek in the maze of rooms and corridors, racing up and down the great hall on bicycles and roller skates, picking apples in the orchard and climbing trees on the driveway. Visions of the past raced before her eyes; the Manor House had always been a happy place for Meg.

"Miss Abby is in the library. Please go through; she's expecting you," instructed Darrow, motioning towards the large, panelled doors to the left of the grand oak staircase.

"Darling, it's been far too long!" Abby rose from the leather winged-back chair by the fireplace and embraced Meg for several minutes. "I couldn't believe it when you emailed to say you were coming back to the village, I thought I'd lost you to the big city forever."

Abby stood back and took a good long look at her old friend. "I've missed you so much; the last ten years have been so boring."

Abby hadn't changed at all. She was the image of her mother: girlish figure, lightly bronzed skin tone with cascading golden hair and eyes the colour of tanzanite. The years had been kind to her, yet Abby had never married.

They sat together on the old leather Chesterfield and

chatted for hours.

Darrow brought sandwiches, cupcakes and buttered scones, coupled with pink champagne in crystal flutes.

The years of separation melted into insignificance, and the time ticked by rapidly.

The hours were crammed with missed conversations and updates - they had both been hopeless at keeping in touch. Odd emails and text messages had passed between them on the rare occasion, but communication had been relatively scarce. There was so much to catch up on and by the time Darrow served a third round of coffees, the light outside was beginning to dim.

As a curtain of grey veiled the Manor House window, it was time for Meg to leave. Manston Moor was spooky enough by daylight, so Meg did not relish the thought of being there alone after dark.

Unlike the Manor House, Molecatcher Farm had always had an uneasy feeling. Ben and Alice Cross, Joby's parents, were friendly enough, but there was a shroud of mystery that surrounded the farm, most of all the farmhouse, into which Meg and Abby had rarely been invited.

Meg continued her hike across the route she and her friends had trampled so many times before. The rugged terrain of the moor was now a maze of unfriendly brambles, tugging at Meg's jeans as she struggled forward. Then, in the distance, she caught sight of the silhouette of Molecatcher Farm. It sat like a smudge of ink against the canvas of the night sky, cold grey stone, windswept and crumbling, an untidy structure as unnerving and formidable as she remembered.

She reached the cobbled, overgrown driveway that led to the house and stopped to draw breath. The house was lifeless; no smoke was puffing from the chimney and no light shone in the windows. Meg prayed silently that Joby had remembered her visit.

CHAPTER 6
Molecatcher Farm

Sitting at the highest peak of Manston Moor, Molecatcher Farm was surrounded by nothing but wilderness on three sides. Acres of bracken and heather stretched as far as the eye could see, broken only by the white dots of grazing sheep.

At the back of the farm, far into the distance sat Weaver's Wood, a graveyard of enormous pine and fir trees that dominated the horizon, spreading over a massive area of land that terminated beside the lake where Meg had swum as a child.

The wood was avoided by most villagers and Aunty June had kept Meg away with stories of forest monsters and missing children.

The moor was eerily quiet and still as if nature had suddenly taken a holiday. Cooper, the family's border collie, was not barking. The farm felt abandoned. A shiver coasted down Meg's spine; she had that uneasy feeling again.

Just as Meg had given up hope, she spotted the sole of a red wellington boot protruding above the driveway wall. She smiled inside. Joby was a trickster, so he would most likely be attached to the other end of it.

She approached with caution hoping to catch him off

guard, but as she got closer, the boot never moved. 'Joby would have been on his feet by now,' thought Meg. Was it just an abandoned boot wedged into the wall? However, as she reached the red wellington, she discovered there was indeed a leg attached to it. Meg's heart skipped a beat. Police or not, this was a vulnerable situation. Anyone could be waiting for her behind the wall and she was defenceless.

Meg searched the ground for a sizeable stone and gripped it tightly. She edged towards the wall again and hit the bottom of the red boot hard with her newfound weapon. The stone bounced back, but the boot didn't move.

This time, Meg moved closer to the wall and peered over the other side. In the dim shadow of fading light, she realised that the boot was attached to a body that was lying on its back in the grass on the other side of the wall.

Meg searched for her phone. She lit the torch and looked again. Passing the light over the red boot and down the attached leg, she found the other leg twisted against the stonework. She scanned upwards - a plaid shirt was heavily stained, and then the torchlight settled on the face of a young man, eyes fixed, skin a tinge of pale blue with a deathly stare.

Meg knew instantly he was dead, the culprit a gaping wound across his throat. The stain on his shirt was blood, his blood. Meg recognised him as the young man who had greeted her that morning by the pond.

She shone her torch around searching the shadows for movement. She needed to report her find immediately, but the latest technology had not yet reached the moor and she had no signal. She raced towards the farmhouse for help.

The moon was rapidly disappearing behind a cushion of dark grey clouds as Meg knocked feverishly on the weather-beaten back door but the farm still felt abandoned. Meg was on her own. She knocked again, louder, and waited. She glanced around the yard - the old pickup was resting by the haystack and a much smaller, slightly newer vehicle sat beside it.

Meg was beginning to feel desperate. The silence was deafening, and she needed to think. Switching her torch back on, she searched the porch steps for a key. Perhaps she could just let herself into the farmhouse, use the house phone and leave a note to explain her actions.

The cracked uneven steps of the farmhouse were suddenly illuminated. There was no sign of a key, but Meg's gaze was drawn to a pool of dark liquid leaking out from one corner of the wooden door. The substance flowed down the steps and onto the gravel beneath.

Meg dropped to her knees and ran a finger through the liquid. She had encountered its thick and sticky texture before and she knew instantly that it was blood.

Rising slowly, Meg pulled a woolly glove over her hand

and reached cautiously for the door handle. It turned with ease and she stepped carefully inside, following the bloody river that flowed from the depths of the room.

It was dark and cold; the fire was dead. An unsavoury odour hung heavy in the air. Meg knew instantly its significance. Her breath quickened as she moved carefully, every step calculated with precision. When she was sure she had reached the centre of the room and the floor beneath her was clear of blood, Meg began to scan the wall behind her. She reached out for a single switch and suddenly the whole room was bathed in harsh cool light.

Meg stood for a moment, her breathing heavy, blinking her eyes to adjust to the brightness. She felt a burning pain of anguish engulf her. She didn't dare to turn around, afraid of what she might see, but she had to.

Moving in slow motion, she hesitantly faced the room and paused, eyes fixed firmly on the ground. Taking a deep breath, she began to lift her eyes upwards, but she wasn't prepared for the scene of unprecedented horror that lay before her.

Meg stumbled back against the wall, pressing her body against it to steady herself. Her eyes were stinging from the harshness of the light. She felt dizzy and gagged uncontrollably, the contents of her afternoon tea ready to spill forth, but she placed a shaky hand across her mouth to stop it, and through a haze of tears, she slowly stepped forward into the light.

Meg had witnessed murder scenes before, but nothing in comparison to the level of depravity that she was looking at now.

For a moment, Meg imagined that Joby was one of the victims, but closer examination revealed that the mutilated bodies belonged to Ben and Alice Cross, his parents.

Meg couldn't draw her gaze away from the elderly couple. They were sitting on either side of the fireplace in matching wooden rocking chairs, the remnants of fruit cake and half-drunk coffee mugs beside them.

In any other situation, this would have been a tranquil scene, but the reality was very different. Feeling less inclined to throw up, Meg moved forward for a closer look, being careful to preserve the scene.

Alice was sitting to the right of the fireplace. She had been stabbed from behind - easy access between the slats of the wooden chair had allowed the knife to thrust deep into her spinal cord with precision. Instant paralysis would have occurred, and death would have followed quickly as the blade was withdrawn and thrust upwards through her heart.

Her blood pooled generously around her feet and flowed freely along the stone-flagged floor towards a gap beneath the back door and out into the darkness.

The killer hadn't stopped there. Alice's head had then been severed and placed upon her lap, and a knitting needle inserted into each eye.

It was a macabre act by the killer, which felt symbolic and very personal.

Ben Cross had also been beheaded. His torso bore the wounds of a frantic knife attack, his clothes bathed in his own blood and his head sitting between his legs. His eyes were intact but judging by the amount of red liquid that had poured from his mouth, his tongue had been removed.

She tried hard to compose herself, but the whole scene was overwhelming, even for Meg.

Meg searched for the house phone hoping that it still lived in the same place in the kitchen area. A dial tone, thank goodness. She placed the emergency call and waited for the police to arrive.

There was no sign of forced entry. Cooper, the family dog, was missing, as were Gully and Joby Cross. Could Ben and Alice have known their assailants, even invited them in? Meg shuddered at the thought of what they had endured. It was hard to stay professional under the circumstances but she wanted answers. She needed to know who would have done this to the people she once considered family.

A hazy glow of blue lights flashed across the window, and Meg headed for the door to introduce herself. She needed to explain her presence at the farm and prepare the village officers for what they were about to see. It was not a sight for the faint-hearted and Meg was certain these guys would never have encountered such a crime before.

As she suspected, green-faced officers ran, one by one, from the farmhouse to expel the contents of their stomachs in nearby bushes. Meg knew the images of this crime scene would haunt their nightmares, and hers, for years to come.

Molecatcher Farm was soon buzzing with the white suits of crime scene investigators.

Joby and Gully Cross were missing and, therefore, in the eyes of the police, they were persons of interest and their descriptions were distributed across the police network.

Meg knew in her heart that Joby could not have committed such heinous acts, and Gully, though strength was his only real attribute, did not have the mental capacity to even contemplate such a scene of utter horror.

This felt premeditated; someone wanted the couple dead, wanted them to suffer. Their deaths were committed with anger and hatred, but by whom and why?

And what of the hiker? Was he just caught in the crossfire, wrong place, wrong time? The questions haunted Meg; she needed answers.

CHAPTER 7
Monty and Pepper

It was around midnight when Meg finally climbed the stairs of Pebble Cottage and slumped into bed. The softness of the pillows was comforting, but as sleep enveloped her, the horrors of the night invaded her dreams.

Her night had been restless and she woke around 6 am.

The removal truck was due today, so Meg fuelled herself with coffee, showered quickly and dressed appropriately for the long day ahead.

Even though she was excited to be reunited with her possessions, and most of all, Pepper, her canine companion, she couldn't stop thinking about the gruesome scene at Molecatcher Farm.

Monty Harris, her London BFF, arrived bang on time. Pepper, a mottled chocolate and white miniature dachshund, was uncontrollable, kissing Meg's face with a long, wet tongue, then racing up and down the garden path and in and out of her new home with barks of approval. It was lovely to have her home at last; she was good company. Monty had taken her for the last few days so that Meg could settle into her new surroundings.

Montgomery (Monty) Harris had a condition known as verbal diarrhoea, but his heart was huge and his intentions only ever honourable. Having met at university several years earlier, they had hit it off immediately and spent many happy hours of student life together.

Despite a First in psychology, Monty had abandoned his passion for serial killers and set up an interior design business with his sister-in-law. He felt it was a more prudent and safer path to follow, but Meg knew where his heart really lay, and that he would be intrigued by the murders at Molecatcher Farm.

After hours of unpacking, arranging and rearranging, Meg called time for a lunch break. They sat by the kitchen window with an over-indulgent lunch and several glasses of pink Prosecco.

Meg recapped the events of the previous evening, while Monty hung on her every word. He asked sensible questions and offered plausible scenarios of how and why the murder had been committed. Monty encouraged her to get involved with the local police and keep him updated on the progress. He had contacts at Scotland Yard if she needed expert help, so she only had to call.

It was around 7:30 that evening when a knock at the door halted the conversation.

Meg could see the blue uniform she knew so well through the hazy glass panes of the cottage door. A young officer, clean-shaven and looking just about old enough to hold a driving licence, stood on her doorstep.

"Megan Quinn?" he enquired.

Meg nodded. "My name is Will Thackeray, Constable Will Thackeray. I'm with the local station. I've been sent to ask you a few questions..." His cheeks flushed slightly. It was obvious to Meg that Constable Thackeray was a probationer and he hadn't yet mastered the art of control, as he added sheepishly, "...if that's ok?"

Meg loosened her grip on the door and invited him inside. "Excuse the mess, I'm still moving in," she said.

Thackeray entered the living room where Monty had taken up residence in the armchair by the fire and Pepper had taken up residence on Monty's lap.

Monty needed no introduction; he offered his name immediately and extended a hand from the armchair where Pepper held him captive. He was a larger-than-life character, bubbly and fun, and his clothes matched his persona, bright and loud. A slightly tipsy Monty was even louder than usual and Meg wasn't sure what Constable Thackeray thought of him.

"What's your name?" Monty demanded with a slight slur in his voice. "Not the Constable Thackeray bit - what do your friends call you?"

Thackeray blushed again at the direct question.

"Please don't mind Monty, he's a terrible tease and very nosy," interrupted Meg, as she threw a disapproving look in Monty's direction. "Now, what did you want to ask me?"

Thackeray withdrew a shiny new notebook from his

pocket. Meg smiled - probationers, you could spot them a mile away!

Thumbing to the third page, Thackeray began his questions.

Meg's answers were the same as she'd given to the sergeant at the scene, but Thackeray wrote them down with great enthusiasm. He declined a hot beverage and bade them goodnight, leaving a number where he could be reached should Meg recall anything that might be useful.

"Biggest case of his career, I shouldn't doubt," proffered Monty. "Don't suppose they get many crimes here, let alone a murder, or two, or three!"

Monty was right - the biggest scandal that had ever hit Brightmarsh was way back when Herbert Cooke, the ex-postmistress's husband, rode his bike through the village dressed in his wife's clothes. It was a talking point for many years. The postmistress left the village never to be seen again. Her husband moved in with the choir master and changed his name to Sylvia.

Monty was thoroughly amused, and, after a third bottle of pink fizz, opted to spend the night before heading back to London the next morning.

Monty had not been an asset as far as unpacking boxes was concerned, but he was incredible company and Meg was sorry to see him leave.

With Monty gone, Meg's thoughts turned to Joby and

Gully Cross. The longer they were missing the more they would become suspects in their own parents' murders. Meg would not allow herself to consider that either of them was capable of such crimes. She needed to find them as quickly as possible; the question was, where should she start?

CHAPTER 8
Minnie Jessop

After Pepper's morning walk, Meg headed to Holcombe, a neighbouring village with a larger population than Brightmarsh.

Gully had been a pupil at the school there, as it catered for Gully's special needs.

Miss Jessop had been the teacher for the last two years of Gully's school life. Perhaps Miss Jessop could help Meg understand where the brothers may have gone. It was a long shot but definitely worth investigating.

Minnie Jessop had retired years ago, but she still lived in the village beside the school where she had taught for 30 years.

She had never married but devoted herself to the needs of the children in Holcombe and the surrounding areas.

Meg stopped at the village post office for Miss Jessop's address. After all, if anyone would be privy to such information it would be Bea Tilley, the current postmistress. Bea was a pleasant woman, short in stature with a massive personality. She walked with a limp and carried a little too much weight around her middle. Grey hair and wrinkles placed her in the post-retirement bracket, but her mind was sharp and her memory sharper. She had an uncanny ability to speak for long periods of time without pausing for breath. Her penchant for gossip made her more than happy to divulge the teacher's whereabouts, informing Meg that Miss Jessop was suffering the early stages of dementia, so any information she provided could not be entirely relied upon.

Nevertheless, Meg set off undeterred.

Miss Jessop lived in a modest cottage which looked onto the grounds of her old school. A faded blue door with a novelty knocker and a garden yielding an abundance of overgrown weeds was where she called home.

Meg knocked hard and waited. Several minutes later, she heard the faint tone of an elderly voice responding. There was quite a lapse of time before Minnie Jessop appeared at the door. She was a frail old lady with snow-white hair piled in a bun on top of her head, however, short strands had teased their way free and fell softly against her cheeks. She squinted through steel-rimmed spectacles and smiled politely. Meg explained the reason for her visit and Miss Jessop invited her inside.

Shuffling at a snail's pace with a stick in each hand, Miss Jessop directed Meg into what she referred to as her 'parlour'. The room would once have been fashionable, but like its occupant, it was now old and faded.

"Gully Cross, you say..." Miss Jessop pondered on the names as she eased herself down into a well- worn leather chair.

"I was hoping that you might be able to give me some information about him."

"Is he in trouble?" enquired the old lady.

Meg shook her head and replied, "No, but he could be if I don't find him."

"It's such a long time ago, my dear, and my memory is not what it used to be," replied Miss Jessop.

"Anything at all that you can tell me about him could be valuable," reassured Meg, and she waited for Minnie to respond.

"I taught Gully for two years. A shy boy, mute, as I recall. He had a younger brother."

Meg urged Miss Jessop to continue and praised her ability to recall one of her pupils so many years later.

"Gully was a hopeless case though," she continued. "My deepest regret was not being able to coax him to talk."

"I didn't know that Gully had ever talked!" Meg was feeling confused, or was it Miss Jessop who was confused? She couldn't be sure.

"Oh no, dear, Gully talked his way through primary school. Then something happened and the boy wouldn't utter another word."

Meg was intrigued; "Do you know what happened to him?"

"No one does. There were rumours, but I really couldn't say."

Miss Jessop paused to rub a bony knee. A loose

stocking hung around her ankle like ageing skin that had surrendered itself to gravity. She caught Meg watching her; "Old age, dear," she informed her and tugged the stocking back into place. She straightened the wrinkles in her skirt and offered Meg refreshments for a third time.

For a moment, her mind seemed to wander. She lost her concentration until a large ginger cat suddenly leapt from nowhere onto her lap and she snapped back into the moment and began to stroke the cat.

"You were saying about Gully Cross...." Meg prompted.

Miss Jessop adjusted her glasses as they teetered on the end of her nose. "There was nothing to be done with Gully. He had a child's mind and would never be any different. He found comfort in nature; butterflies and birds intrigued him. In the end, he left the school and went to work with his father on the farm."

"And the rumours, Miss Jessop, what were they?"

"If memory serves," began the old woman, "and it doesn't always these days, you know, it was something that he witnessed; something awful." Miss Jessop's gaze was suddenly drawn to the window, and her mind began to wander.

"How old was he when this awful thing happened?" pressed Meg. She could see that Minnie was beginning to tire.

"Young; around 8. That wasn't the reason for his diminished intellect, though. He had been starved of oxygen at birth. It was the trauma of whatever happened years later that left him mute."

"Is there anyone who could give me more information about him?" pleaded Meg.

Miss Jessop sat trancelike for several minutes. Meg wondered whether she was okay and watched her chest to make sure she was breathing. She was just about to touch her when Miss Jessop raised a finger in the air as if prompting a lightbulb moment. "Hegarty Baxter," she said as she wagged the finger towards Meg. "You need to speak with Hegarty Baxter - she was the social worker for the Cross family. Every child with special needs is assigned a social worker and Hegarty was theirs for many years."

Miss Jessop had been more helpful than Meg could have hoped and she left the old lady in good spirits with a tray of tea and biscuits.

Perhaps Hegarty Baxter was worth a visit.

CHAPTER 9

Driving back towards Brightmarsh, Meg received a call from Sergeant Castleton requesting her presence at the station.

Sergeant Castleton ushered her into one of the briefing rooms and offered her lukewarm coffee in a paper cup. Meg accepted with a smile, though she knew that police coffee was weak and tasteless. She pretended to sip at the beverage as Castleton brought her up to date on what he referred to as 'the farmhouse murders'.

"We've combed the farmhouse, outbuildings and surrounding area, but as yet, revealed nothing. No prints were found at the house, except those of the victims and two extra sets, which we presume are those of the missing sons."

Castleton cleared his throat, then continued; "That brings me to conclude that one or possibly both sons were involved in this crime and that's why they've done a runner. There was no forced entry and the dog is missing too, probably with them. I asked you here today to give me as much background on..." he flicked through the file in his hand floundering for the names, "...Joby and Gulliver Cross as you can."

"With respect, Sergeant, I don't think the lack of evidence can be used to assume that Joby and/or Gully

Cross are responsible. I've known the family for years. Gully would be too afraid to do something like this; besides, he couldn't cope without his parents. They did everything for him, and he honestly would not have the capacity. Joby is the nicest, kindest person in the world, and I refuse to believe that he would be capable of something so evil. I think you're missing something here. What if the brothers are being used as a decoy to throw you off the scent and stop you looking for anyone else?" Meg drained her coffee in desperation.

"I appreciate your loyalty, but in fairness, you have only recently returned to the village. You've had a gap of however many years. You couldn't possibly know what Gully or Joby Cross are capable of."

Castleton rose from behind the desk. "As I see it, we have two missing suspects and until we find them and can rule them out of our investigation, they will remain at the top of the suspect list." Meg was disheartened by Castleton's narrow-minded attitude. The man was not equipped to deal with a crime of this ferocity. She would continue her own investigation and prove that her friend and his brother were both innocent.

Surely, he could see that the murders were personal; the knitting needles in the eyes and the frenzied knife attack were symbolic. This was a deeply personal crime committed by someone with a motive, someone with a score to settle, someone very dangerous.

Meg suggested a criminal profiler might be helpful, but Brightmarsh Police Force was not yet ready to enter the 21st century.

Castleton did, however, suggest that Meg's previous experience could be helpful to the investigation and she reluctantly agreed to make herself available when needed.

She could hear him breathing, soft and slow, a deep inhale, a pause followed by a long exhale. She lay still listening and waiting. When the snoring stage began, she knew it was safe to move. Sliding from beneath the soft satin sheets, she dressed quickly. Black casuals for ease and training shoes for stealth.

She disappeared through an open window, sprinting over the balcony onto the soft earth below. She raced through the darkness, heart rate rising, morphing into the shadows like a phantom in the night.

The house was cloaked in darkness just as she had hoped. An old-fashioned lock, easy to tease with her fingers, a click and the door opened inviting her into the void beyond. The woman was sleeping in an armchair, glasses balanced on the end of her nose, an open book across her lap. She reached down the leg of her pants and withdrew a razor-sharp blade.

It glinted for a moment in the spark of light from the dying fire.

One quick wrist movement and it was done. The woman stirred momentarily, her eyes wide with shock, her hands desperately gripping at the gaping wound across her throat. Blood flowed with speed, soaking into the pages of her paperback, engulfing her life, and, in a moment, Hegarty Baxter was gone.

The cool night air caressed her cheeks; the road was clear, so it was safe to leave. This kill hadn't invoked the same satisfaction as the old couple, but it was vital and another name off her list. Now to make it back into bed before he noticed she was gone.

She smirked as his hand reached out to her beneath the sheet. She closed her eyes and invited sleep to devour her.

CHAPTER 10

Back at the cottage, Meg paced uneasily.

It was almost time for bed, but she knew sleep would not come without a struggle.

Perhaps a late film would help? She couldn't concentrate. A tasty supper? She wasn't hungry and she'd drunk so much coffee that she'd drained the jar. Tomorrow, she planned to visit Hegarty Baxter, but tomorrow was a long way away.

Suddenly, Meg's phone lit up with a message. She didn't recognise the number.

'IN THE CAR PARK NEED HELP, JOBY'

Meg's heart rate quickened. She threw on some clothes and headed for the Snooty Fox public house, which sat within staggering distance of her cottage.

The pub was in darkness, with only the security lights illuminated as she cautiously prowled the perimeter of the car park.

If the text hadn't come from Joby, Meg could be in danger, so she must stay alert. A second lap revealed nothing and Meg was beginning to feel uneasy.

"Joby, are you here?" her voice whispered into the darkness. She stood for a moment awaiting a response.

Suddenly, there was a rustling sound behind the huge commercial bins and then, out of the shadows, Joby emerged.

Meg sighed with relief.

He was dirty and dishevelled and wearing a pungent odour of rotting trash. As Joby stepped into the light, his slender physique silhouetted against the moonlight, his mass of black hair fell in an unruly fashion around his face, and his hazel eyes still twinkled.

Meg wanted to embrace him, but her senses wouldn't allow it.

Joby was clutching a leather strap in his hand and on the other end, looking equally dishevelled, was Cooper, the family's working canine.

Meg had so many questions, but Joby needed a shower, food and a warm bed first.

Without uttering a word, she beckoned him to follow her behind the Snooty Fox and into the open field beyond. From there, they could gain easy access to Meg's cottage without arousing suspicion from the twitchy curtain brigade.

They lifted Cooper over the wall and Joby followed close behind. Meg entered from the front and soon Joby and his dog were comfortably inside.

In the light of the cottage kitchen, Meg could see the grief on Joby's face and the searching look in his almond eyes. He was not the murderous son the local police were looking for.

When Joby emerged from the bathroom fresh and

clean, Meg was able to embrace him at last. He felt thinner than she remembered. Meg suspected that he hadn't eaten recently and the stubble grazing his chin indicated he hadn't used a razor either. Joby had been living rough for several days, so he was exhausted. The questions would have to wait.

She fixed a bed for him on the sofa and placed a blanket on the floor for Cooper.

Joby smiled thankfully and kissed her head. Within minutes, he was sleeping and Meg finally felt ready for bed.

As the sun rose over the village green, Meg descended the creaky stairs of Pebble Cottage to make breakfast for Joby, who was still snuggled under the duvet with Cooper by his side.

It wasn't long before the kitchen came to life as Meg and Joby sat enjoying pancakes with maple syrup, just like the old days.

Pepper had reluctantly allowed Cooper to play in the garden so long as he didn't touch any of her toys.

Meg watched as Joby enjoyed breakfast, but it was time to get some answers. Time was of the essence and she had a duty to contact Sergeant Castleton about Joby's appearance, but first, she had a few questions of her own.

"Joby, do you know what has happened at the farm?" "I know they're dead," Joby replied.

"How do you know that?" Meg enquired.

"I heard people talking about it. They said they'd been murdered." Joby's eye pooled as he fought hard to hold back the tears.

"Is it true, Meg?" Meg nodded.

"But how and by who?" Joby begged.

Meg knew in that moment that her intuition had not failed her and that her friend was innocent.

Meg explained how she had found his murdered parents that evening at the farmhouse, sparing him the grisly details.

"That's what we're working on, Joby. I have no answers for you now, but I promise you I will find whoever did this."

"There was also the body of a young man found in the meadow on the approach to the farm; a hiker. He had pitched his tent there and his throat had been cut. Would you have any idea who he was?" Meg waited for Joby's response, his mouth gaping in disbelief. He paused in the moment trying to process the information - the discovery of another body.

"Oh god... that would be Dalton, Dalton Emery." His hands were shaking and his face grew pale. For a moment, Meg thought he might faint; Joby was overwhelmed.

"A friend of yours?" Meg enquired when the colour had returned to Joby's cheeks.

"Not specifically, but he was a regular visitor, always pitching his tent in the north corner of the meadow." Joby smiled slightly. "He was into bugs; researched them for the University. He came each year around the same time to check on them. We got quite chatty; he was a knowledgeable guy, especially about bugs."

Joby's insight into the hiker had been useful. Dalton Emery would be easy enough to trace at the local university and his loved ones could be informed.

Joby then recounted the events of the last few days starting with the day of the murder. Joby had gone over to the Manor House to shoot vermin with the groundsman, Teddy Gimp.

He headed home around 10 pm having eaten his fill of a hearty rabbit pie in the Manor House kitchen, followed by a few rounds of cards with the Manor House staff. As he exited the forest with the farmhouse in sight, he saw someone running from the building and heading in his direction.

Joby hid himself in the forest for several hours until he was sure it was safe to come out, but, by the time he did, the farmhouse was swarming with blue lights, police dogs and officers. Joby retreated back to the forest and hid there while he decided what to do. Cooper had been with Joby the whole time.

The story was plausible, but Meg asked, "Why were you afraid of the person running from the farmhouse?"

"They were covered in blood," answered Joby. "You could see that from a distance?" Meg queried.

"They stopped for a moment on the steps and the light

from their phone came on and I could see red stains on their clothes. I hid when they headed in my direction, but, as they ran past, I could clearly see that the stains were blood."

Meg was satisfied with his answers, but one important question remained before she rang the police station; "Where was Gully?"

Joby recounted his story virtually word for word. He had no idea about Gully's whereabouts, stating that he had left him at the farm that morning as he headed off to meet Theodore Gimp at the Manor House.

After contacting Mr Gimp for confirmation, the sergeant seemed happy with Joby's statement. He allowed Meg to take him back to her house as the farm was still off-limits.

The sudden appearance of Joby meant Meg had not had time to visit Hegarty Baxter. After dropping him back at the cottage with a rather long 'to do' list, she made her way over to visit the social worker.

CHAPTER 11
Hegarty Baxter

Hegarty Baxter was a widow. Born and bred in the village, she had not been blessed with children of her own but spent her life helping children and families in the neighbouring villages as a social worker. She was well known for her determination, organisation and ability to communicate with children from all walks of life. She was an invaluable part of the social welfare team.

It was early afternoon when Meg forced her way past Hegarty's rusted garden gate. Once past the obnoxious barrier, the rest of the property appeared to have been well loved. A square of lawned area was neatly trimmed, window boxes exploded with colourful blooms and a bright red front door with a shiny bee-shaped knocker welcomed visitors to Hegarty's home.

Meg knocked and waited. She tried again and waited some more, but Hegarty never answered. Perhaps she was out in the village, but her curtains were closed and a fresh bottle of milk sat warming on the doorstep.

Meg's instincts were heightened; something felt wrong. The neat presentation of Hegarty's house did not fit with the psyche of a person who would leave home without first drawing back the curtains or taking in the milk.

Meg felt her detective training suddenly kick in.

She tried the door handle but it was locked. She headed for the back of the property.

The door was already ajar. Meg stepped inside cautiously, recalling in vivid detail the nightmare that had unfolded the last time she had entered an unlocked dwelling.

The hallway was dark with no hint of light to ease the way. She edged along slowly watching her step. She called out but there was no response.

The house was silent. The only movement was that of the hairs standing to attention on the back of Meg's neck.

At the end of the hallway was an inner door which she pushed aside and stepped forward into Hegarty's living room.

A large ginger tabby rushed past in a sudden bid for freedom, startling Meg in the process. She composed herself and moved further into the room.

One look at Hegarty Baxter and Meg knew she was yet again in the centre of a crime scene. She was slumped back in her armchair, a wide gaping wound across the width of her neck, a blood-stained book across her lap and reading glasses swinging from one ear. Hegarty Baxter had met death in a quick, yet brutal way.

A rainbow of blood splatter decorated the wall behind her - she had been slain where she sat.

The ginger cat had left a frenzy of bloody prints around

the room in its attempt to escape its deathly prison. The blood was dry, and Hegarty's body rigid, so time of death had been hours earlier under the shadow of darkness.

Thackeray and Castleton arrived at Hegarty's house together.

"We must stop meeting like this," mused Castleton as he entered the old woman's cottage. There was a definite undertone in his seemingly innocent comment.

'Understandable,' thought Meg, who had arrived in the village just a couple of days ago, and not one but three murders had then occurred within a very short space of time. Not only that but Meg was first on the scene on both occasions. She had to admit that if Castleton had his suspicions, they were indeed well founded.

Feeling the pressure, Meg explained her presence at Hegarty Baxter's home. Castleton listened but made no comment.

The crime scene boys arrived and Meg felt the need to withdraw herself from the situation.

She paused by the back door surveying Hegarty's perfectly appointed rear garden area. Some of her clothes were still pegged to the washing line, and just beyond, at the end of a well-worn pathway, sat a little wooden shed.

Meg followed her instinct to the garden structure and peered inside.

Hegarty had grown her flowers here; trays of yellow and purple pansies that filled the window boxes at the front of the cottage sat in rows on a potting bench. Garden implements, a lawn mower, bags of lawn seed and a collection of brooms were all neatly packed inside.

Just as Meg turned to leave, she noticed something poking out from beneath the bags of seed. Its position was such that its existence was partially hidden, but the execution was poor. Meg tugged at what revealed itself to be a cardboard box squashed under the weight of seed bags and disintegrating with age.

The box had once been heavily sealed with layers of brown tape, though the edges were now peeling and the box itself was no longer secure. Meg ripped through the tape by hand and it gave way easily, allowing its treasure to be revealed.

Inside lay a set of files indexed alphabetically. Meg recognised the header on the paper to be that of the local Social Services. The files were photocopies of the ones belonging to each child that Hegarty Baxter had been assigned. All, that is, except one.

One file was obviously the original. Meg was confused. Why would Hegarty retain the files when the sensitive information within them should have remained within Social Services?

For some reason known only to the recently deceased Mrs Baxter, she had removed the files on her retirement and had hidden them away in her garden shed.

Meg handed the files to Thackeray, saying, "Take a look

at these - not sure if they're relevant, but call me if you find anything." Thackeray nodded in acknowledgement and Meg left while Castleton was still inside the house.

CHAPTER 12

Back at the cottage, Joby had thrown together a hearty meal with wine and candles. He was the perfect house guest and very useful at fixing things, gardening and decorating. The cottage path was clear of weeds and the fence was a welcoming shade of blue. He had cooked a delicious meal and even drawn a bubble bath for Meg to relax in.

Joby was disturbed to hear of another murder in the village. He knew of Hegarty Baxter, though he'd had little contact with her.

"I remember Mrs Baxter visiting our house when I was small," revealed Joby. "Why was that?" Meg questioned.

"Don't really remember, but she visited quite a lot." He shrugged his shoulders. "Perhaps she and Mum were friends." And that was all that Joby Cross had to say on the subject.

A couple of days later, Constable Thackeray arrived at the cottage to talk with Meg. Joby made himself scarce; policemen made him nervous anyway.

The files retrieved from Hegarty Baxter's garden shed had yielded some interesting information. Why she had kept the files was a mystery and the penalty she risked by breaching data protection laws would have been a hefty one. Whatever her reason, Hegarty had felt it necessary to copy the files and hide them away.

Most of the files were insignificant; even Gully Cross's file had been dismissed, but a name Meg had never heard before, Ayda Cross, was the focus of Thackeray's investigation.

Thackeray explained that Ayda was the Cross's second child, who had been placed in care by Hegarty Baxter and Father Maloney of the nearby catholic church.

Meg browsed the file. Violent tendencies, feral behaviour, psychotic episodes - these had been typed on every page.

She checked the girl's birth date; Gully would have been eight and Joby would not yet have existed.

Meg was shocked by the revelation that the Cross's had another child. Photographs around the farm only depicted a family of four. There were no baby pictures of a girl nor any evidence that a girl had ever lived there. Joby would have been a newborn by the time she was taken into care, but Gully should remember the presence of a sister in the house. If only they could find him.

The file bore little else of interest except for the child's birth certificate.

"Any clues as to whether the girl is still alive and, if so, where she might be now?" Meg asked. Thackeray shrugged.

"Sarge is making enquiries, but we have very little to go on as most of the file has been destroyed. Her information is minimal in comparison to the others."

Meg thought this very odd; destroying a file was ominous behaviour and suggested there was something about the child that someone wanted to keep secret.

Thackeray returned to the station and Meg called Aunty June. If anyone would know about Ayda Cross, she would.

CHAPTER 13
Aunty June

Aunty June and Uncle Tom had been married for almost forty years. Both were born in the village and met after Uncle Tom returned from National Service.

They had courted for several months and married at Brightmarsh C of E church in December 1967. Uncle Tom had been the village constable, a much different way of policing back then. He had teased Meg on more than one occasion when she spoke of profiling and DNA tests. Uncle Tom followed his nose and always listened to his instincts. He policed the village with friendly banter and a keen eye, knowing its occupants by name.

He rose to the position of sergeant, which he held until his retirement. In all his years of policing, he had never dealt with murder or sexual assault. A sign of the times nowadays, no doubt.

In 1998, Uncle Tom was mentioned in the local newspaper when the story of Herbert Cooke's cross-dressing incident hit the headlines. Brightmarsh claimed infamy as the scandalous village that housed the disreputable Herbert, and his partner, the local choirmaster.

Uncle Tom revelled in his new-found fame and always

had a knack of telling that story with just the right amount of comedy to send its listeners into raucous fits of laughter. It was his party piece at Christmas and even found its way into the after-dinner speech at his retirement party.

Sadly, COPD claimed Uncle Tom's last breath two years later and Aunty June was left alone. Tom and June had been the only parents Meg had known, and she was the daughter they had longed for.

Meg wondered what Uncle Tom would have made of the murders and what advice he would have given her. She smiled fondly as she remembered the old man who she had been lucky enough to call Dad.

Rather disappointingly, Aunty June was not able to shed much light on Ayda Cross. She had known that Alice was pregnant, but word had spread around the village that the child had died at birth.

She suggested that Meg visit Mary Mackie, the local midwife, who would certainly have attended the child's birth, given that she was the only midwife in the area at that time.

Aunty June was vague on the whereabouts of Mary Mackie or if she was even still alive, but she would consult with Bea Tilley.

A few days later, Aunty June was able to report that Miss Tilley had recalled Mary Mackie in an instant, and quickly provided her last known address, though she warned that Mary's residence was not a place to visit alone.

Joby had been an invaluable asset around the house. He had rebuilt the garden wall, mowed the lawn, weeded the borders, painted the shed, fixed the gate and every evening he had prepared the most delicious meal for Meg to come home to. He was a regular Cinderella.

Tonight was no exception; the waft of beef stew bathed in red wine and aromatic herbs met her at the door. The table was set, flowers as the centrepiece and the Châteauneuf breathing beside two glasses. Joby had harboured dreams of becoming a chef, but his difficulty with reading and understanding weights and measures had shattered his dream.

CHAPTER 14
Mary Mackie

The following day, a thick veil of fog had descended on the village, and visibility was particularly difficult. Undeterred, Meg set off on her quest to find answers about Ayda Cross from the midwife, Mary Mackie. Meg had shared her information with Constable Thackeray the night before, and he was going to meet her there.

The journey was confusing; even the GPS was puzzled. A maze of winding lanes, barely a car's width wide, was particularly difficult to navigate through plumes of thickening haze.

Meg's old jeep limped along at the pace of a blind snail, and the mist was suffocating and visibility almost extinct.

Finally, they reached a turning with the hint of a dirt track and labelled by a broken sign which read 'The Gables'.

Meg followed the track, ploughing through a tunnel of fog, which eventually dispersed to reveal a cobbled courtyard. At first glance, it had the appearance of a scrap yard, and Meg wondered if she had made a mistake. This graveyard for redundant machinery, carcasses of rusty cars and an avalanche of discarded metal scattered in mounds like enormous mole hills was surely not the residence of

Mary Mackie. In the distance, there was the faint outline of a building, perhaps the one she had been looking for.

Meg felt she had stumbled onto the set of the next major horror film. The atmospheric fog and abandoned dwelling were the perfect backdrop for a gruesome murder or malevolent spirit to inhabit.

Meg was uncertain she was at the correct address and she wasn't sure she wanted to find out. Perhaps she should wait for Thackeray to arrive, if he could find it.

Ten minutes later, compelled by her own curiosity, Meg found herself negotiating a cautious path through the iron jungle, heading in the direction of the distant building. The unknown outline soon became recognisable as that of a simple mobile home. It slotted into the picture so easily that Meg was uncertain from its appearance whether it belonged to the metal graveyard. She ventured closer to find out.

Shabby grey nets cloaked the windows, and cardboard covered the panes that were broken. There was no sign of life here; everything was still and silent.

Meg was silently praying that Thackeray would make his appearance. The situation was beyond eerie and Meg sensed danger.

Two large gas canisters were attached to the dwelling and Meg had spotted canine faeces around the area, both signs that someone visited, if not lived here.

The caravan looked fragile. A strong gust of wind

would have crushed it with ease; it had certainly seen better days. Meg found the dinted, claw-marked door and knocked briskly.

From inside, a muffled voice responded. Meg waited, but no one appeared. She was just about to knock again when the caravan door flew open and the frame of a small dishevelled woman shuffled into view.

Meg was slightly stunned by her appearance. Thick grey hair shrouded her face, her eyes were engulfed within the frizzy mess, deep-set and black, and only the rim of silver glasses defined the boundaries between hair and face. If this was Mary Mackie, she had done an impressive job of hiding from society, as the twisted old hag that stood before Meg looked nothing like the photograph she had seen.

"Mary...Mary Mackie?" Meg forced the name from her lips.

"Who wants to know?" came the reply. Reassuringly for Meg, the voice sounded far more human than the entity it came from.

"I'm Meg; June Watson is my aunt. I'm investigating a murder and I believe you may have some information that might help."

The figure stepped back into the shadow of the caravan and signalled with a bony finger for Meg to follow.

In the background, Meg heard the sound of a car and the welcome voice of Thackeray calling for direction in the distance. Meg felt relieved; Thackeray had arrived just as she was about to enter the witch's lair, so his timing was perfect.

Thackeray soon appeared and the look on his face told Meg that he was equally disturbed by the woman's appearance and the squalor in which she lived, but he followed Meg into the van. The inside was equally as unattractive as the outside. There were no discernible boundaries between where the seating began and finished, rubbish spilled from every nook and cranny, and the smell was indescribable.

There was not an inch of unused space on the worktops, and dog excrement was smeared into the threadbare carpet. Meg wanted to gag, the odour burning the back of her throat and stinging her eyes. She glanced towards Thackeray - his face was a pale grey and he was desperately struggling to keep the contents of his fried breakfast in situ.

The woman lurched forward. Meg and Thackeray stepped aside as clutter flew in their direction from the fixed seating and scattered around their feet.

"Sit down," she ordered. Meg took a careful step forward and perched cautiously on the edge of the grubby material. Thackeray declined the invitation, choosing to hover in the doorway where he had access to fresher air.

"I know nothing about a murder," scolded the old woman.

She was now partially hidden behind a stack of cardboard boxes, where a tiny ray of daylight had forced its way through a rip in the tattered curtain, revealing Mary's shrivelled features and unruly grey hair with more definition. Her eyes were black, sunken and cold. She scratched at her skin with claw-like discoloured talons, but the voice was soft with a hint of an Irish accent.

Meg pondered on why this woman had succumbed to a life such as this, but she wasn't there for Mary's life history, nor did she want to spend a moment longer in her hovel than was needed. "Are you the Mary Mackie who was once the village midwife?"

"I am," came the reply.

"Do you remember a birth at Molecatcher Farm, a baby daughter born to Alice and Ben Cross?" The woman dropped her head and studied her hands as if looking for the answer in her wrinkled palms.

"A child was born at the farm, a girl, a monster! Born with the mark of the devil," Mary hissed. Meg felt a chill creep down her spine, goose bumps popped and she shivered inside.

"They paid me to keep it quiet, say the child had died at birth. They couldn't handle her; she should have died at birth."

The statement was bold and uncaring for one whose profession was delivering babies, but Mary's words were spoken with fear.

Meg threw a glance in Thackeray's direction. He was teetering on the edge of the caravan step, looking as disturbed as Meg was feeling.

"When you say born with a mark, what exactly do you mean?" questioned Meg.

The woman lurched forward and stooped to within inches of Meg's face. Her breath was warm and acrid, her words spilled forth like a toxic substance, and Meg inhaled every word.

Suddenly, she felt a little dizzy and rushed towards fresh air and daylight. She gasped for breath; the stench of the old woman's words still lingered around her senses.

Thackeray was beside her, strong arms guiding her across the treacherous iron jungle to safety. Meg's head was spinning, so she stood for a moment waiting for the motion to steady. Thackeray had reached for a bottle of water and handed it to her.

"What the hell happened in there?" Thackeray asked.

Meg gulped the water in a bid to eliminate Mary Mackie's fetid words.

She shook her head, trying desperately to make sense of the old hag's whispers. "It was something about death, a raven, danger and the girl. It didn't make sense; it's jumbled in my head like the fragments of a dream."

Meg still felt disoriented. Her experience with Mary Mackie was unforgettable. Why the woman chose to live as she did, an outcast from society, was puzzling. Perhaps she had an explanation, but Meg was happy not knowing; she never wanted to visit Mary Mackie again.

Soon, the dingy caravan was a blur in the rear-view mirror and Meg was winding her way back to the safety of Pebble Cottage.

The visit to Mary Mackie was never really spoken of again. Both were uncertain of what they had encountered that morning and both preferred not to talk about it, at least not now anyway.

Castleton was told that the midwife had provided no valuable information, which he accepted.

Meg thanked Thackeray for his assistance and offered him coffee, as he had kindly followed her home, but he, like Meg, felt a desperate need to shower and wash away any trace of Mary Mackie and her appalling lifestyle.

"Just one thing," queried Meg. "What do you think is the mark of the devil?"

Thackeray paused, contemplating the question, "I think Mary Mackie's words were senseless, the ravings of a lonely individual. I wouldn't lose any sleep over it, Meg." Thackeray jumped into his car and drove away.

The night seemed endless and sleep didn't find Meg until dawn. Even then, it was haunted by Mary Mackie's words. Meg awoke to a voicemail message from Castleton asking her to meet him at Molecatcher Farm that morning.

CHAPTER 15

When Meg arrived, Castleton and Thackeray were in discussion with a posse of men in white suits. The scene of a week ago came rushing back in vivid detail and Meg's head began to spin. She took a moment to let the feeling pass before joining the sergeant on the steps of the back porch. Castleton explained that the farmhouse was being searched again and he wanted her to accompany him as a fresh pair of eyes, but also someone who knew the property. He passed her a forensic suit and gloves and she followed him inside.

The victims of the horror scene were resting in the Police morgue, but the room still bore the scars of bloody murder. The stone-flagged kitchen floor was heavily stained with the contents of Alice and Ben Cross's lifeforce. Also, the two rocking chairs where their headless bodies had sat and the blood-spattered walls remained chilling features of the victims' sadistic demise.

The house was chaotic; ghostly figures filled every room. Castleton disappeared and Meg was left to wander through the lifetime of memories absorbed within the walls of this home. Framed photos portrayed a happy family unit, trophies won at local shows for prize ewes sat proudly on homemade wooden shelves and Gully's attempts at art were taped to the dining room wall.

It was impossible to believe that the Crosses had hidden the existence of a child inside this building and kept it secret from the rest of the world.

Meg reminded herself that nostalgia was not why Castleton had brought her here, so she swapped persona from long-time family friend to trained detective.

It was in that moment that Meg was drawn to the hallway, and, in particular, to the hanging jumble of coats and the glint of something shiny hidden in the depth of waxed jackets.

Pushing the clothing aside, Meg discovered that the shiny object was a keyhole. It belonged to a small door purposely cut out of the plasterboard wall and cloaked by the turmoil of outer garments. It had obviously been constructed for a reason and Meg was eager to find out why.

At the end of the hallway just beside the front door sat a wall-mounted wooden box which housed a variety of different-sized keys. Meg grabbed a bunch of them and hurried back to the enigmatic keyhole.

Her first attempts were futile, but then, a perfect fit slipped into position and unlocked the little door. Meg lit her torch and pulled the door aside. It opened outwards revealing a black space beyond.

On the inside of the door hung a pink horseshoe crudely painted with the name 'A-Y-D-A' in black letters and a piece of Gully's artwork beside it.

Meg felt the flutter of butterflies as she poked her torch into the black space illuminating the outline of a structure no bigger than a standard kitchen cupboard. The find had been handmade, a makeshift addition attached behind the wall.

Meg could not imagine being locked inside it. There was no light, no heating, no comfort of any kind. Small holes had been punctured along the top of one side for ventilation, and one hole had been gouged away to make it bigger than the rest. The carcass of a decaying rat lay in one corner, while remnants of faecal matter stained the floor. The air was stale and stuffy like removing the lid of a sarcophagus after a thousand years.

Meg could not fit inside the cramped space, nor did she want to, but she covered every inch with the glow of torchlight. If Ayda Cross had been forced to live in this wooden prison, then the probability that she might have issues was all too clear.

Then suddenly, her torchlight fell on a black furry-looking object. Meg feared it was a live rat waiting to retaliate if she poked it, but, on further investigation, it turned out to be nothing more than a pile of black feathers.

It was time to show Castleton her find.

He surveyed the dingy cell and instructed his ghostly colleagues to scour it for forensic evidence, as there were many questions to be answered.

"Looks like the Crosses were hiding a secret," he said.

In the doorway, he paused; "Good work, Meg. You always seem to be in the right place at the right time!"

Meg had known Ben and Alice Cross most of her childhood life, growing up around the farm with Joby and Abby. They were hardworking people who lived a simple existence.

Ben was a man of few words; he worked the farm from dawn to dusk seven days a week.

Alice rarely ventured outside, but when she did, she wore the look of a sickly woman, weak and weathered by anxiety.

Meg had never questioned why she was seldom allowed in the farmhouse or why the Cross family chose to live such a reclusive life, but now she knew the answer. They had harboured a deep dark secret, one they hoped would never be revealed.

Sitting outside Pebble Cottage, Meg ruminated over the possibility that Joby had any knowledge of his sister, Ayda. She could see his busy little figure passing before the window, and she knew a delicious aroma would be waiting to greet her as she opened the cottage door.

Perhaps Joby could offer an explanation for the room, but it wasn't a subject that could easily be discussed over dinner.

Meg's self-debate was suddenly interrupted by a text message from Thackeray, which read, 'Forensics have lifted three sets of prints from the hidden room, two were a match to Alice and Ben Cross, the third was unknown. The database came up with no match, but DNA yielded one clue, the third set of prints belonged to a female'.

Meg checked her watch; dinner would have to wait. She abandoned Joby and headed for the Registrar's office in Ambleton.

On the second floor of the council building, Meg was greeted by a peaky-faced woman behind a large wooden desk, who glanced over rimless glasses but said nothing.

"I'm looking for a register of births for 1991," stated Meg.

"Those registers are not available for members of the public to view," replied the woman with a rather smug tone.

"I'm a police officer, so if you would be so kind as to point me in the right direction, I would be very grateful." Meg couldn't hold back a wry smile as she watched the expression on the woman's face disintegrate. She rose silently from her desk and signalled for Meg to follow her down a passageway of huge mobile shelves, where a library of ledgers was stored. The woman parked a small step ladder beside the dusty shelves and climbed up. She withdrew a leather-bound book from the third shelf and handed it down to Meg.

"This is what you're looking for," she mumbled, and with that, she scurried out of the room.

Setting the register down, Meg thumbed hurriedly

through the pages until she reached the required year. There she found the written proof that Alice Cross did indeed have a child, born on 6 June, a daughter named Ayda Rose.

Ben, however, was not registered as the child's father. That honour belonged to none other than Sir Henry Attwood, Abby's father. Meg was astonished. Did Abby know that she shared family ties with Joby in the form of a half-sister? Meg was certain that she didn't. A quick snap of her iPhone and the evidence was shared with Castleton and Thackeray.

Ayda Rose Cross had survived, just as Mary Mackie had said. Evidence showed that she was imprisoned in a secret room at Molecatcher Farm, but what had happened next and where was she now?

Arriving back at the cottage, Joby was waiting to serve his culinary delight. Meg was not much company though, as her mind was focused on the whereabouts of Ayda Cross and what kind of life she had endured at the hands of Ben and Alice Cross. Did Sir Henry know of her existence? One could only assume that he did since his name was cited on the birth certificate.

Meg was desperate for answers, but Joby could not provide them. Gully was still missing and Hegarty Baxter was dead.

A message from Abby invaded the moment. It was a dinner invitation to the Manor House and Joby was invited too. He was beside himself with excitement, though Meg couldn't share his enthusiasm. She had far more on her mind than a dinner party, but she reluctantly agreed to accompany her friend the following evening.

Adrenaline was rushing through her body like a high-speed train; pulse racing, blood pumping, she had never felt more alive than in these moments. Murder was a drug far superior to any synthetic potion; revenge its humble partner.

The aftermath was never as sweet as the kill, though she still felt a tremor of delight whenever she remembered the look of horror on the faces of her first. She must focus now; she had a date night with her next victim.

CHAPTER 16
Father Maloney

The church was empty. Only the flicker of dying candles cast a shadowy eye across the altar. The powerful smell of polished wood and musty hymn books brought back a flood of tearful memories. She had always hated the church, its teachings and everything it stood for. Most of all, she hated Father Maloney.

She stood before the figure of Mary; a symbol of divine motherhood, worshipped and adored by millions. She had knelt before her on many occasions and prayed to her for help, but Mary, like everyone else she encountered through life, had shown her no mercy.

Father Maloney, a thin, decrepit little man who stank of whiskey and smoked like a chimney, had sealed his own fate when she was just a child by encouraging her parents to lock her away like a rabid animal, and filling their minds with images of the devil. He offered to perform an exorcism, but the only things he performed were non-consensual acts of sexual depravity on children.

Her parents, devout followers of the church, believed every word that spewed forth from the priest's dishonest mouth. They feared her for what she had become, a victim of circumstance in the hands of the weak and naive. They created the monster that lived inside her and they had paid the price; now it was Father Maloney's turn.

The church afforded her no sympathy and provided no sympathy.

In truth, Father Maloney had helped to create the worst version of herself. Her experiences in life and those within the walls of social institutions were the foundation on which she had built her pathway to revenge. It was that and that alone that gave her the strength to survive, and survive she did!

The sound of footsteps caught her attention. An aged, slow-moving Father Maloney came into view. He bowed awkwardly before his God, pain and stiffness ravishing his bones. His God couldn't save him now - she stepped out of the shadows, and, as Father Maloney snuffed out the last candle, she snuffed out Father Maloney.

Meg awoke the next morning to a terrible noise resounding across the village. A distressed wailing echoed in the distance. Grabbing a robe and rushing downstairs, Meg crossed the village green in the direction of the alarming sound. She soon realised it was coming from inside the catholic church.

Running through the church gates and the open door ahead, Meg halted just inside.

The noise emanated from a young woman who was standing beside the altar, on which the body of Father Maloney was splayed, like a human sacrifice.

Joby, who had followed Meg, entered the church just behind her, so she grabbed his arm and asked him to call Sergeant Castleton. Joby's face paled as he glimpsed the lifeless body of the clergyman lying across the altar.

Meg embraced the young woman in an attempt to console her, but she was almost frantic.

Father Maloney lay like a wax sculpture cloaked in his own blood. His throat had been sliced with such ferocity that his head had almost parted company with his body. A large crucifix lay across his chest and the words 'I repent' had been carved across his forehead. His penis had been removed and wedged inside his mouth. He'd been dead for several hours judging by the discolouration and rigidity of his body.

Castleton arrived with a female officer in tow. She was assigned to comfort the young woman who had entered the church to arrange flowers as she had previously on many occasions.

Castleton surveyed the crime scene. "Four murders in six days," he said, circling the altar. Meg nodded, then added, "You do realise this is no coincidence; we have a serial killer in our midst."

Castleton stopped circling, the grim realisation of Meg's words depicted by the animated look of horror on his face He bit at his lip. He knew she was right.

Meg had profiled serial killers as part of her training when she joined the murder squad after Michael's death. It was her last attempt at staying with the police, a change of scenery, a new direction, but even that was no match for the overwhelming void that Michael had left in her life. Serial killers were extremely difficult to catch, well-organised, intelligent individuals who relished the art of leaving no trace evidence. Masters of disguise, blending seamlessly into the community, they were neighbours, colleagues, family members; human chameleons adapting to their surroundings, everywhere and nowhere, unseen and unheard, and exceptionally dangerous.

Castleton headed to the station to interview the flower arranger who had been treated by a local doctor and was now able to recount the traumatic discovery of Father Maloney's body.

She had arrived early that morning to decorate the church with colourful flowers for the upcoming Mass. She worked in the village at the local florist's and had been tasked with the job of dressing the church three times a week.

On arrival, she was surprised that the church door was already open as, usually, she would have to visit the local verger's house for the spare key. Father Maloney was never up and about before 9 am; his arthritic bones just wouldn't allow it.

As the young woman entered the church, she did not notice anything unusual, but the morning light was still shy and she had only peered inside expecting to see someone there. By the time she had unpacked the flowers, sunlight was illuminating the stained-glass window above the altar, and it was then that she made the gruesome discovery.

Castleton closed the file. "You okay?" asked Meg.

"Yeah, I will be. Just never faced anything like this before." Castleton paused then went on, "Think I'm going to need your help, Meg, if you're up for it."

"Of course," replied Meg. "I'll be here in the morning, but right now, I have a dinner to go to."

CHAPTER 17
The Dinner

The Manor House was even more magnificent at night. Its windows danced with light beneath heavy regal drapes, the garden was flooded by moonlight throwing shadowy shapes across perfectly manicured lawns and a thousand stars twinkled overhead like a diamond-studded backdrop.

Joby was beside himself with excitement. He was not blinded by the opulence of the Manor House; he probably hadn't noticed it as they rolled up the driveway. Instead, he was tingling with anticipation at the culinary delights that awaited him. Mrs Hobson and her team of kitchen staff were famous for their Michelin star menus and tonight would be no exception.

By 8 pm, they had arrived, Meg in a shimmering top and faux leather jeans, Joby in a checked shirt and waistcoat, well-fitting trousers and leather boots. Abby was delighted to see them both and ushered them into the drawing room for pre-dinner drinks. The conversation flowed freely; the three friends, reunited after all these years, were totally immersed in recapping historic moments from their youth.

About half an hour later, the roar of a sporty engine bellowed outside - Theo had arrived. Always one to make an entrance, Theo strode into the drawing room with a leggy, red-haired beauty on his arm. He hadn't changed much, a little fuller in the face with a slightly different hairstyle, but there was no mistaking the arrogant, pompous and overly confident Theo Attwood.

When Isobel Atwood left the family mansion and waltzed off into the horizon with her new beau, Theo and Abby were essentially orphaned. Henry, injured by the fact that his wife had found herself a much younger model, retreated to their apartment in London and immersed himself in work.

He employed a housekeeper/nanny to care for his children, but they were desperate for Henry's attention and a long line of nannies were no match for the Attwood children.

Henry sent Abby to Cheltenham Ladies' College, where he hoped she would transform into a lady befitting of her title.

Abby, desperately unhappy but also very stubborn, wouldn't allow herself public displays of emotion. She dealt with her feelings in the secrecy of the college bathroom late at night in the form of recreational drugs and alcohol. Fuelled by vodka and heroin, she would hit the social scene with a vengeance, but when she finally returned to the Manor House, she had transitioned into the woman Henry had hoped for.

Her relationship with Henry was never going to run

smoothly. She felt betrayed by him, but living back at the Manor House, she had allowed herself to tolerate the man she called Father. It was hard to forgive a man who had selfishly cast his children aside and continued a bachelor lifestyle. Abby was never going to forget his misgivings, but, for the sake of her own harmony, she had learnt to forgive.

Theo, on the other hand, made it his life's ambition to make Henry suffer.

Desperate for love and security, Theo became an intolerable and disobedient child. He was loathed by the staff and the army of nannies could not reform him.

An exasperated Henry sent Theo away to a boot camp for boys. Surprisingly, Theo felt more at home there than anywhere else in his life and eventually, he settled and allowed the boot camp to serve its purpose. He came home a reformed young man.

When Theo finally returned to the Manor House years later, Sir Henry tried desperately to atone for his paternal desertion and showered the young man with everything he desired.

Theo, of course, ensured he took full advantage of his father's generosity. He flew between a penthouse in London and a luxury yacht in Monte Carlo. Henry allowed him an unlimited credit card and turned a blind eye to his disregard for the law. The spirited young Theo purposely crashed his sports cars, accumulated parking fines and continued to act like a spoilt brat, all in the pursuit of his father's atonement.

Henry, however, continued to play the dutiful father by paying the fines, repairing the cars and settling misdemeanours out of court at great expense to himself.

Theo continued to enjoy his playboy lifestyle still feeling nothing but resentment for his father. Nothing on earth could cost enough to make up for his abandonment and he was never going to let him forget it.

As the giant antique grandfather clock in the hallway chimed nine, Darrow appeared in the doorway of the drawing room and invited everyone to take their places for dinner.

Joby, with an excited glint in his eye, led the way.

He was seated beside Theo, who immediately introduced his dinner guest as Madison Pope, an American glamour model. Joby, it's safe to say, was slightly distracted from the dinner menu by Miss Pope's overly generous breasts. They spilled from her spaghetti string dress towards him, held captive by the mere strength of the strappy fabric. Meg suspected Joby was hoping for the flame-haired beauty to encounter a wardrobe faux pas, as he would be on hand to retrieve her dignity. The glamorous Miss Pope had a totally unglamorous southern drawl, loud and high-pitched, with an annoying snort when she laughed. Joby, of course, had not noticed.

Fortunately for Meg, she was seated at the opposite

end of the table between Sir Henry, who had not yet taken his seat, and best friend Abby. Thankfully, there were no voluminous body parts on display, just mature, champagne-fuelled conversation.

Eventually, Sir Henry appeared and took his seat at the table. He hadn't changed much over the years. Age had only enhanced his rugged good looks, and he had kept his athletic figure and charismatic smile. It was understandable how women found him attractive; even Meg felt the flutter of butterflies when he entered the room. His greying hair was plentiful and cut to display his profile to its best advantage, and below it, piercing blue eyes still sparkled with a youthful glint. Henry Attwood was an extremely handsome man, who, despite having neglected his fatherly duties, had definitely blessed his children with his biological genes.

He was a powerful man with an ego to match. Raised in a male-dominated family, it was inevitable that the departure of his previous wife would have dinted his ego considerably. His second wife, Lilia, was his recompense.

"He has been frequenting the gentlemen's clubs of Soho again," informed Abby, "no doubt on the lookout for the next Lady Attwood," she joked.

Abby was right; Henry had certainly been on the hunt for a perfect specimen and he'd found it in the guise of Lilia Czechova, a Hungarian pole dancer, half his age and twice as good-looking.

Henry was smitten from the moment she sashayed onto the stage and caressed her pole with sexual dexterity.

It was his mission to woo her and one evening, as they dined in the heart of the capital, Henry dropped to one knee and proposed to Lilia with a ten-carat Tiffany diamond.

A month later, Lilia Czechova became Lady Lilia Attwood and the latest addition to the family. Henry flaunted his new wife throughout Europe and eventually brought her home to meet his children.

Theo despised her as he had all of Henry's previous dalliances. He knew that in months, or, if she was lucky, years, Henry would grow bored and the whole process would begin again.

Abby accepted Henry's conquests without argument. So long as she remained the recognised, true lady of the Manor House, then they would get along fine. She avoided them at all costs and, for the most part, her strategy worked.

Henry placed a warm comforting arm around Meg's shoulder and pulled her towards his chest. He gave her a soft kiss on the forehead and whispered, "Welcome home." Meg felt a rush of emotion flood her body and a slight blush tinted her cheeks. He smelled so good. Meg wanted to stay in the warmth of his hug, as the memories of the last few days and the brutal murders she had faced melted into oblivion.

Suddenly, the hug ended as the sound of a door closing caught everyone's attention.

Lilia Attwood, the new Lady of the Manor floated seamlessly into the room. Silence descended and all eyes were on her. A low audible gasp could be heard as her mesmerising figure glided across the floor.

She paused beside Henry, kissing his cheek with a passion Meg had only ever read about. Henry grinned appreciatively, and, taking his wife's hand, introduced her to her unknown dinner guests.

The American was first in line. Lilia afforded her a slight tilt of the head and moved past her to where Joby was sitting with his mouth now open, and the remnants of red wine dribbling from one corner.

Poor Joby; he was awestruck. His first real close encounter with women was just too much for him to handle. Miss Pope, feeling slightly abandoned by her new friend, was able to regain his attention by offering to wipe his mouth with a silk handkerchief. She and her bosom moved closer, and his gaze returned to her cleavage once again.

As she moved along the line of guests, Lilia's eyes met Meg's. Henry introduced her as a friend of the family. Lilia smiled approvingly. Her eyes were a striking shade of hazel, beautiful yet intimidating. The gaze felt awkward and difficult to break, as if Lilia was controlling the situation. It was only when she fluttered her eyelashes back in Henry's direction that Meg was released.

Lilia was hypnotic, intriguing and obscenely beautiful and Meg, like the other guests, found it hard not to stare at her. She was elegant and confident, clad in a figure-hugging silver gown. Her dark hair swept upwards into a loose bun and her face was framed by fine wavy wisps that she had carefully positioned.

Despite the string of diamonds that sparkled around her neck, it was she who drew the attention. She was simply stunning, like a priceless masterpiece, now sitting at the head of the table.

Of course, essentially, that's what she was. By definition, she was no more than one of Henry's prize trophies.

Abby leaned towards Meg; "Breathtaking, isn't she? By far, Father's best effort to date," she joked. Meg couldn't remember much after that. She had tried so hard not to stare at Lilia that she had drunk more than her body weight in champagne.

CHAPTER 18
The Morning After

The evening had been a complete success, as far as Meg could remember.

She woke the next morning with church bells ringing in her ears, literally. She managed to drag her champagne-soaked carcass out of bed and head downstairs to find Joby. They hadn't talked much on the journey home and she was interested to know what he thought of the dinner menu and his new American friend.

Joby was otherwise engaged in the downstairs bathroom. His first dinner party had yielded his first hangover and it was a couple of hours before he managed to stop throwing up and join Meg.

Coffee was Meg's hero; hot, strong and plenty of it. It was mid-afternoon by the time the alcoholic cloud cleared over Pebble Cottage.

Meg could not help but think about Lilia Attwood. She had been a gracious host; she had laughed at ridiculous jokes; she had raised her glass to numerous toasts and she had complimented the staff on the success of the dinner menu. Her accent was ill-defined. She hailed from Budapest but said her childhood had been spent in several exotic and European places, which accounted for her unusual brogue.

Monday began with an over-enthusiastic alarm clock. Meg prised herself from the warmth of her duvet and prepared to join Castleton at the station. The murders would not solve themselves and Castleton had asked her to officially become part of the investigation.

She had accepted, partly because she had nothing else to do and partly because she wanted to establish a link between the victims and, ultimately, solve the crimes.

It was a pleasure to hear Joby milling about in the kitchen again and the smell of pancakes was wafting up the stairs.

Meg arrived just in time for the briefing. Castleton, who looked as though he had slept in his clothes all weekend, was recapping on the dates of the murders.

Photographs of the victims were plastered across the wall, their horrific injuries displayed in full colour. Ben and Alice Cross, Hegarty Baxter and Father Maloney. Four victims in six days and not a suspect in sight.

"We have no obvious link between the victims, except that they all live in the vicinity of Brightmarsh and Ambleton. They appear to have been killed by the same person, which means we probably have a serial killer in our village. We have no DNA, no discernible clues and no murder weapon.

In short, people, we are f**ked!"

The room fell silent. It was obvious from the sea of shocked faces that Castleton was not known for his use of profanities. He was visibly frustrated and rightly so.

Thackeray, realising the awkwardness in the room, barked instructions and he and the team dispersed immediately.

When the room had cleared, Castleton poured two coffees and sat down opposite Meg.

"I've got to be honest with you, I've never dealt with anything on this scale before. I have no witnesses, no murder weapon and no motive. I'm working in the dark here, Meg, so I need all the help you can give."

Castleton sipped his coffee slowly. Meg realised the magnitude of stress he was suffering by the nervous tremor in his hand. He wanted Meg's assurance that they would catch the culprit, but Meg could give no such guarantee. Finding such a killer was like finding a needle in a haystack.

"In my experience," she began, "serial killers don't always choose their victims randomly; they plan meticulously and they're motivated. They usually don't leave clues or DNA and that's what makes them so difficult to catch, but something drives them to murder - they usually have a back story."

Castleton changed position and drained his cup. "And this is supposed to make me feel better?" Meg grinned; "It's difficult enough with a team of a hundred officers, but we're a team of six. So, don't be too hard on yourself; this is no mean feat."

Several cups of coffee later, Meg suggested they should start by exploring a link between the victims. Did they know each other or were they just random kills?

Castleton began creating a list of all the people known by the victims; any names that cropped up more than once was the place to start. Then they went through the evidence they already had.

The Crosses lived a secluded life in an equally secluded location. A second search of their house uncovered a purpose-built secret cupboard. The house and the cupboard were reluctant to give up much in the way of DNA, other than that of Mr and Mrs Cross, their two sons and a third person, that person being a female.

The link between the Crosses and Hegarty Baxter was that she was their assigned social worker. Father Maloney was their priest and he and Hegarty had helped rehome Ayda Cross, if that's who was assumed to have lived in the cupboard.

Gully Cross was still unaccounted for and, so far, was top of the suspect list. They needed to widen the search for Gully, possibly with Joby's help.

Castleton's nerves had settled and he was feeling more positive. He thanked Meg for her help and returned to his desk.

"Oh, I was wondering," began Meg just as Castleton had picked up his phone, "the feathers, anything come from them?"

Castleton replaced the receiver. "That's where we got the female DNA from. There were three hundred of them in total."

"What species?" "Raven," he replied.

CHAPTER 19

That afternoon, they picked up Joby from Pebble Cottage. Meg and Castleton drove him back to Molecatcher Farm for the first time since his parents' murders. Meg had spared him the gruesome details of their demise, and Joby had never asked, though the farmhouse bore the scars of that fateful night and Joby was about to enter it.

The farm stood alone at the peak of Manston Moor, encircled by acres of desolate moorland. Only the dense mass of Weaver's Wood, cutting across the landscape to the north side, interrupted the view.

In the midst of this wilderness, sitting like a doll's house on a football field, was Molecatcher Farm. This once-productive smallholding had turned into a house of horrors.

Joby was hesitant at first, clinging to the handle of Castleton's car door, anguish and sadness flashing across his face and fear glinting in his eyes.

He gazed at the old farmhouse as if recalling the memories. "What is he doing?" Castleton growled, pacing with frustration.

Meg knew the situation was delicate; after all, she was asking him to visit the place where his parents had been slaughtered.

Meg, with a little gentle persuasion, helped him to

step inside.

Joby stood statuesque in the doorway. He found no voice, but the expressions on his face spoke volumes. Meg, recognising his pain, grabbed him by the arm and guided him through the kitchen area and into the hallway. She hurried him past the bloodstained walls trying to keep his gaze fixed anywhere but the murder scene.

Castleton pointed out the hidden cupboard behind the area where coats once hung. Joby stared in amazement, trying to absorb the information Castleton was reciting.

Poor Joby; he had no idea about the little cupboard, or the girl who had reportedly lived there. He searched Meg's eyes for answers, his own pooling with uncontrollable tears.

Meg hugged him tightly. Joby wasn't the killer - his reaction had cemented any doubts she might have had, but Castleton wasn't convinced.

As the sun settled above Molecatcher Farm, it was bathed in a halo of light. It brought back memories of summer evenings chasing rabbits across the moor, paddling in the brook and climbing trees in Weaver's Wood.

When it was really hot, Mrs Cross would serve homemade lemonade and Mr Cross would allow them to hitch a ride on the back of the hay-laden trailer.

Meg escorted Joby back to the car and then returned to speak with Castleton out of earshot.

It was in that moment, as she turned back towards Castleton, that a bright flash in the distance caught her attention.

She waited for a moment; Castleton followed her gaze, and, as he turned, there was another flash. A tiny speck of sunlight was hitting something in the doorway of the old shed.

Castleton and Meg headed towards the shining beacon to investigate.

"Careful, Meg," warned Castleton as she gathered pace. She glanced back at him acknowledging his warning but didn't change her speed. Just beyond the barn door, a dart of light appeared again, coming from just inside the doorway.

Meg stepped closer signalling to Castleton that she was going to open the door, but before she could, a pitchfork lunged in her direction. She jumped clear and the pitchfork hit the ground beside her stabbing the earth with deep intent.

Joby had also seen the object fly out of the barn towards Meg. He recognised it instantly and ran to her aid, shouting loudly, "Gully, is that you?"

A moment later, the giant figure of Gulliver Cross stepped into the sunlight. He was dirty and dishevelled with a strong smell of body odour and urine emanating from him. He stared at Joby for a moment, his eyes adjusting to the light, then a slow stream of tears began to flow as he recognised his brother.

Meg had a million questions for Gully, all of which she wanted answered now, but she would need Joby's help to coax Gully to cooperate with the police.

Castleton was staring in awe at the colossus that was Gully Cross. He requested a police van to pick up Gully and allowed Joby to ride with him back to the station.

He asked for a local GP to assess Gully's health and ordered Thackeray to supply him with food and drink.

A quick search of the barn revealed a makeshift bed, where Gully had been hunkered down. The area was peppered with empty cans and crisp packets, sweet wrappers and apple cores, the evidence of Gully's fight to survive.

The barn had been searched on previous visits but Gully was not discovered there. Perhaps he had been hiding somewhere else and only recently returned.

Meg felt a sigh of relief as she journeyed back to the station. Gully was alive and hopefully able to give them some answers.

A hot meal later, with approval from a doctor that Gully was fit for interview, and with Joby by his side, the process began.

CHAPTER 20
Gully Cross

Castleton invited Meg to join him. He felt a female presence would comfort the situation and Gully might be more liable to co-operate amongst people he knew.

Gully had entered the world starved of oxygen, and this deprivation of vital human necessity had left him with mental incapacity. Physically, his growth was off the charts, but mentally, he equalled the intelligence of a young child.

His loss of speech occurred years later following an incident that Gully was never able to explain. Gully was taught sign language, but his ability to remember this meant his vocabulary was limited. Meg, though somewhat rusty, was able to sign her name and introduce Castleton by spelling out his name on her fingers. Gully seemed to recognise her and signed back.

Joby was fully adept at communicating with his brother and would act as interpreter during the interview.

Gully sat hunched over in his chair, eyes focused on his hands. He rocked backwards and forwards in a slow gentle rhythm.

The interview began with Gully answering simple questions openly.

When Castleton's questions turned to the newly discovered cubby hole at Molecatcher Farm, Gully became visibly anxious, rocking vigorously and hugging his arms tightly around his chest. Joby couldn't explain his brother's distress, but it was obvious that this was not Gully's first knowledge of the place.

Gully was asked if he was ever placed in the cupboard, but he shook his head in denial.

When Castleton placed photographs of the cupboard itself on the table, Gully stood bolt upright, sending his chair speeding across the room. He retreated to a corner and sank into a ball with his hands over his head and resumed the rocking motion with distressed ferocity.

"I think we better leave it there for today," said Joby.

Castleton nodded. "He knows something, Joby, so if you can find out what that is, it will spare him a repeat of this, but if not, I'm afraid we will have to continue interviewing him until we find out what he's not telling us."

Joby understood completely and asked to speak outside. They left the room while Gully continued to self-soothe in the corner.

"Just an idea, but if you can give me a couple of days with my brother alone to settle him down, I might be able to get him to talk to me," Joby suggested.

Castleton pondered for a moment. He threw Meg a questioning glance, which she answered with a nod of approval.

It was decided that Joby and Gully would spend a couple of nights at the village B&B. It was a stone's throw from Pebble Cottage and was owned by Castleton's Aunt Imelda.

Castleton made a call, and in no time, Meg was driving the brothers into the village centre to deposit them with Imelda Carter at the Old Oak B&B.

A jolly, grey-haired lady answered the door and invited them inside.

"Welcome, welcome, please come in. I'm Imelda and I'll be looking after you for the next couple of days."

She ushered them into the kitchen where she had prepared a fresh pot of tea with homemade scones just out of the oven.

To say Imelda was a talkative woman was an understatement. Her cherry-red lips never stopped moving, and Joby was loving every minute. Gully, though slightly subdued, was excitedly tucking into his scone, which Imelda had lavished with cream and jam.

"I've put you in Room 5 - it's the biggest, with two single beds and its own bathroom. Breakfast is served between 7 and 10, and I provide daily newspapers free of charge. You're free to come and go as you please, but I do ask that you're home by 11 as I lock the front door at that time on my way to bed."

Imelda seemed just as excited to have the brothers'

company as Gully was about her home-baked scones.

Meg knew they would be safe and said goodbye, promising to look in on them in a couple of days' time.

She felt irritable; trapped, even. It had been a few days since she felt the cool grip of the knife in her hand. She removed it from the leather sheath and caressed it with a finger, smiling proudly. There was more work to do, another life to claim, but this time the silver blade would not be needed. She wanted to dabble and expand her portfolio by introducing different methods in her quest for murder. After all, variety is the spice of life!

Her fourth victim awaited. She wouldn't count the skinny, young man as a significant kill; he was not on her list. He was an unfortunate necessity, who she hadn't anticipated. She didn't spare a thought for him; his death was meaningless. She construed no pleasure in spilling his blood, and there was no wave of exhilaration as he lay dying on the ground, but her next victim would be different. She shuddered with orgasmic excitement at the thought.

In Brightmarsh, the investigation was yet again at a standstill. Castleton was scratching his head with frustration. Gully had so far been a useless witness, confirming his name and his knowledge of the secret cupboard at Molecatcher Farm, but little else. Joby was trying desperately to make a breakthrough, but progress was slow.

Meg suggested bringing in a criminal psychologist, and Castleton, having very little option, reluctantly agreed.

Meg knew just the man for the job - Spencer Gould, an ex-colleague from London whose knowledge of the science was invaluable. Meg knew that Castleton would probably butt heads with Spencer, being suspicious of outside intervention, but Spencer was a highly qualified professional with letters after his name, so what could possibly go wrong?!

The link between victims pointed unequivocally at Ayda Cross and it was imperative to find out more about her and whether she was still alive.

Spencer arrived the following day on the evening train from Euston. A short, athletic man with closely cropped hair, tattoos and an ear piercing jumped enthusiastically onto the platform and waved his arrival at Meg.

He carried a colourful backpack and a black briefcase. He was exactly as Meg remembered and they exchanged a hug and mandatory small talk.

Spencer appeared more akin to a university student than a high-achieving doctor of psychology, but to judge a book by its cover in his case would be a huge mistake.

His Scottish drawl and cheeky sense of humour had sealed their friendship years earlier, and Meg felt perfectly comfortable inviting Spencer to stay at the cottage.

Spencer was more than happy to spend a few days in the country with his old pal and had soon made himself at home.

That evening, over pizza and wine, Spencer studied the files Meg provided. He stewed over each victim: the cause of death, the timescale. He flicked back and forth through the folder and paused over photographs, muttering and scribbling notes simultaneously. He completely immersed himself in the case and Meg became invisible for a couple of hours, but she didn't mind; few people saw this side of Spencer and the intensity with which he worked.

She drained the bottle and waited patiently.

Eventually, he closed the file and pushed it back in Meg's direction.

"It's a difficult one, Meg," he said, rubbing his eyes beneath the thin metal glasses that perched on the end of his nose.

"It's definitely personal; your killer has a motive, though it's not obvious, I grant you, but killings of this nature are always motivated, be it by a past experience or childhood trauma; they are driven and your job is to find out by what. Whoever it is, they are highly organised, disciplined, focused. These are not random killings; these have been years in the planning."

"I worked all that out for myself," said a disgruntled Meg, emptying the remains of a second bottle of Merlot, "so what can you tell me that I don't know?"

Spencer looked pensive. He sat back in the chair, sipping at the remnants in his wine glass.

He closed his eyes, a symbol of his deep concentration, and then, without opening them, stated, "There will be more killings, Meg. This person has unfinished business, so you need to be very careful because the closer you get, the more dangerous it will become. This person will stop at nothing to finish the job no matter what it takes."

As Spencer opened his eyes, Meg saw the haunting look of fear staring back at her. A sudden chill descended her spine, and almost instantly, Meg felt the cold hand of fear grip her shoulder.

Much to the protestation of Castleton, Spencer spent a couple of days at the station.

He asked to visit each crime scene. He was certain that the killer attacked in the cloak of darkness and that the victims were unaware of their fate.

He felt that discovering the whereabouts of Ayda Cross was imperative to the investigation and that Gully probably knew more about the existence of the cupboard than he was prepared to say. He agreed that Joby was probably not involved, but warned that removing him from the suspect list at this stage was fruitless.

After studying the blood splatter patterns and the wounds across Hegarty Baxter and Father Maloney's throats, Spencer deduced that the killer was left-handed.

He visited the victims at the morgue and subjected each to a rigorous examination.

Spencer's profile indicated that the killer was most likely a man, as the majority of serial killers were, though he struggled with certain aspects of the crimes where he felt a woman could fit the profile better.

"You've a very dangerous person loose in the village," he said solemnly, "so my advice is to tread carefully with this one; a psychotic serial killer will do whatever it takes to avoid capture. Their focus is nothing more than achieving their goal and woe betide anyone who gets in the way.

These killings are personal, not random or sexual, and they WILL kill again."

Castleton shook Spencer by the hand and thanked him for his help. Spencer headed back to London on the 6 o'clock train and Meg headed off to meet up with Joby and Gully Cross.

CHAPTER 21

Joby and Gully were now ready to head back to Molecatcher Farm. All police cordons had been lifted and the farm was ready to call home again.

Though the macabre murder of his parents was still foremost on his mind, Joby was thankful to sleep in his own room away from the continuous grunts and snorts of Gully's nasal inhalations. Gully was not the easiest roommate and sharing such close proximity to his brother was beginning to weigh heavy on Joby.

Meg drove up the moor towards the farm. Her happy childhood memories had been replaced with stark images of the fateful evening when she had found its occupants slaughtered in cold blood. Her visits were tainted with sadness and she knew that Joby and Gully were going to find it significantly more difficult to live in the shadow of their parents' deaths.

In the rear-view mirror, Meg watched for Gully's reaction. He stared from the car window, expressionless and still. She hoped that Joby had made some progress with his brother, though she wouldn't hold her breath.

As they passed through the gate and rumbled over the cobblestone driveway, Meg stopped the car beside the back door. Gully's face was now pressed against the window, like a small child excited to be home. He jumped from the car and disappeared inside.

Meg turned to Joby. "Good luck," she joked.

Joby rolled his eyes. "At least I can get away from him here. That bedroom was getting smaller by the day. I couldn't breathe, Meg."

"Did he open up at all?"

Joby shook his head; "Sadly, not yet, but maybe being back here might help."

"I really hope so, Joby. Gully is our main suspect at the moment and unless you can get him to talk, pardon the pun, Castleton will drag him back to the station where he could possibly be charged."

Joby looked horrified; "You know Gully wouldn't hurt a fly," he protested.

"I do, but Castleton doesn't. He's just doing his job and he's been more than reasonable in allowing Gully these few days. By rights, he could hold him in a cell at the station for a considerable amount of time. You need to come up with something, and soon."

Joby acknowledged Meg's advice.

"Anything, Joby, even if you don't think it's relevant. We need to rule Gully out of our enquiries." Joby exited the car. "One last thing," said Meg. Joby turned; "Is Gully left-handed?"

Joby studied his own hands weighing up left from right, then he shook his head. "No, he's right-handed, but I am."

A couple of days later came a small breakthrough when Joby called with an update. Gully had admitted to knowing about the secret cupboard. Meg encouraged them to call at the station for coffee and an informal chat.

Joby did most of the talking, while Gully sat staring at Meg. He winked playfully and drained his coffee. There was no anxious rocking. Gully seemed much more relaxed and Meg suspected it was because he had regained his routine at home.

Gully knew that a little girl had lived in the cupboard, not all of the time, but most of it, and then one day, she had disappeared. Gully had been forbidden to visit or speak to the girl when she was locked away, but, as a baby, he had cradled her, even loved her.

The girl outgrew the cupboard and then she was gone.

Gully had been introduced to the girl soon after her birth. He knew she was his sister, though the word had no meaning to him.

"Is any of that useful?" Joby asked.

"Well, it confirms what we suspected, that someone had been caged in that wooden box, but other than that..." Castleton rubbed his neck vigorously. Gully's confession had been somewhat disappointing.

"Does he know the girl's name?" "Yes, it's A-Y-D-A," Joby spelled it aloud.

"Okay!" Castleton paced the office floor, then grabbed a file off his desk. He removed a see-through bag, which contained a single black feather. He held it in front of Gully. "Ask him if he knows what this is?"

Gully spotted the black object and let out a high-pitched scream. He rose from his seat and moved backwards, grimacing with fear as he backed himself against the wall.

"I think we have our answer," Meg stated.

"Yes, but what's the significance of it, and why is he so afraid?"

Joby grabbed the bag from Castleton's hand. "It's a feather, a raven feather," he said studying it closely.

He signed to Gully, who was frozen against the wall. Gully didn't reply. "Where did you find it?" Joby enquired.

"There was a pile of them in the wooden box where the girl was kept," answered Meg. "Strange, we don't usually see them on the moor."

With the feather out of sight, Gully took his seat. Meg quickly changed the subject. "Where did you go when you left the farm, Gully - where had you been hiding?"

Gully had spent a few nights in the barn where he was eventually discovered, daring not to approach the house as it was overrun with policemen.

Before that, he had spent a few nights in Weaver's Wood, a place he often retreated to when the atmosphere at the farm was unbearable.

Ben and Alice Cross were not averse to malicious rows, physical altercations and abuse. They raised their children in a God-fearing atmosphere, but on the odd occasion, the devil would make an unwelcome appearance.

Ben had always chastised the boys with his belt or fists, while Alice defended them with the first weapon that came to hand, but Ben was always able to overpower her and Alice would retreat more battered and bruised than her children.

Meg was astonished to hear this, as the shy, reticent Mr Cross and his meek-minded wife were the last people she would have labelled abusive.

"Don't be so naïve, Meg. They kept a child in a box - doesn't that scream abuse?" growled Castleton. He was right; the farmhouse had more than its fair share of secrets, but Meg had never seen that side of its inhabitants and Joby had never divulged such information.

The look of shame on Joby's face was all the confirmation Meg needed.

When Joby and Gully left the office, the mood became sombre. Gully's information was superfluous to the investigation and they were no nearer knowing anything about Ayda Cross. Heads were scratched, files re-read, and keyboards tapped through databases in a desperate bid to uncover one shred of vital information.

Suddenly, Thackeray rose from his seat, a look of possibility on his face. Meg and Castleton looked at each other and rushed to Thackeray's desk.

Thackeray had been going through the census of

births. He already knew that Ayda Cross existed, so he filtered the search to include Alice, and there, on the screen, was the recorded birth of a female named Ayda ATTWOOD, not Cross. The mother was stated as Alice Cross and the father as Sir Henry Attwood, as was already known.

They stared at the screen in amazement. Perhaps now their search for Ayda Attwood would be more successful than her counterpart, Ayda Cross.

Meg still found it hard to believe that Sir Henry and Alice Cross had created a child together. Had Alice been raped at his hand, or was the copulation consensual? It was difficult to imagine two extremely different human beings in such an intimate situation and Meg shook the thoughts from her mind. The question still remained - why was the child kept hidden from the world and where was she now? That was what they needed to find out.

"Ayda could have changed her name, left the country... she could be anywhere in the world, so how are we going to find her?" pondered Castleton.

"She could be dead," added Thackeray.

"Check the register of deaths for both names," Castleton ordered.

Thackeray jumped to attention. They were looking for a needle in a haystack, but now they were looking for Ayda Attwood, not Ayda Cross.

"The school database!" shouted Meg. "If she went to

school, there should be a record." Meg hurried to her desk and began typing. She searched the local area first, then widened the search by twenty miles, and then fifty.

Ayda was an unusual name and Meg hoped that the list would be minimal. Her first attempt yielded three hundred Aydas, but a swift alteration brought the total down to one hundred; still a fair few names to trawl through, so it was going to be a long night.

As midnight came and went, Meg had whittled her list down to six possibilities, leaving only the Aydas with the middle name of Rose.

Discarded pizza boxes and empty coffee mugs, an indication of their late-night activities, were strewn around the office, alongside the six possible sitting on the table. In a couple of hours, the domestics would enter to clean up their leftovers; for now, it was time to go home and recharge.

Meg found it difficult to switch off. That night, sleep was an inconvenience. As daylight broke, she was back in the office.

As Castleton and Thackeray arrived, they glanced at each other - all wore the baggy signs of sleep deprivation, but all were desperate to get on with the investigation.

Coffee bubbled in the corner, cup after cup fuelling their thirst, energising their search and driving them forward through the list of possibilities.

There was a renewed buzz around the office, a quiet,

understated excitement that Ayda Attwood was on the list.

By lunchtime that day, the first two Aydas had been eliminated - one had died in a car accident in Scotland and the other had moved to Australia. Once it was certain that these two were definitely not the Ayda in question, the remaining four became suddenly more important.

Thackeray took the third Ayda and gave Meg the fourth.

It was nearing 5:30 when Meg received a call back regarding Ayda number four. Her pen doodled nervously as the voice on the phone spoke promising words about a girl called Ayda Rose Cosward. She scribbled down the address for St. Agatha's Convent in Brooker Cross and, within no time at all, Meg and Castleton were en route.

CHAPTER 22
St. Agatha's Convent

Ten miles outside of Brightmarsh, the countryside morphed from open meadows and moorland to areas of thick, overgrown forest. A canopy of ageing oak trees arched above the roadway, clad in coats of ivy, so thick that even daylight struggled to make an impression.

Ahead in the distance, as the veil of trees thinned, the gothic structure of St. Agatha's Convent came into view. A tedious stretch of driveway led to a grey and white stone dwelling, the neglected remains of a bygone era. Nature had clawed her way through the immense depth of stonework and ravaged the building's facade.

It was as old as it looked; originally built to house the Order of St. Cuthberts, it had been abandoned by the monks and left to decay for almost a century.

Cardinal Pius Batista had ordered that the convent be reopened in the early sixties and sent an order of nuns from the Sisters of Charity to live there. It was named after the first Mother Superior, Sister Agatha.

"This looks like a fun place to have grown up," joked Castleton as he exited the car. He wasn't wrong; the place had an eerie vibe and that was just the outside.

The grand doors of its entrance were slightly ajar allowing Meg and Castleton to slip inside uninvited.

The gothic decor mimicked the set of a horror movie. Wooden crucifixes adorned the walls and religious statues occupied every nook and cranny along the length of a cold, desolate corridor. In stark contrast, an ornately carved staircase wore a warm shade of mellowed oak. In any other setting, it would have been considered an artistic triumph, yet here, in this building, it was merely the wooden skeleton that held up this monstrous structure.

Passing the portrait of Sister Agatha, Castleton cast Meg an uneasy glance. It was safe to say that Sister Agatha would make anyone feel uneasy - unearthly eyes shrouded in black, a pointed jaw and a twisted expression followed Meg and Castleton as they searched for signs of life.

There was little comfort to be drawn from any part of this place for the girls who were unlucky enough to call it home.

Castleton moved past a door marked 'Office'. He knocked gently and waited for a response. Only silence answered back.

Meg explored the opposite trajectory, lined with faded woven tapestries. Once alive with vivid colour, they now hung as dull and lifeless as the rest of the place.

Suddenly, a nun appeared. She caught sight of Meg and moved towards her.

Meg explained the reason for her visit and the nun, saying nothing, ushered her into a nearby room. She disappeared from view without a word and reappeared with a visibly older nun beside her.

"I am Sister Clair, the Mother Superior; how may I help you?"

Castleton had joined them and gave the nun a brief summary of the investigation.

Sister Clair guided them back along the hallway to the 'Office'. She removed a ring of keys from beneath her cassock and unlocked the door.

The air inside hung heavy with a damp and musty odour. The room held a regimented line of filing cabinets blanketed in thick dust, and it was obvious the room had been unused for quite some time.

Sister Clair, unfazed by the huge spider that hung between the handles of the top two drawers of the first cabinet, tugged at the top drawer, sending the spider and the remnants of its delicately woven home hurtling towards the floor. The spider scurried away taking refuge beneath the cabinet, the remaining fine strands of its demolished web left dangling, all of which remained unnoticed by Sister Clair.

She coaxed a couple of files from the front of the drawer and passed them to Castleton.

Visible black ink written on the side of the files displayed Ayda Wood on one and Ayda Cosward on the other. Castleton soon discarded Ayda Wood's file and handed it back to the patiently waiting nun.

He opened the second file and placed it on a nearby

desk. Inside, the photo of a young girl stared back.

She was aged around 7 with mousy brown plaits framing an angelic smile. Amazing hazel eyes sought out the camera lens with confidence and her image was immortalised forever.

The child in the photograph had the face of an angel, but her file showed otherwise. A bundle of detentions and incident reports accompanied the young girl's image.

Castleton looked towards the Sister and enquired, "She was a problem child?"

The Sister nodded and sighed; "I'm afraid she was much more than a problem - she was a curse upon this Convent. The other children were afraid of her. She wreaked havoc in the classroom and disruption wherever she went."

"But she looks so ..."

"So innocent?" Sister Clair scoffed. "Don't be fooled by her angelic features. There was more of the devil in that child than any other I have come across in my thirty-something years working with children." Sister Clair spoke with desperation in her voice. "It was a relief when she was transferred away. The day Ayda Cosward left St. Agatha's was an enormous relief to everyone." Castleton threw a questioning look towards Meg, plucked a black feather from the girl's file and held it up before Sister Clair. "Why is this in her file?"

The Sister shuddered visibly, her face gaunt as she

mumbled, "I...I didn't realise that was still in there. It belonged to her."

"And what is the significance of it?" questioned Meg.

"She had a kind of pet; a raven. She talked to it constantly. Whenever she had done something bad, she would always be holding a black feather; then she would grin and say 'he made me do it', pointing at the bird."

"Where did she get the bird from?"

"It came with her, or rather, it followed her here. Apparently, it lived with her and she wouldn't leave without it. She was a very disturbed child."

Meg and Castleton exchanged glances. The feather was not a total surprise, after all, they had found handfuls in the makeshift cupboard, but the fact that one had turned up at the Convent suddenly gave their investigation an eerie turn.

"Do you know where she was transferred to and by whom?" queried Castleton. The Sister nodded. Castleton shot a hopeful glance towards Meg.

"She was assessed by several different professionals and they all concluded that the child needed specialist mental care. She was relocated to an asylum." Sister Clair's memory failed to recall the name, but she knew the district. It wouldn't be too hard to track it down.

Castleton thanked the nun for her help and tucked the little girl's file under his arm as they headed for the exit. Once outside, Meg turned back; "One last question, Sister

- who was responsible for the transfer of Ayda Cosward?"

Without a flicker of hesitation, the Sister replied, "Hegarty Baxter and Father Maloney from the church at Brightmarsh."

Meg threw a thankful nod in her direction and turned back towards Castleton. Finally, there was the hint of a connection between the murders.

The car journey back was mostly silent. Both were deep in thought over the information Sister Clair had provided and both were slightly shocked to discover that the two people involved with Ayda Cosward were now lying in the hospital morgue.

Back in the office, Thackeray set to work searching for the asylum that Ayda Cosward had been transferred to.

There were five listed in the district Sister Clair had named.

Thackeray got a hit immediately - Ayda Cosward had been an in-patient at The Good Samaritan Asylum in Lancaster.

Meg drove home that evening feeling a sense of achievement for the first time since she had found the unfortunate Mr and Mrs Cross. She walked Pepper across the green before bed. She was certain that sleep would come easily tonight.

Meg was just about to retire to bed with a glass of red wine and a good book when her phone began to vibrate silently. The number was not recognisable and Meg ignored the call, settling under the duvet with Pepper beside her. The book, though perfectly readable, brought with it the uncontrollable urge to sleep.

As she reached for the bedside lamp, she noticed a voicemail symbol lighting up her phone. Meg, forever inquisitive, could not ignore it. The voice, female and eventually recognisable as Lilia Attwood, was inviting Meg to another evening soirée at the Manor House. Meg checked her calendar; the date was a Saturday. She sighed heavily. The last thing she wanted to do on a weekend was play social butterfly in a room filled with pretentious strangers.

On the other hand, though, it would be rude to decline, after all, the last dinner at the Manor House had been incredible fun.

CHAPTER 23
The Good Samaritan Asylum

The following morning, Meg rose earlier than usual. She felt refreshed, though slightly fuzzy, the after-effects of too much wine. A brisk walk in the chilly air would soon remedy that, and by eight, she was showered and on her way to pick up Castleton.

He looked as though he hadn't slept a wink, his curly untamed hair desperate for the attention of a comb, and his lower jaw sporting far more stubble than usual.

Meg thought it best not to pry into his personal life, so she handed him a homemade latte and they headed off to Lancaster.

The journey took longer than anticipated - the usual volume of slow-moving traffic, motorway repairs and speed restrictions meant that it was almost lunchtime when they reached their destination.

They stopped beside an old-style Inn and lunched al fresco in the midday sun. Castleton had missed breakfast and hunger made him grouchy. That explained a lot, thought Meg silently.

She knew very little about Castleton, nor he about her. Their conversations had strictly adhered to work, but a pint of ale seemed to lighten his mood. He even removed his jacket and loosened his tie.

It seemed that Castleton had been the victim of infidelity and his marriage had broken down because of it. He had lost trust in love and had thrown himself into work, refusing to be distracted by a pretty face or sexy figure.

He knew that Meg was widowed, and was sympathetic as Meg unburdened herself and reminisced about the man with whom she had expected to live out her life.

With the table cleared away and the last drops of liquid drained, the reality of their visit came back into focus. The lunch had been a success in terms of getting to know Castleton and understanding his seemingly brisk manner. They walked back to the car and Meg found herself looking at Castleton with a faint fluttering inside.

Twenty minutes later, they had reached the gates of the Good Samaritan Asylum.

It was an imposing, purpose-built structure mounted on three floors of grey concrete, with barred windows and security cameras aplenty, mounted like technical spies on every facet of the building. On first impression, it looked more like a prison than a hospital.

An intercom system allowed Meg to announce their arrival and they were greeted by a dark-haired little man with a slug-sized moustache who introduced himself as the Manager, Dr Frobisher.

Once inside, Meg and Castleton were escorted to Frobisher's office.

The smell of cleaning fluids was overpowering; the sharp acrid odour of disinfectant clawed at their nostrils with a burning ferocity.

Frobisher offered coffee and biscuits, a tour of the facility and help in any way that he could. When Ayda Cosward was mentioned, Frobisher became fidgety and visibly anxious. He crossed and uncrossed his arms, his voice pitched slightly higher and beads of perspiration formed on his brow. He opened a window and gulped a glass of water with a trembling hand.

"I hadn't realised you had come to talk about Ayda," he stuttered.

"Any information you can disclose about her would be most valuable, Dr Frobisher." Castleton looked towards Meg and then back to Frobisher.

"Ayda Cosward is not a person one wishes to remember," spluttered Frobisher reaching for more water. "I had hoped never to hear that name again."

Frobisher reached for his telephone and pressed a button that connected to a secretary in a different office.

"Ms Appleton, could you page Sister Maguire for me, please."

A polite woman's voice answered, "Of course, Dr Frobisher." He wiped a discoloured handkerchief across his brow.

Frobisher nervously explained, "Sister Maguire is the best person to speak to with regards to Ayda Cosward.

She has had first-hand experience of the girl and no one knows what she was capable of more than her."

Sister Maguire bustled into the room minutes later. Greying hair cut as a sharp bob around her ears, thick pink glasses and a generous figure was the best way to describe her. She had a no-nonsense attitude about her, an authoritative manner and a brusque tone to her voice. Meg could not imagine anyone getting the better of Sister Maguire.

"You asked for me, Darryl?" she queried.

"Yes, yes, Bunny, these police officers need some information on…" he hesitated for a moment as if the name would send Sister Maguire running in the opposite direction.

"Spit it out, man, I haven't got all day."

"A-A-Ayda Cosward," stuttered Frobisher, his eyes not daring to look in Sister Maguire's direction.

Sister Maguire's cheeks drained from a rosy glow to ghostly white in seconds. Meg offered the nurse her seat, as the poor woman looked on the verge of collapse. Bunny Maguire sat down and placed a shaky hand to her cheek. Whatever problems Ayda Cosward had caused here, the mere mention of her name had had an incredible effect on these two individuals.

Castleton grew impatient; sympathetic as he was to Sister Maguire's visible shock, he craved answers.

"I assume from your reactions that Ayda Cosward was

a memorable patient, and not in a good way?" questioned Castleton.

The Sister fanned her face with a file from Frobisher's desk as the colour slowly returned to her cheeks.

"Ayda Cosward," Bunny began, "was the patient that no one will ever forget. She was the most evil child I have ever had the misfortune to nurse, and I cannot deny that I for one was more than happy when she disappeared."

Dr Frobisher nodded his agreement. "Please elaborate?"

Bunny shot a look to Frobisher. "Tell them, Bunny, tell them everything," he said.

Bunny Maguire poured herself a glass of water, took a deep breath and began. "Ayda Cosward came to us from St. Agatha's Convent at the request of Father Maloney and a social worker, whose name I can't recall. She had wreaked havoc on the nuns and children of St. Agatha's for three years with feral, uncontrollable behaviour. It was impossible to keep her isolated and she became obscenely violent when locked in her room.

Professional assessment concluded that she needed care in a facility for the mentally insane, hence her arrival here.

She accused Father Maloney of sexual abuse.

She set fire to Sister Maura's habit and it was only the swift actions of the other nuns that saved her. The child was seen roaming the corridors at night sneaking into other rooms and convincing her peers that horrible things were going to happen to them. One girl threw herself from the roof of the convent after sharing a room with her."

Bunny paused for breath. It was obvious from the strained look on her face that recalling the escapades of Ayda Cosward was not only mentally, but physically draining.

"You're doing great," encouraged Meg, "please continue."

Bunny took another sip of water and began again. "Dr Frobisher reluctantly agreed to admit the child to our care. She had been refused by several other hospitals and institutions. We were, I suppose, her last resort and he," she flashed a disapproving scowl towards Frobisher, "did not feel that an eight-year-old would be too difficult for us to manage!

On first meeting, she was withdrawn, pale and appeared undernourished. Bright almond-shaped eyes peered from beneath a bush of matted hair. We suspected she had been sedated for the journey and we were right.

As she regained total consciousness, her issues became spontaneously apparent. We placed her on mild sedation; it was the only way to keep her under control, and she had sessions with our resident psychiatrist, Amelia Beddoe."

"Did the sessions work?" interrupted Castleton.

"Not to begin with, but eventually, she began to calm down and even communicated on a couple of occasions, which was a massive step forward.

Then, just when we thought there was a breakthrough she filed a complaint with Dr Beddoe about Dr Frobisher, accusing him of sexual abuse."

Bunny flashed a troubled glance towards Frobisher, who sat quietly with his head in his hands. "She described the events in such explicit detail that Dr Beddoe found it impossible not to report the matter."

"It happened more than once?" Castleton probed. "According to her, yes."

Frobisher's face was now redder than the scarlet handkerchief poking from his jacket pocket. "Of course, there was no truth in it at all," he exclaimed, "but when the child was interviewed, she gave an Oscar-winning performance and I was suspended from duty with immediate effect."

Meg could see that Frobisher had been devastated by the actions of the eight-year-old.

"I lost everything because of that girl," he sobbed. "My wife left me and she wouldn't allow me to see my own children. I became a social pariah and yet, I never touched her,"

Bunny patted his hand sympathetically as his eyes welled with tears. She placed a box of tissues within reach and Frobisher wiped the sadness from his face.

"He's been to hell and back, poor man, but he's slowly rebuilding his life."

Dr Frobisher requested tea and biscuits for his guests; it lightened the mood slightly and he was able to regain his dignity before the next round of questions.

"That must have been an incredibly difficult time for you, Dr Frobisher, but besides that incident with yourself, did anything else happen?" Meg began the questions again once the plate of biscuits was empty.

Bunny sat forward in her chair. "How long have you got?" she scoffed.

"As long as it takes," came the reply.

"She would steal and deny it even though the item would be found in her possession. She would bite her own arm and blame the person nearest to her.

She broke one patient's arm when she wouldn't pass the tv remote.

One lunchtime, she stabbed another patient in the eye with her fork, and she disembowelled our resident cat.

She dismembered a rat and added it to the dinner-time soup. We had three patients hospitalised because of it.

She tried to strangle her roommate so that she could have a room to herself and she told one of our paranoid schizophrenics that she had put a spell on her. We found her the following morning hanging in her bedroom.

Need I go on?" Bunny sank back in her chair, visibly drained.

"We have a whole cellar full of her shenanigans if you

care to take a look," added Dr Frobisher. Castleton shook his head. "No, thanks, just a few more questions then we will leave you alone. How did she escape?"

"Well, there's a question we cannot answer," replied the doctor. "We feel she had inside help, but don't quote me on that; it's pure speculation."

"No CCTV?"

"Yes, but it had failed; power cut, apparently." Frobisher rolled his eyes in disbelief. "Did anyone contact her at all?" probed Castleton.

Frobisher paused for thought; "Yes, but no idea who it was. One day, a mobile phone was delivered addressed to her. We don't allow them and it was never given to her and as far as we knew she had no knowledge of it, but that phone disappeared from the office a couple of days later and we never found it."

"The night staff reported that they had heard her talking to someone, but she always maintained it was to her imaginary pet."

"Did that pet happen to be a black bird, a raven?"

Bunny looked confused. "Yes, that's correct. You mean it was real?"

Castleton explained the relevance of the raven and Bunny's face turned a paler shade of white once again.

"I wondered where she got the feathers from," Bunny muttered. "You found feathers?"

"It was her calling card of sorts. Whenever she had

done something bad, she would leave a black feather at the scene. She would never talk about the reason behind it, but maintained that it was the bird that made her do it."

It had been a long afternoon and the interview was over. Dr Frobisher suggested they visit the local police station, as they had investigated Ayda's disappearance and instigated an extensive manhunt.

Meg and Castleton headed for the car.

"We need to contact Lancaster's cold case unit and missing persons," stated Castleton. "Ayda Cosward should be an unsolved case, and it could be useful to check their file on her. You never know, we might find something helpful."

"You think she's still alive then?" questioned Meg.

Castleton nodded. "Yes, but where?"

He grabbed the keys from Meg's hand. "I'll drive back," he smiled. "Don't trust my driving?" she joked.

There went those butterflies again!

She felt a new sensation; pride! The village coppers had discovered her artwork - everyone was talking about it. Her gallery of murder scenes had caused quite a stir.

She smiled wryly imagining the horror-struck faces of the discoverers. She wished she had been there to see them in person. It would have been so satisfying. She would put Brightmarsh on the map, and her murders would become iconic studies for budding psychologists. She would be written and talked about for years after her death. She would never be forgotten about again.

NEVER!

She was needed. A deep breath, a wand of lip gloss and a last fleeting glance in the mirror and she vanished down the corridor. She paused in the doorway, painted on her smile and entered the room.

CHAPTER 24
The Next Victim

That Saturday night invitation from Lilia Attwood had caught Meg by surprise. It was marked on her calendar, but somehow, it had managed to creep up on her and tonight was the night.

Meg had been smiling a lot more since her return from Lancaster. She had fallen asleep in the car. Castleton had thrown a thoughtful blanket over her and driven home in silence.

Outside the cottage, Meg offered to drive Castleton home, but he politely declined and headed off to his aunt's B&B.

Meg showered, curled her hair, painted her nails and even applied a little makeup. It was the first time since she lost Michael that she had taken the trouble to pamper herself. Pearl earrings and a sequinned dress completed the look. She glanced in the mirror. "My god, Meg, you look half decent for once!" She smiled and headed out of the door.

Just as before, Abby greeted her with squeals of excitement. Champagne was flowing and the house looked and smelled amazing.

Joby had not received an invitation and, from the look of the guests arriving, Meg could see why. Lilia had brought together an intimate evening of influential and celebrity VIPs. Lilia's message had cited, 'just a small soirée, darling, intimate, with a handpicked selection of guests.'

Perhaps Lilia, with her limited understanding of the English language, had not fully grasped the meaning of 'small'. The soirée appeared to be quite the party as guests continued to arrive over the next hour.

Theo and his latest conquest, Verity Hobbs, an Irish folk singer from Dublin, had made the guest list. There were a handful of celebrities, a couple of MPs and Sir Henry's business partner, the billionaire, Adam Cornish.

Meg felt a little lonely without Joby, as Abby had abandoned her for the arrival of her favourite singer. Abby, fuelled with champagne, opted to spend the evening hanging on the singer's every word. Meg could not deny her friend the chance to meet her idol and she slipped into the drawing room to acquire another glass of bubbly.

It was quite unexpected, but, in Meg's opinion, marvellous timing as Sergeant Castleton entered the room.

He looked extremely uncomfortable as he surveyed the splendour of the Manor House. Darrow approached him with champagne. He gratefully lifted a glass and sipped cautiously from the exquisite crystal stem.

"Quite something, isn't it?" Meg whispered, standing just behind his left shoulder.

Castleton spun around spraying champagne in every direction. Meg giggled as he searched himself and the Persian rug beneath his feet for spillage.

"Relax, these floors are practically coated in champagne," she joked.

Castleton was speechless for a moment. "Meg, I didn't expect to see you here."

"Well, I'll have you know that I have rubbed shoulders with the rich and famous before, even if it does seem hard to believe," she teased.

Castleton blushed slightly, spluttering in his attempt to find the correct response.

"Relax, I'm joking. Abby Attwood is one of my best friends. I'm practically part of the family. I grew up here." Castleton shrugged away the anxious tension in his shoulders and smiled.

"I would never have recognised you. You look so... so... different!" His eyes surveyed the length of her body and he blushed again.

Meg wouldn't have believed that Castleton could blush if she hadn't seen it with her own eyes. He had always seemed so confident, even bolshy, especially in the workplace.

Tonight, there was a tenderness about him, a side she hadn't seen, a side she definitely liked. Their eyes were locked in hypnotic contemplation.

Suddenly, the moment was gone as Sir Henry and Lilia Attwood entered the room. All eyes turned to greet them.

Henry was debonair and handsome in white tuxedo and black tie, and Lilia, breathtaking in floor-length lurex gown.

Meg threw a glance towards Castleton, who was visibly mesmerised by Lilia's beauty, as all men usually were.

She worked the room with grace and poise; she laughed in the right places, she listened with interest, and she welcomed her guests with a kiss or a handshake.

As she moved towards Meg, Castleton shuffled beside her, his eyes glazed over, a bead of sweat on his forehead and a boyish grin on his lips.

"Meg, so lovely to see you! I'm so glad you could make it." Lilia's purring accent was an aphrodisiac in a voice; even Meg felt light-headed. She leaned in for a fake kiss then turned her attention to Castleton, extending a perfectly toned arm towards him.

"Who do we have here?" she teased. "You must be the detective who works with Meg." Castleton, now smiling like a Cheshire Cat, eyes glinting with excitement, took Lilia's hand in his and bent to place a kiss upon it.

Lilia ran her other hand through the thick tussle of hair in a soft stroking movement. Castleton, resuming an upright position, was almost dribbling. Meg wanted to retch as Castleton morphed into a pubescent teenager beside her.

"Please enjoy the evening, Mr Castleton. I'm sure we shall meet again."

Lilia floated away in the direction of her husband,

leaving Castleton in a catatonic state.

Suddenly, the sound of a gong bellowed through the room and Castleton regained his composure. Darrow announced that dinner was served and everyone made their way into the dining room.

Meg was seated to the right of Sir Henry with Abby sitting opposite. Abby's infatuation was seated to her left. Lilia, as usual, took her seat at the other end of the table and Castleton was seated to her right. Meg had a clear view down the table.

Theo and Verity were sitting opposite Castleton. He looked as uncomfortable as Meg felt, but she knew the secret to surviving an evening at the Manor House was never to refuse a drink, which was usually offered at very frequent intervals.

By the time dessert was served, Meg had lost interest in Castleton and was deep in conversation with her neighbour, the Right Honourable Percy Hough, QC.

Percy drank like a fish, and, at this point in the evening, was absolutely bladdered, but his stories of cases he'd tried in the High Court were considerably amusing and Meg found him a most entertaining dinner fellow.

The evening was now in full swing, intoxication peeling back the complex layers of human beings. The shy became bold and the loud became louder; the stuffiness of aristocracy vanishing with each swig of the grape. Even Castleton had shed the awkwardness of the evening and was fully immersed in conversation at his end of the table.

Darrow, dutifully filling drained glasses, circled constantly like a hapless vulture.

Sir Henry took to his feet with champagne in hand and raised his glass to propose a toast to the success of Lilia's dinner party. He drained the crystal flute with practised ease, proud and satisfied with his new wife's achievement. The table roared with rapturous applause and all eyes turned to Lilia, but her appreciative nods and smiles quickly dissipated and grimaces of anguish and despair replaced them. She rose slowly from her chair, eyes never wavering from her husband, and she let out a blood-curdling scream.

The room fell silent. All eyes turned back towards Henry, who was slumped sideways in his chair. A chaotic moment of shock ensued as chairs scattered and crystal glasses hit the ground, in the realisation that Sir Henry Attwood was dead.

Lilia rushed to his side, shaking him violently, ordering him to respond.

Meg searched for Castleton, who was talking on his mobile and heading in her direction.

"I've called for an ambulance," he said, as he passed behind Meg's chair. Pulling Lilia aside and dragging Henry to the floor, he began CPR. Another guest, Dr Razma, a renowned pathologist from the Royal London joined him, then, placing a hand on Castleton's arm, he shook his head slowly. The procedure was futile; Henry was already gone.

Lilia, sobbing uncontrollably, was comforted by Theo

and his girlfriend. Abby sat in stunned silence, unable to move from her seat. Meg was there to console her friend, whilst keeping her eyes on Castleton and Sir Henry.

It seemed like an age before sirens broke the silence of the evening. Two paramedics attended, but there was little they could do but confirm Henry's demise.

Castleton took Meg aside. "I can't be certain, but I think Henry was murdered," he whispered. Meg looked back at him in shock. "What do you mean, murdered, how?"

"Look at his face; I think he's been poisoned," was Castleton's reply.

Meg had assumed Sir Henry had suffered a sudden and massive heart attack.

His lifeless body was being zipped into a black bag ready for its journey to the morgue, but Meg stepped forward just in time to see the bluish tint of Henry's face disappearing beneath the plastic, and just like that, he was gone.

Lilia had been taken to her room with Dr Razma administering a dose of sedation to calm her distress.

Abby and Theo were consoling each other in a warm embrace.

Darrow was handing out shots of brandy for the shattered nerves of the evening's guests. "What do you suppose we should do now?" asked Meg.

"Well, we need an autopsy to confirm my suspicion, but that could take days. If Henry was indeed murdered, then this room is a crime scene and all of these people are suspects!"

Distraught guests were ordering taxis to take them home. Furs and overcoats were distributed. The smokers retreated outside to calm their nerves with a puff of nicotine.

Castleton jumped into detective mode and sensibly compiled a list of guests and their contact details as they each exited the Manor House.

Soon the dining room was empty. Darrow began collecting glasses. Castleton caught his eye; "Please, don't touch anything," he ordered.

Darrow glanced at Meg, who nodded her agreement.

Darrow, confused and very tired from his twelve-hour shift, asked to be excused from his duties. "Grab Henry's glass," instructed Castleton.

Meg took a clean napkin to wrap around Sir Henry's flute, but as she arrived at Sir Henry's placement, she noticed a dark object float quietly from the damask material of his carver to the polished oak beneath.

It was a feather, black as the night, laying on the floor where Henry's lifeless body had rested.

The arrival of forensics was formidable. Castleton was guarding the dining room like a soldier on patrol.

Meg was feeling drained; the sobering event of Henry's death was beginning to take its toll. She crashed on a sofa by the roaring fire of the drawing room and closed her eyes.

When she awoke several hours later, daylight lit the room and the cold pile of ashes in the grate was a vivid reminder of why Meg had spent the night at the Manor House.

For a moment, she hoped that last night had been a bad dream, a sleep-driven nightmare, but the reality of Castleton's voice echoing down the majestic hallway confirmed it was not.

Castleton was in the kitchen drinking coffee with Thackeray and Abby who had struggled to find sleep following her father's sudden death.

Meg approached with caution, uncertain as to what Castleton had disclosed to her friend, though surely Abby had questioned his presence almost twelve hours later.

Castleton reached for the coffee pot and refilled his mug, the signs of sleep deprivation evident in his bloodshot eyes.

"Good morning! Fancy a coffee?" he asked as he caught sight of Meg.

"Yes, please."

Meg perched on a stool beside Abby at the kitchen island and hugged the coffee mug for comfort. She reached for Abby's hand and squeezed. No words were needed. Abby smiled with gratitude through tear-filled eyes.

Meg, Castleton and Thackeray left the Manor House an hour or so later and headed back to the station, detouring for a much-needed change of clothes on the way.

Thackeray rang Lancaster police for information on

the missing Ayda Cosward. Castleton disappeared to the forensic lab eager to confirm Sir Henry's cause of death and Meg was left to view the guest list that Castleton had compiled.

She had no idea what she was looking for, but Castleton was adamant that Sir Henry had been murdered and the culprit's name was on that list.

The Manor House staff, apart from Darrow, had been given the evening off unless they worked in the kitchen. There were only two cooks working on the menu that night and statements had been taken from both. Neither left the kitchen until the last dish had been served and both left for home at the same time. Food samples had been taken for analysis, as had drink samples, of which there were many.

The list comprised of Darrow, five celebrities, Abby, Theo, Theo's girlfriend, Lilia, Dr Razma and his wife, Castleton, Meg, Percy Hough QC and his partner, Hugh Brightman, Henry's business partner Adam Cornish, his girlfriend, Swedish model Inge Stoltz, MP Jackson Coulby, MP Sebastian Brogan and Brigadier Alec Darling.

Meg crossed out her own name, Castleton's, Abby's and Theo's. She could vouch for Abby and even Theo, who might be an egotistical prick but was not capable of murder.

She split the list into two and passed one to Thackeray, who, whilst waiting for Lancaster police to forward their missing person's file on Ayda Cosward, had agreed to help.

"What exactly am I looking for?" he asked.

Meg wasn't sure herself, but someone who was willing to kill another person usually had a reason for doing so, whether it was justified or not.

"Look into their history, how they knew Attwood, if they had money problems, that sort of thing." Thackeray nodded and set to work.

First on Meg's list was Dr Razma and his wife, Suriya, also a doctor. They both worked at the Royal London Hospital, had a small family, no debts and no motive. They met Henry at Oxbridge and had remained good friends.

Adam Cornish had made his money on the stock exchange. He met Henry at a gentleman's club in Soho, where they bonded over whiskey and formed a friendship. Fifteen years ago, they had set up an internet business, the yields from which were fruitful and both lived a lavish lifestyle on the proceeds, sharing a penchant for shooting, fast cars and beautiful women.

Adam never married, preferring to take the bachelor approach to love and changing his women as often as he did his cars, his current girlfriend being a Swedish supermodel.

He had more money than he could ever spend, he raced around Europe in obscenely expensive yachts and had more homes than he did cars.

Adam Cornish was not likely to be the murderer since he had no motive or violent tendencies.

Percy Hough, QC and his partner, Hugh Brightman

lived a modest life in London's Hampstead in a third-floor apartment overlooking the heath.

For two successful barristers, their lifestyle was meagre by comparison. Percy was once a married man with three children living in a large house in Chelsea. He led a double life with Hugh under the cover of darkness. Mrs Hough, fearing her husband's late-night absences were the product of extramarital dalliances, employed the services of a private investigator.

When photographs of Percy and Hugh dropped through her letterbox, the jig was up and Percy had to come clean about his sexuality. Divorce followed and Percy, feeling disgraced and embarrassed by his actions, pledged most of the settlement to his wife and children.

He moved in with Hugh, acquiring two spaniels, who he happily walks across the heath twice a day, while Hugh continues to practice law and bring home a necessary salary.

A poignant story and a definitive explanation for the two barristers' unglamorous lifestyle, but no motive for murder, and they were crossed from the list.

The last name on Meg's list was that of Verity Hobbs. The Irish folk singer had met Theo on holiday in Thailand. There was nothing in her history to suggest that she had ever met Sir Henry before that night and no reason to consider that she would have committed his murder.

Thackeray was enjoying himself rummaging through the lives of the rich and famous, but the five celebrities on his list were far too immersed in themselves to have taken the time to plan and execute a murder. Apart from a couple of drug violations, none had a history of violence or had done time in jail.

"We don't think Henry's murder is linked to the others, do we?" enquired Thackeray.

Until that moment, the thought had never crossed Meg's mind. She and Castleton were treating this as a separate incident. She pondered a while before answering.

"Not unless you find something that makes us think otherwise."

The question was now planted deep inside Meg's head. Henry Attwood was the biological father of Ayda Cosward, and that linked him indirectly to all the other victims, save the unfortunate hiker.

It was now even more imperative to find the elusive Ayda and quickly.

Thackeray rummaged through the lives of the two MPs who attended Lilia's dinner party. They were both minor back-benchers who had been introduced to Henry at the gentleman's club that he and Adam Cornish frequented. There were no financial or business links between them and Sir Henry, and it appeared that their only crime was an appreciation of smooth whiskey and fine women.

Brigadier Darling was an old army friend. His family tree showed distant connections with the Royals. The Brigadier was old school; raised by aristocracy, he was an Englishman to the core. He had nothing to gain from Sir

Henry's death; in fact, Henry had saved the Brigadier's life back in Ireland when a bomb exploded on the Irish border and Sinn Fein opened fire. The Brigadier was visiting barracks that day when Henry's lightning response pushed him to the floor to avoid a bullet.

He was crossed from the list.

"Should I look into Darrow?" asked Thackeray.

"If he's on your list, then yes," replied Meg.

She felt certain that Darrow wasn't involved. He, like the Brigadier, had met Sir Henry during his time in the Army, when he was assigned to be Sir Henry's 'batman', an old term for a modern-day valet.

A batman acted as an officer's driver/bodyguard. Darrow was responsible for serving Sir Henry's meals, preparing his uniform and any other miscellaneous tasks as required. In battle, he would have carried his rifle. An officer and his valet formed a strong bond, hence, when Sir Henry announced his retirement from the army, he brought Darrow to live at the Manor House in his continued service.

Darrow had never married and considered the Attwood family to be his surrogate relatives. He had served them dutifully for decades, loving every moment, and was honoured to have been considered worthy enough of the position by his Commanding Officer.

Daylight was waning; the guest list had taken up most of the day and the colleagues were tired.

"Shall we call it a day, Thackeray?"

"I just have one last name to check," he replied.

Meg began closing down her computer and tidying her desk. She had promised Thackeray a ride home that night, his usual mode of transport sporting a recent puncture.

Castleton came rushing through the door waving the lab report. "I was right! Henry was poisoned!" Catching his breath from the excitement of his prediction, he placed the report in front of Meg.

It confirmed that Henry had died from cyanide poisoning; high levels were detected in his plasma and blood lactate levels.

The amount ingested would have caused an immediate heart attack.

"If you wanted to kill someone and make it look like a heart attack, this is what you would use," explained Castleton.

"And hope that you didn't have two detectives at your dinner table," added Meg.

"If you guys hadn't been at the party that night, then Henry's death would not have been attributed to murder, but to a massive and sudden heart attack," said Thackeray.

"The big question is how was the cyanide administered?"

They looked from one to the other. Meg sighed and rebooted her computer; they couldn't leave now, there was too much information to investigate.

Thackeray set the coffee machine in motion - it was definitely going to be needed.

Oh, what a night! She laughed malevolently. It could not have gone better. The planning, the preparation - it was all worth it. Henry Attwood was dead. He had deserved a more painful ending but circumstance forbade it.

She hadn't felt the rush of exhilaration that her previous killings had emanated, but the theatrical ambience and the unsuspecting audience with their shocked reaction had allowed a certain feeling of closure and satisfaction for a job well done.

CHAPTER 25
Inge Stoltz

The last name on Thackeray's list was that of Inge Stoltz, Swedish model and current girlfriend of Adam Cornish.

He was complacent that her background checks would yield nothing of interest or indeed any link between the Swedish beauty and Sir Henry, but he continued nevertheless.

Inge had grown up in Sweden, began modelling at a very young age, travelled the globe and amassed her own extensive fortune. She had walked the world's most famous catwalks for the world's most famous designers, and dated some of the world's most eligible men.

Thackeray was about to strike her name off his list when he noticed a photograph of Inge and Adam Cornish exiting a gentleman's club in London's Soho. Enhancing the image, he discovered that the club was the same one frequented by Henry and his male acquaintances.

The photo itself was uneventful, but the headline was most interesting. It read: "BILLIONAIRE ADAM CORNISH DATES GENTLEMAN'S CLUB DANCER, INGE STOLTZ."

The story had broken several years earlier, when Inge, who was living in London, had, by her own admission, taken up a resident dance position at the famous club in her search for a wealthy husband. She was, at that time, relatively unknown in the modelling world, and it was Cornish who had propelled her to catwalk stardom. They had a very public on/off relationship and stories about them frequented the news on an almost weekly basis.

Inge was reported to have a very fiery temper and her jealousy turned to rage at the mere mention of another woman's name. Adam, who had never had a monogamous relationship in his life, was smitten by the leggy model and swore to remain faithful to her, and her alone.

Thackeray trudged through the plethora of articles that made any mention of the Swede's name, but Inge had graced the cover of the world's most renown magazines which made his work extremely time-consuming.

Eventually, he discovered a photograph of Sir Henry and Inge Stoltz together at a glamorous hotel in New York. Inge was hanging from Sir Henry's arm, posing for the paparazzi who had gathered inside the hotel to catch a snap of her. On closer inspection, the article revealed that she had once dated the infamous Sir Henry Attwood, but in an interview at a later date, the eligible Lord had described her as, 'not marriage material'.

Thackeray pulled the team together to exhibit his findings.

"That's very interesting," stated Castleton, "but it doesn't give her motive." "A woman scorned and all that," proffered Thackeray.

"Keep digging. I doubt she's a killer, but see if there's anything else to connect Inge with Henry. Perhaps a visit to the gentleman's club would be in order, Thackeray?"

Thackeray's grin gave Castleton his answer.

Meg rolled her eyes and continued with her work.

The night had turned into morning before they realised it.

Desperate for a shower, a change of clothes and a couple of hours' sleep, they disbanded. Thackeray and Castleton would head into Soho later that day and Meg would revisit the Manor House in search of evidence with regards to the cyanide used to kill Sir Henry.

CHAPTER 26
The Buccaneer Gentleman's Club

The back streets of Soho housed many clandestine establishments frequented under the cover of darkness. Thackeray was intrigued.

The Buccaneer's Club was among its most famous. It was a private establishment, set up in the 18th century by men, for men of the British upper classes to be able to socialise in an enclosed environment with their equals, away from the prying eyes of the public.

It offered a formal dining room, a bar, a library, and a billiard room amongst its amenities, allowing its members to escape the stresses of their everyday lives.

In later years, the birth of the suffragette movement forced membership rules to relax allowing the introduction of women into the enclave of well-heeled gentlemen, whilst still maintaining a mahogany veneer of exclusivity. Whatever happened inside the club was known only to a privileged group of individuals.

Thackeray and Castleton had secured an appointment with the manager of the club. On arrival, they were met by a security man who checked their badges and directed them to the manager's office on the second floor.

Inside, the club was much as Castleton had imagined, but to Thackeray, it was a whole new experience and one that he was eager to explore.

A couple of dancers, clad in scanty outfits, were rehearsing, hanging from poles in the centre of the stage. The innocent and youthful Thackeray was easily distracted by the provocative moves and sexual gestures thrust in his direction. His puppy dog eyes and the naivety with which he salivated at the sight of the half-naked girls made them want to play with him some more, but as one girl crawled seductively towards him wearing nothing but a thong and a glossy pout, Castleton whisked him away in the direction of the manager's office.

Herman Van der Broek was the current manager in situ and he greeted the officers warmly, offering them tea or coffee and seats on a leather Chesterfield.

"Now, how can I help you, gentlemen?" Herman questioned. "We just have a couple of questions to ask you, if that's okay?" Herman stirred his coffee and nodded.

Castleton produced an image of Inge Stoltz from the inside pocket of his jacket and placed it on the desk.

"Do you know this lady?"

"Of course," replied Herman without a second glance, "everyone knows Inge." "How do you know her?"

"She's a very famous model, and apparently, she worked here many years ago, before my time. She is also a member now and dates a billionaire."

"Quite," agreed Castleton, retrieving the photograph and returning it to the safety of his pocket. "In what capacity did she work here - waitress, dancer?"

"I'm pretty sure she was a dancer, but like I say, it was before my time. I would really have liked to watch her performance though, if you know what I mean!" The Dutchman grinned salaciously. "Do you have an employment record for her?" Castleton continued, ignoring the man's lewd comment.

Herman thought for a moment. "I don't think our records will date back that far, though they could be archived somewhere. I can find out." He scratched his ear with the biro he was holding, then, throwing it onto the desk, he reached for his phone.

"Abel, it's Herman, are you working today?"

A distant voice was heard to respond with a positive acknowledgement.

"Can you come straight to the office when you arrive, please?" Herman hung up without waiting for a reply. He reclined back in the chair, nursing his coffee cup, both eyes on Castleton.

The room fell silent, both police officers waiting for an explanation after Herman's brusque telephone conversation.

"Who or what are we waiting for?" enquired Thackeray, piercing the veil of uncomfortable quietude. "Abel Costa, he's part of our clean-up team. He's worked here for decades, and he was here around the same time as Inge."

About an hour later, as the atmosphere in the

manager's office was becoming intolerable and the coffee machine was empty, the door opened and in shuffled Abel Costa.

He was a grey-haired, bearded gentleman of ethnic origin, with an excruciatingly twisted posture. He looked much older than he was, and a deep furrow of wrinkles ravaged his forehead, the signs of intense discomfort and pain rather than age.

Castleton wondered how the poor man managed to drag himself out of bed in the morning, let alone hold down a cleaning job at the club.

Castleton reached for Inge's photograph once more and handed it to Abel. The old man's face lit up with pleasure as he perused the picture in his hand.

"Miss Inge was just 18 when she came begging for work here," Abel recalled. "Mr Humphrey, who was the manager back then, took a real shine to her. He gave her a prime-time slot on the stage. She was a real hit with the gentlemen, pretty and young, the two essentials for a club like this." Abel paused for a moment, keeping Inge's photograph gripped tightly in his hand. Even his fingers were disease-ridden, gnarled and disfigured, but any pain he felt had momentarily melted away as he continued to stare at Inge with a wide, toothless smile.

"So, Ms Stoltz was a dancer?" questioned Castleton, retrieving her picture from Abel's aged grip. Abel rubbed his hands together slowly, as if the pain had suddenly returned, then he glanced from Thackeray to Castleton and said, "Oh yes, she was a dancer alright."

"If she was as popular as you say, what made her leave?"

"Well, I suppose you're only popular 'til you ain't," came the reply. "And why was that, Mr Costa? Did something happen?"

"What happened was simple; Mr Humphrey replaced her." Abel shuffled forward and took a seat on the arm of the Chesterfield beside Thackeray.

"I see; can you remember who he replaced her with?"

"Of course," sniggered Abel. "Mr Humphrey was a fickle man with an insatiable lust for women. Ms Inge had been top of his list for a long time, and nobody thought he would find anyone else to take her place, but oh boy, when Ms Lilia arrived, she caused one hell of a stir. Mr Humphrey thought he had died and gone to heaven!" Abel laughed loudly.

Castleton and Thackeray looked at each other. "Would that be Lilia Czechova?"

"The very same," replied Abel.

At this point, Herman joined the conversation. "Lilia was here when I arrived, but by then, her dancing career had ended and she was engaged to Sir Henry Attwood."

"Yes, sir," added Abel, "Ms Lilia could have whoever she wanted, but for some reason, she chose Mr Henry."

"Perhaps it was love?" Thackeray pontificated. Everyone turned to look at him, making him blush uncontrollably.

Herman laughed raucously at Thackery's remark. "Love has nothing to do with it, Constable," he growled. "It's this they're after," and he rubbed his fingers together indicating wealth.

Thackeray shrank back on the sofa feeling small and insignificant. Castleton patted his shoulder in a show of support.

"So, when Lilia arrived, what happened to Inge?" Castleton asked.

Abel took the lead; "Ms Inge was keen on Sir Henry herself - they'd had a few dates and I think she was hoping he'd propose, but when that article was published, she never spoke to him again. She met Mr Cornish shortly after and he whisked her away. Next thing you know, she's appearing on the front of magazines. She never got over Sir Henry though; broke her heart he did."

"Well, that was a long time ago, Abel, water under the bridge," interrupted Herman. "Now, if you gentlemen have finished, I have a club to run."

Herman, intent on bringing the meeting to an end, wrenched Abel off the arm of the sofa and pushed him towards the door.

"Thank you, Abel, you've been very helpful," said a grateful Castleton.

CHAPTER 27

Meanwhile, Meg had arrived at the Manor House.

It was eerily quiet. Sir Henry's jovial presence was definitely missed; the whole estate was in mourning. Typically, his voice would have been heard bellowing from the dining room as he awaited his morning coffee. The sound of raucous laughter would echo around the room and the waft of his scent would garnish the nostrils. Sadly, Sir Henry had left behind only the sound of emptiness.

The hallway was awash with bouquets of flowers, cards and unopened gift boxes. Theo and Verity had flown off to Ireland and Lilia had retreated to a private spa somewhere in the Alps to grieve alone.

The kitchen staff were idly sat around; with no one to cook for, their presence wasn't required. Meg suggested they take the day off and, of course, they didn't need telling twice.

Darrow was alone in the drawing room nursing a mature malt. He stood as Meg entered the room, but she signalled otherwise.

"Any news, Miss?" asked Darrow, swigging back another mouthful.

"I'm sorry, Darrow; you know I couldn't tell you even if there was. I'm just here to have another look around, see if there's anything we missed."

Darrow refilled his glass, "I still can't believe it. Sir Henry, in the prime of his life, constitution of an ox, gone … never coming back."

Meg nodded her agreement. She had no words of comfort for him. She wanted to hug the sadness from his loyal bones, but Darrow would hate that. "I'll leave you to your thoughts. I'll be as quick as I can; take care, Darrow."

Darrow raised his glass in gratitude.

Meg had no idea what she was looking for or even where to start. She paced the dining room, memories of that evening flashing through her mind like a slide show. The room had been returned to its usual order, the table laid in preparation for family mealtimes, the drapes drawn back revealing huge patio windows that exited into the garden. Daylight bounced upon the crystal glassware and the polished cutlery gleamed spotlessly. Everything was as Meg remembered, but it was not the same; it would never be the same.

She crossed into the kitchen area and headed for the larder cupboard. The cupboard was a full-sized room, housing a huge expanse of wall-to-wall cupboards and shelving. It was stocked from ceiling to floor with all of the essentials befitting an aristocratic family. Fresh pheasant and quail hung from the ceiling, and baskets of freshly picked vegetables and fruit were piled in abundance.

Giant tins of caviar and exotic truffles were stacked in ordered precision next to truckles of cheeses from around the world.

The larder resembled a supermarket, whose contents could have fed a small country. It was hard to believe that one family needed this amount of provisions.

Beyond the expensive supplies was a cupboard marked 'herbs and spices'. Inside, a myriad of miniature pots were stacked in alphabetical order. Every kind of spice and herb from every continent lived within. Meg had read that cyanide could be found in certain foods in the form of amygdalin. Small trace amounts would certainly cause no harm, but high concentrations could be lethal.

Moving aside the regimented pots, she reached to the back of the cupboard. There were a couple of larger jars filled with a variety of different nuts. Meg pulled forward one that caught her interest; it was marked 'prunus dulcis var amara', better known as bitter almonds.

Meg knew that bitter almonds held a high concentration of cyanide, but a significant amount would be needed to warrant a reaction as deadly as Sir Henry's. The jar was half full of content.

Meg pondered for a moment; if the nut was ground down and disguised in food, it would be ingested without the victim realising.

It was a possibility but not without its complications. The food would have to be contaminated over a relatively long period of time, and the powder would need to be administered in small doses so as not to attract the attention of the recipient. Not only that, it would need to be placed in the food before it arrived at the table, meaning that the kitchen staff or Darrow would have to perform the duty.

Meg could not allow herself to consider Darrow as Sir Henry's murderer, nor could she imagine that any of the kitchen staff could be responsible.

She heard movement in the kitchen and stepped outside to find Theodore Gimp unburdening himself of half a dozen dead rabbits onto the kitchen table.

"Pardon me, Miss," said the startled groundsman, "I didn't realise you was here." "That's alright, Mr Gimp, I was just taking a look around the pantry."

Teddy Gimp was the latest in a long line of groundsmen at the Manor House. The grounds were intolerably difficult to keep to Sir Henry's standard and Mr Gimp was the only keeper, thus far, to have managed the task.

"I'll be leaving you to it then," said Teddy and doffed his cloth cap in a gesture of goodbye.

He was just about to exit the back door when Meg thought of a question; "Just a moment, Mr Gimp; perhaps you could answer a question for me."

Teddy Gimp turned slowly back towards her. "I'll try, Miss."

"Do you have any idea where the bitter almonds come from, specifically the ones delivered here?" Teddy stepped forward. "They are generally grown in the Middle East,

Miss; they likes a warm climate."

"So that's where the ones here come from?"

"I couldn't really say, Miss, but I knows they don't come from the almond trees here on the estate." Meg had no idea there were almond trees growing in the grounds of the Manor House.

"I hadn't realised there were almond trees. Where might I find them? Are they the pretty ones down by the lake?"

Teddy lowered his head slightly to disguise the hint of a smile. "No, Miss, they'd be the cherry blossoms; the almond trees grow in the orchard beside the apples and other fruits."

Meg had seldom visited the orchard, but she had seen the abundance of fruit baskets delivered to the kitchen after picking season.

"Thank you, Mr Gimp, that's most helpful." Teddy headed for the door and was gone.

Meg headed upstairs.

As children, the bedrooms were off limits to them and Meg had always longed for a chance to steal a sight of the master suite; now was that time.

To Meg's surprise, she found Abby, stretched out on top of a huge four-poster bed, wrapped in Henry's dressing gown. She jumped up as Meg opened the door, but said nothing.

Henry's death had hit her hard.

Meg sidled onto the bed and stroked her legs. The silence between them was comforting; both knew each other well enough that words were not necessary.

Meg admired the beautifully sculpted posts of the oak bed. In any other setting, it would have dwarfed the room, but not here - here it looked perfect. Dressed in white Egyptian cotton with sumptuous fluffy pillows and an army of different coloured cushions, it was the focus of the room.

Rich velvet drapes hung fluidly from the windows and artwork adorned the walls.

Abby closed her eyes and curled into a ball. Meg understood she wanted to be left alone, so she turned to exit, but found herself, not on the landing from where she had entered, but standing in the opulence of the master bathroom.

His and hers sinks, a large sunken whirlpool bath, walk-in shower, a mountain of fluffy towels and gilt-framed mirrors on every wall. It smelled divine too. Bottles of designer bubble bath, shower gels and creams, and perfumes from every designer, housed in crystal atomisers, flooded Lilia's side of the room.

Henry's side was more modest. Meg picked up his aftershave bottle and sniffed. Instantly, Henry was there, his smell distinct, charismatic and unmistakable. A tear pooled in the corner of her eye; she swept it away and turned to leave.

Then, as if an unknown force had stopped her, she spun back around. She stared at the bottle of Henry's scent, then grabbed it from the shelf.

Cyanide could be absorbed through the skin, so perhaps Henry's aftershave would reveal more than just a delicious fragrance.

At the station, Inge Stoltz was the topic of discussion.

Everyone agreed that although she had once been romantically involved with Sir Henry, there was no evidence or probable cause that she had murdered him. Many years had passed since Inge carried a torch for the man and there were too many unanswered questions to place her at the top of the suspect list.

However, Meg suggested a chat with Inge may be prudent, to clear up loose ends and afford her the courtesy of giving her side of the story.

Castleton agreed and Thackeray set a date for the interview via Inge's housekeeper.

CHAPTER 28
Victim Number 7

Henry's sudden death had thrown the original investigation into disarray and the murders at Molecatcher Farm had been side-lined.

As Lilia was not due to return home for another few days, it gave Meg the chance to reconnect with the file before setting up an interview on her return.

Thackeray had taken a much-needed day off and Castleton had a dental appointment, which left Meg alone in the office.

She re-read the gruesome details of the five murders again. It didn't get any easier to handle no matter how many times she read it, but it made her more determined to find the killer.

The common denominator in the case was, of course, Ayda Cosward. As Meg continued through the file, Castleton suddenly burst through the door, red-faced and out of breath. He was waving his phone in the air and spluttering, through the numbness of a nerve block, something about Inge Stoltz.

Meg failed to grasp the awkward slur of words as Castleton grabbed her keyboard and typed ferociously. There on the screen, in large black letters, were the words: INGE STOLTZ, SUPERMODEL FOUND DEAD.

Meg turned to Castleton, whose eyes were wide with excitement, as he spluttered, "This is getting weird."

Meg had to agree.

The details of Inge's death were not available, but this was no coincidence. "I need to make a phone call," Meg said as she dialled feverishly.

At Scotland Yard, her call was answered and Meg spent twenty minutes huddled over her desk scribbling as she talked. Castleton, breathing heavily over her left shoulder, was reading as she wrote: Inge Stoltz found dead - Adam's penthouse London, this afternoon - wrists slit - possible suicide - no note.

When the call was over, Meg filled the coffee machine; she had a feeling they were going to need it.

Just as she poured two mugs, Thackeray arrived. From the look on his face, he already knew. Meg poured a third coffee and they sat together staring at each other for inspiration.

CHAPTER 29
A Trip To Scotland Yard

The following morning, Meg and Castleton caught the early train to London. It was the first time Meg had visited the city since her move to the country and she was feeling slightly nervous.

Castleton had secured them a meeting with the investigating team responsible for looking into Inge Stoltz's sudden death.

DCI Norman Stratton was there to welcome them. Thankfully for Meg, faces at the Yard were no longer recognisable, which made the situation easier. The Serious Crime Squad was well known for its frequent change of officers as most couldn't handle it and others used it as a stepping stone to other departments.

DCI Stratton had been assigned to lead the investigation, but most of the brief was conducted by DS Andrea Maynard, a middle-aged woman with a husky voice and no-nonsense attitude.

DS Maynard produced an array of crime scene photos which she pinned to the evidence board. From the pictures, a simple suicide would be deemed a reasonable conclusion - a woman in the bath slits her wrists, bleeds out and is found dead by her boyfriend several hours later.

However, there was no suicide note found at the

scene. In the majority of suicides, it is usual for a note of repentance, apology or reason to be placed in plain sight of the victim's body, however, in a small number of cases, no note is ever found.

Adam Cornish, the boyfriend, had been interviewed and gave an alibi which had already been corroborated. He was, therefore, not a suspect.

Castleton was offered the chance to speak and he explained why Inge Stoltz's death was of extreme interest to a small group of detectives from a country village in the middle of nowhere.

DCI Stratton, though convinced the death was suicide, agreed to share information and, after a fair amount of persuasion from Castleton, agreed to DC Hogarth taking them to view the scene of Inge's death.

DC Hogarth had a strong Glaswegian accent, making him markedly difficult to understand. He was a humorous chap who sported a frizz of curly red hair and the early sproutings of a moustache to match.

They drove to Holland Park, an exclusive and expensive borough of London. The building that housed Inge and Adam's penthouse resembled a high-class hotel. In the foyer, they were greeted by a smart, well-spoken concierge. He called a lift for them, shooting them to the dizzy heights of the top floor.

The penthouse was magnificent, though the bathroom was of most interest. DC Hogarth headed straight for the en-suite where Inge's body was found. The scene had been cleaned now and Castleton had to admit that there was nothing to contradict the verdict of suicide.

DC Hogarth walked them through the timeline. Adam Cornish had left home around 7:30 am that morning for a breakfast meeting on the other side of town. The housekeeper, who arrived an hour later, had served Inge orange juice on the terrace. The housekeeper left around noon, as Inge was lounging on the sofa flicking through a magazine, but she reminded the housekeeper to pick up her dry cleaning for the following morning's photo shoot in Hyde Park.

Cornish arrived back at the apartment around 4:30 pm and found Inge dead in the bath. Time of death is estimated to be around 2 pm.

"Why worry about your dry cleaning for a job the next day if you have thoughts of killing yourself the day before?" Meg questioned.

"Valid point," replied DC Hogarth. "Maybe it was to throw the housekeeper off the scent, make her think everything was okay, or maybe she hadn't decided if she was going to go through with it at that point."

"What about visitors?"

"The concierge said no one visited the penthouse that day except for the housekeeper, but we have CCTV tapes back at the yard to plough through yet, and a copy of the visitors' book." Castleton shrugged, "Well, if you come up with anything on them, let us know, otherwise, it looks like suicide."

"One last thing," added Meg. "Did you find a black feather at the scene?"

Hogarth wasn't sure what to make of the question, but the look on Meg's face told him that she was serious. "Not that I'm aware of, but I'll check."

DC Hogarth drove them back to Euston in time for the evening train back to Brightmarsh.

Meg bade farewell to Castleton and walked briskly back towards her little cottage, tired and hungry.

A shrill ping in her pocket told her she had a message. It was from Thackeray - 'lab results on Sir Henry's aftershave positive for trace evidence of cyanide!'

She knew it. Henry Attwood had been murdered. The question was why and by whom?

The following day, Meg called at the Manor House to check on Abby, who was still home alone. Lilia had extended her break at the spa in Austria for a couple of extra days, much to Abby's dissatisfaction. Henry's funeral plans were on hold until Lilia returned to give them her seal of approval and running a home the size of the Manor House wasn't an easy task. Lilia was now its custodian and there were pressing matters that needed her attention, but Lilia was adamant that they could wait whilst she continued grieving for her husband at the luxury spa.

Meg needed to break the news of her father's murder

to an already overstressed and anxious Abby. She, of course, didn't take it well. Fearing her friend was close to breaking point, Meg contacted Theo in Ireland and he promised to fly home the following day.

Back at the station, results were coming in from Scotland Yard. Inge Stoltz had not killed herself. The pathologist reported a puncture mark found on her neck where a paralytic agent had rendered the model incapacitated. She had more than likely been placed in a hot bath and both wrists slit to stage a suicide.

"What the hell is going on?" yelled Castleton. "Seven murders in the space of a couple of weeks; what the fuck?!"

"Do you think they're all linked?" Thackeray queried.

"I don't know what to think," growled Castleton, tossing the lab report across his desk.

He was frustrated, and it was understandable. Meg retrieved the discarded file and left Castleton to his thoughts.

She perused the lab report and photographs of the puncture wound on Inge's neck; the coroner had done well to find it. The swelling and discolouration on the model's neck disguised the tiny mark that only a well-trained eye could have spotted.

There was no mention of a black feather in any report, so Inge Stoltz's death could therefore be an isolated incident totally unconnected to the deaths in Brightmarsh.

By lunchtime, Castleton had received news that forced

him from his broody mood.

The CCTV footage from Adam Cornish's building had yielded nothing significant inside, but an outside camera had captured the image of a hooded figure leaving via a back exit.

The blurry outline displayed no discernible features, and there was no other footage available as this was the only working camera; all the others had been disabled. It seems the suspicious visitor had overlooked this one.

Visual enhancements hadn't helped to reveal the identity of the clandestine guest, although the shape and size were befitting of a female build.

Castleton, with a renewed vigour, called the team together for a briefing. On a whiteboard at the front of the office, he wrote the victims' names, then added that of Ayda Cosward and underlined it twice.

"This is our only link," he said and tapped the name repeatedly to emphasise its importance. "Ben and Alice Cross were Ayda's parents, Sir Henry was her biological Father, Father Maloney and Hegarty Baxter put her in the convent, then the asylum, and Inge Stoltz was her rival at the Buccaneer's Club. This guy," he tapped the name of Dalton Emery, "was in the wrong place at the wrong time and I don't think he is connected in any way to the rest of the victims, or Ayda Cosward. We NEED to find this woman."

"With respect, Sir, we are looking for a needle in a

haystack," groaned Thackeray.

"Then I suggest, Constable, that instead of whinging about it, you start going through that haystack until you find that needle." Thackeray looked deflated.

"Where was the last place she was seen?" asked Castleton, then, without waiting for an answer, he replied to his own question, "The sanatorium. So that's where your haystack begins, Thackeray.

First thing, you go back there and question anyone who knew Ayda Cosward, shared a room with her, treated her, fed her; surely someone knows something of significance about her. Is that clear?"

"Yes, Sir," nodded Thackeray.

"Did we ever do a background check on Ayda Cosward, run her through the database?" asked Meg. "Was she reported as a missing person?"

"Worth a shot," grinned Castleton. "Do we have a photograph of her? I'm thinking Mike in forensics could use his age progression software to give us an idea of what she looks like now." Castleton was thinking out loud and was already dialling Mike.

Meg found her attachment to the brusque, dark-haired Sergeant growing steadily each day. She stayed late in the office if he was there, she would follow him down the corridor like a lovestruck teenager to share an empty lift, she liked the feel of his breath on her neck as he stood over her and the way he ran his fingers through the thickness of his hair whenever he was thinking.

Aside from their journey to Lancaster, when each had opened up about their past lives, they had never spent any other time alone. Meg felt unsure whether Castleton was interested in her at all, but there was an electricity between them when their hands had touched over coffee and she'd caught him looking at her when he thought she hadn't noticed.

Meg shook her head. 'I haven't time for this right now', she thought and turned her attention back to Ayda Cosward.

The list was getting shorter; one by one, the names were disappearing, so what would she do when she was finished?

The thrill of the kill was not going to leave her - she may need to quench her thirst from time to time. A drifter, perhaps, a rapist or paedophile. She could become a vigilante, eradicating the scum from other people's lives, but would it feel the same? For her, it was a personal quest, payback, revenge.

She couldn't think beyond her next victim and stroked the jagged edge of her trusted knife, a speck of blood staining her finger. She grinned sadistically. This one had been hard to find but it would be worth the wait. She slipped the knife away safely and left the room.

Meg ran Ayda Cosward through the database and found nothing.

Ayda had been reported missing by Dr Frobisher and her photograph had been distributed in the usual way. Her angelic face stared back at Meg. It was hard to believe that this child had caused so much trouble for so many people. What had really happened to her? Was her behaviour comprehensible - was she a victim of abuse, or had she experienced terrible events in her life? Without finding her, they would never know the answer. Hopefully, Castleton and Thackeray would have some luck.

Castleton had called to see Mike in forensics. His request was possible but the waiting list was huge. "Backlog, Finlay, too much work and not enough staff," joked Mike.

"Any way you can hurry it along?" begged Castleton, but Mike shook his head; "More than my job's worth to do that. You'll have it as soon as we can do it and that's all I've got to offer you, so take it or leave it," shrugged Mike.

"What about headquarters?" proffered Castleton.

Mike sniggered; "Not a chance! It's me or nothing, I'm afraid."

Castleton unwillingly accepted Mike's service. "I'll be in touch," shouted Mike, as Castleton strode from the office.

CHAPTER 30

Meanwhile, Thackeray had travelled back to the Good Samaritan Asylum. He met briefly with Darryl Frobisher and Bunny Maguire and asked if he could interview individuals who had had any contact with Ayda Cosward during her stay.

Frobisher set up a makeshift interview room in a back office and rounded up the staff members who had experienced Ayda Cosward in one way or another. For the most part, there was little information available, except for their common disdain for the girl.

Next, Thackeray asked to speak with any patients who Ayda had spent time with, whether it be good or bad. Bunny Maguire was hesitant at his request.

"It could do a lot of damage," she explained. "These patients all have a mental illness and to some, the mere mention of Ayda's name could action a regression."

Thackeray assured her that he understood, but he was investigating a series of murders in which Ayda Cosward was the common denominator. Deliberations later and a further conversation with Dr Frobisher and Bunny Maguire reluctantly agreed, but she requested to be present at the interviews to deal with any traumatic reactions first-hand.

Thackeray agreed. Most patients were too heavily sedated to answer any questions and didn't react at all at the mention of Ayda's name. Thackeray, fearing his journey had been thankless, waited to meet the last patient, Mercy Wilkes.

Mercy, like her fellow residents, was dressed in a pale blue jogging suit. She had porcelain skin, light green eyes and flaming red hair that pooled around her shoulders. In any other setting, she would have been most attractive, and yet the healing scars of self-harm and dark circles beneath both eyes were evidence that Mercy, like the others, was no stranger to mental illness.

Mercy, however, was more astute than her counterparts. Sedation for her was only administered on a PRN basis.

Thackeray explained the reason for his visit and why he had to speak with her. She smiled and nodded politely.

"Did you know Ayda Cosward?" he asked cautiously, not sure what reaction the name would elicit. A quiet whisper of a voice replied, "Yes."

"Were you and her friends?" "Yes," said Mercy.

"Did you like Ayda?"

The response was a slight nod of the head.

"Was she kind to you, Mercy?" Again, Mercy nodded with the slightest hint of a vocal response. Thackeray needed to up his game; his preliminary questions had not sent Mercy spinning out of control, so he continued, under the watchful eye of Bunny Maguire.

"Did Ayda tell you things, like secrets?"

Mercy lifted her head and Thackeray could see the

slightest hint of expression in her eyes. She rubbed her hands together vigorously.

"Steady now, Mercy." Bunny placed a hand on her shoulder. "Don't get overexcited."

Thackeray threw a surprised look in Bunny's direction - this was overexcitement?! Bunny gave him the go-ahead to continue.

"What things did Ayda tell you, Mercy?"

Mercy, still wrestling with her 'overexcitement', replied, "I'm not supposed to tell."

"That's ok, you can tell me, I'm a policeman," Thackeray explained.

Mercy was silent for a moment as if contemplating Thackeray's words. Then, in a clear and much louder voice, she answered, "She told me she was going to kill!" Mercy began to laugh uncontrollably.

Thackeray, feeling slightly uneasy by Mercy's amusement, continued, "Who was she going to kill?"

"People, people, people..." repeated Mercy, her voice growing louder and louder until the tone was hysterical.

"Which people?" Thackeray continued above the volume of craziness. "Many people," Mercy stated as she regained composure.

"Why did she want to kill people?" "She was told to, silly."

"By who?"

"The raven, of course." Mercy lifted a hand into the air

mimicking a soaring motion above her head. Thackeray glanced towards Bunny who shrugged her shoulders. "Ayda always talked about a pet bird, said it lived outside her window. She blamed every wrong thing she did on that bird."

"Did you see the bird, Mercy?" Thackeray continued.

"Yes, but she was very protective of it. She wouldn't let me talk to it." "So, Ayda talked to the bird?"

"All the time."

"Did you hear it talk?"

Mercy thought for a moment before answering, "Not talk exactly, but I heard it sing." Thackeray wasn't aware that the raven was a songbird.

"Ayda said, 'When the raven sings, it's telling me what to do, and I just do it.'"

"You've been very helpful, Mercy, thank you." Thackeray rose from his seat. Mercy grabbed his hand; her grip was tight, almost painful.

"She gave me this on the night that she left," said Mercy, holding a silky black feather towards Thackeray. She began to laugh uncontrollably as Thackeray backed away and headed for the door.

He could hear Bunny's voice desperately trying to calm her down as he travelled a long corridor in search of the exit. A man in a white uniform ran past. Looking back, Thackeray saw him enter the room and a moment later Mercy was quiet.

Searching the corridors for a way out, Thackeray increased his pace.

Suddenly, a face popped out from behind a door to his right. "Psst ...come here," said a voice, then a hand appeared and beckoned him into the room. Thackeray checked the corridor for signs of life then headed towards the mysterious voice.

Once inside, a little man with rimless glasses, a belly bulging over the top of his joggers and a head as bald as an egg, pulled Thackeray abruptly into the room. Thackeray, unsure whether his situation was dangerous, backed up against the wall with one eye focused on the door. The man retreated to his bed and puffed on an electric cigarette as he checked Thackeray up and down. "Want to know about Ayda?"

Thackeray, slightly relieved that the man had not accosted him for more insidious reasons, slowly relaxed.

"That's right. Did you know her?"

"Oh yes, I knew her; everyone did," he replied. "It was hard not to know Ayda; she made you know her." The man rolled his eyes momentarily; he was gone for a second, perhaps a product of his medication or a sudden TIA. Thackeray knew the signs from his grandmother's own affliction. "Have you found her?" demanded the man.

"No, not yet," replied Thackeray.

"You need to..." the man was gone again briefly.

"Any idea where I might find her?" Thackeray asked.

"How should I know?" chortled the man, eyes rolling again. "Overseas, that was her plan." "Overseas," repeated Thackeray.

"Ask Ernie, he knows." And with that, the man jumped into bed and pulled the covers up over his head.

Thackeray, slightly unnerved by the man, retreated for the door and continued down the corridor. As he waited for security to let him through, he noticed the man walking towards him was wearing an identity badge displaying the name Ernie.

As Ernie punched the keypad and the door opened, Thackeray stepped through. "Thanks .... Ernie!"

"Anytime," was Ernie's reply.

Thackeray turned towards the car park, then turned back just in time to catch Ernie before he locked the door.

"Forget something, Constable?"

Thackeray shook his head. "No, just a quick question - what do you know about Ayda Cosward?"

Lilia had returned from her spa retreat just in time for Sir Henry's funeral.

She stood at the graveside in black silk and fur surrounded by Henry's family. Meg thought she was the most beautiful sad person she had ever seen. Even grief did not overshadow the mesmerising widow.

She wiped a solitary tear from her cheek as she placed a single red rose onto Henry's coffin. He took his place in the family crypt beside his forebears, encased within its walls forever. Theo and Abby, drowning in emotion, clung to her side as the trio headed back to Sir Henry's classic Silver Shadow. Darrow, in the driving seat, took a moment to doff his hat towards the granite mausoleum.

Back at the Manor House, the staff had been busily preparing afternoon tea for the many guests who had attended Henry's service.

"He was a popular guy," stated Castleton, looking around at the large numbers of people who now filled the Manor House's many entertaining rooms.

"He certainly was," acknowledged Meg. "Who would want to kill him?"

"The killer could be right here standing amongst us," added Castleton. They looked at each other and then around the room as if the murderer was suddenly about to be revealed.

Meg recognised some of the people as guests from around the dinner table on the fateful night when Sir Henry died. Adam Cornish had not made an appearance, though it was not surprising; he was grieving the loss of his girlfriend.

Abby and Theo seemed to cling to each other's sides. Meg had only been afforded a solitary wave of acknowledgement.

Lilia was immersed in conversation with a tall, handsome-looking man, younger in years than herself.

'Probably her next husband,' thought Meg to herself.

The wake ended with a champagne toast in Henry's honour and the crowd dispersed slowly. Meg went to find Abby but she had already retreated to her bedroom and Theo seemed to think it was best to leave her with her thoughts. Meg agreed and set off to walk home.

About halfway down the Manor House drive, a car pulled up beside her; it was Castleton. "Fancy a lift?"

Meg hesitated for a moment. She lived within walking distance of the Manor House, though, it was a decent walk back to Pebble Cottage.

"Thanks," she eventually replied and hopped in beside the sergeant.

The car journey took a little less than ten minutes and she was back at the cottage gate. Castleton had been quiet throughout, not even discussing details of the case. There was a definite vibe in the air, but Meg wasn't quite sure what it represented. She didn't want to read the situation wrong, though the butterflies were doing somersaults again.

As she exited the car, she looked back. "Want to come in?" Castleton nodded and followed her up the path.

They chatted and drank wine. Meg drained the bottle. "Another?" she quizzed waving the bottle in the air.

Castleton rose from the table and removed the empty bottle from her hand. He pulled her close, his breath heavy against her cheek, and the scent of wine and sandalwood cologne enveloped her. She felt light-headed, giddy; the butterflies had flown, replaced by a deep longing and a desperate need to be held.

Castleton's lips closed around hers, his arms hugging her body close, the soft warm touch of his skin on hers.

Within a moment, he had released her and they were climbing the stairs to heaven, ripping at each other's clothes with uncontrollable passion, twisting and writhing in a frenzy of ardent love-making. The night came and went, but Meg did not notice.

Held in Castleton's strong arms, she reached the climax of sexual excitement, again and again.

As the first light of dawn broke, Meg stirred slowly. She turned to find her bed fellow staring back at her. "Good morning," he said as he stretched towards her for a kiss. Meg felt her body tremble at his touch as she melted once again beneath him.

A fervent hour followed, then an X-rated shower scene, and Meg was ready to leave for work. She floated down the gravel path towards Castleton's car.

"Best if you drive yourself, Meg - don't want tongues wagging," Castleton closed the window and drove away.

Meg was left puzzled by the sudden change in attitude. What did he think she would do - sit on his knee whilst he worked, drag him into the nearest cupboard to rip his clothes off? Meg was a professional - she could handle a relationship with a colleague. After all, Michael had been her husband and colleague.

Perhaps Castleton was nervous by the sudden development in their relationship, but Meg refused to allow him to remove her inner contentment or the ridiculous grin that she was sporting.

Ernie, shocked by Thackeray's question, took a moment to answer. Ushering Thackeray to one side of the building, out of earshot of the security team, he asked, "What do you want to know about Ayda Cosward?"

"One of the patients told me to ask you about her," replied Thackeray.

Ernie began to twitch nervously, rubbing his nose and pulling at his ear, the way someone does when they feel uncomfortable.

"Come on, Ernie, don't make me come back again and take you in for questioning. Just tell me what you know," Thackeray insisted.

Ernie fumbled for the words, but in short, he had become a victim of Ayda Cosward himself. She had promised to expose him for inappropriate behaviour, discredit his impeccable record and lose him his job. Ernie knew that once accusations had been made, his career would have been over. Even if you're innocent, mud sticks, so, in return for Ayda's silence, he followed her instructions.

Ernie had a key cut for Ayda - not just any key, but the master key. On the night she made her escape, Ernie was to turn off the power to the security cameras, wait for twenty minutes and then reboot the system. That would give Ayda the chance to break free. Ernie would report a power cut and nobody would be any the wiser. Ernie never heard from her again, his job was safe and everyone was more than happy to see the back of the girl.

Thackeray thanked Ernie for the information, though he could not promise him that there wouldn't be repercussions from his actions.

Ernie looked deflated.

Just as Thackeray reached his car, Ernie caught up with him. Breathing heavily, he panted, "I just remembered that she was heading for the coast, picking up a boat there to take her across to Europe. I think someone was helping her," he added.

"She told you that?" Thackeray queried.

"No, I overheard a conversation she had. She never had a visitor but she talked to someone regularly on a mobile. I don't know where she kept it; it was never found on routine searches."

Thackeray left the asylum with a sense of relief. If Ayda had a mobile phone, perhaps it could be traced, expose her accomplice and answer some of the many questions that Ayda Cosward had instigated.

CHAPTER 31

Castleton arrived at the Manor House around lunchtime. He had an appointment to speak with Lilia, who had graciously invited him to dine with her.

The table on the patio was brimming with dainty sandwiches and cakes, fruits, pastries and all manner of petits fours. Champagne bottles were chilling in a silver bucket and jugs of non-alcoholic juices were cooling on a tray of ice.

Castleton sat eagerly awaiting the arrival of Lady Attwood. The growling and gurgling in his abdomen told him and anyone in the vicinity that hunger was the first thing on his mind.

Eventually, Lilia graced the patio, a vision of enchantment in a long, floaty white dress and sandals. Her hair was tied in a sleek ponytail and her face masked by designer sunglasses. The hint of a small tattoo was visible beneath the silky material that caressed her ankles as she moved.

"Sergeant, how lovely to see you again," she said, reaching out her hand towards him.

"Thank you for taking the time to see me, Lady Attwood."

"Lilia, please!" Lilia positioned herself across the table from him so they were looking directly at each other.

"Now, what can I do for you?"

"I'm sure you already know that Sir Henry's death was not a heart attack."

Lilia removed her sunglasses and poured herself a glass of pink champagne. She continued to gaze at Castleton but said nothing.

"We suspect … Well, we know, that Sir Henry was murdered," stuttered Castleton, Lilia's beauty setting him slightly on edge.

"I can't believe it, Sergeant," Lilia sobbed. "Who would do such a thing to Henry?"

"Well, that's the question, and the main reason why I wanted to see you today," replied Castleton. "Do you know anyone who might have a grudge against Henry, a feud or suchlike?"

"I have only known Henry for a couple of years, so I can't speak about his past acquaintances, but I know that the people he introduced me to loved him as much I did. Henry was a giver, Sergeant, although he never boasted about the charities he supported or the philanthropic work he was involved in. I cannot think of anyone who had a bad word to say about him."

Castleton was relieved when Lilia instructed him to help himself to the luncheon feast. It was divine and he could happily have spent the whole afternoon eating and drinking with the beguiling widow.

"Did you hear about Inge Stoltz?" Castleton asked,

biting into his second cream horn. "Dreadful, isn't it? Adam is distraught. Such a beautiful life taken far too soon."

"You knew her well?"

"I knew her; I wouldn't say well, though," replied Lilia, refilling her flute for the third time. "Didn't the two of you meet at the Buccaneer's Club?"

Lilia's lip curled, and she threw Castleton a look of displeasure. His knowledge of her historic night-time exploits agitated her. "Yes, Sergeant, we did, but like I say, we weren't close."

Realising her sudden sharpness, Lilia apologised. "I'm sorry, I'm still not myself. Henry's death has hit me harder than you can imagine."

"I understand completely, so I'll make this as brief as possible. Anything you can tell me about Inge Stoltz, however trivial you may think it is, could help with our investigation."

Lilia looked confused. "Investigation... is that usual in a suicide?"

"It wasn't a suicide; Inge was murdered," declared Castleton.

Lilia's eyes lit with surprise. "Oh, my goodness, that's terrible," she exclaimed. "Does Adam know?"

"Yes, of course he does." Castleton detected Lilia's sympathy lay slightly more with Adam Cornish than the late Inge Stoltz.

Lilia sat back pensively, nursing the champagne-filled flute.

"Inge and I were merely acquaintances, dancers at the same club. I don't really think I can tell you anything you don't already know."

"Did Inge have, shall we say, a romantic interest in Henry?" Castleton asked tentatively.

Lilia set down her flute and refilled it again. "I believe she did, but that was years ago, all water under the bridge, as they say." She lifted the flute towards Castleton. "Besides, the best woman won," she asserted, winking playfully. "Cheers!"

Castleton munched his way through dessert, tossing questions between mouthfuls of tasty, calorific delights. Lilia, unsurprisingly, drank more than she ate, but she was an affable host, charming and attentive.

"One last thing before I go. A black feather was found with Henry's body on the night he was killed. Does that mean anything to you?"

Lilia's body language didn't change. "Black feathers can be found all over the estate, Sergeant. We are surrounded by a maze of trees, and all manner of wildlife and birds live amongst us. It's perfectly possible for a black feather to have blown in through an open window," boasted Lilia.

"I suppose you're right," Castleton acknowledged, "though the feather came from a raven - not a usual inhabitant of Brightmarsh."

"How fascinating that you can name the actual bird," sniggered Lilia, "and its significance to Henry's murder is...?"

"No significance," answered Castleton, "just a quirky discovery, that's all."

"I should think you can cross the bird off your suspect list, Sergeant," laughed Lilia, tossing her hair playfully.

Castleton smiled and grabbed a third cream horn.

"Now, if there's nothing else, I have a prior engagement to attend," exclaimed Lilia. "Feel free to stay and enjoy the food. Darrow will see you out when you're finished and if you need any more information on killer birds, I suggest you speak with Mr Gimp," Lilia mocked as she crossed the patio and disappeared.

Castleton finished lunch and thanked Darrow for his hospitality.

CHAPTER 32

Joby and Gully were settling back into life at the farm.

Gully had busied himself repairing fencing and gateways. They'd bought a flock of sheep from the local auction house to keep him happy, while Joby redecorated the downstairs of the farmhouse, erasing the physical evidence of the grisly crime that had happened there.

Meg had been invited to join them for dinner.

The outside of the farmhouse looked immediately warmer and more inviting than her last visits. Inside, Joby had decluttered and painted the walls a pale shade of sunshine; everything sparkled with cleanliness and smelled divine. Flowers on the large oak kitchen table and an array of church candles added to the ambience.

"You'd make someone a good wife," joked Meg.

The aroma of Joby's dinner menu wafted delightfully throughout the house. Finishing a tour of his decorative skills, Joby poured two glasses of wine. "You've done a great job, Joby," praised Meg. "How has Gully been?"

"His usual inhibited self. I never know what he's thinking, Meg. We were never close as children, the age gap saw to that, but nowadays, we seem to be drifting further apart. I thought the two of us living here would strengthen our bond, but Gully is just happy in his own world. Half the time I don't even know where he is. He can be gone for days, then he will suddenly turn up and carry on as before."

"Have you asked him where he goes?"

"Oh, I've tried, but he's as secretive about that as he was about that .... prison cell, for want of a better word. Fancy being able to keep that hidden from me all these years."

Joby looked disheartened. Gully was a difficult individual to get to know; he never exposed his feelings, and he kept everyone at a distance.

"You've tried, Joby," Meg said in an attempt to comfort him. "What have you done about that secret room?"

"I've padlocked it for now, but once the case is closed, I'll probably board it up and paint away all traces of it."

Gully arrived just as Joby pulled a golden roasted chicken from the oven.

"You must have smelled dinner," joked Meg, but Gully didn't acknowledge her presence. He took off his boots and disappeared. A moment later, he took his place at the table and tucked into the culinary delights that Joby had slaved over.

The atmosphere was uneasy. Meg found herself waffling just to break the silence. She revealed all about her night of passion with Sergeant Castleton. Joby was intrigued. Gully wasn't paying attention. He was feeding bits of the gourmet feast to Cooper under the table.

Meg could see that Joby was beginning to fidget.

Gully feeding his hard work to the dog was insulting. Meg desperately tried to keep his attention on her conversation, but finally, Joby bawled, "Gully, stop feeding the dog!"

Gully looked up, pushed his chair aside and stormed out of the room. Meg suddenly realised how intimidating Gully's enormous physical structure could be. She had never thought about it before, Gully had just been Joby's older brother, silent and nondescript. He lurked in the shadows of the barn when she played at the farm, but he had always been irrelevant. Aunty June had said that Gully was a mute, but, despite his huge size, he was a soft and gentle boy. She had said that Meg needn't be afraid of him as he wasn't the violent type.

Tonight, Meg thought differently. She had seen a side of Gully that she had never witnessed before. "See what I mean?" Joby exploded, as he began ferreting around the kitchen.

"I've never seen him like that," admitted Meg. "Is it because I'm here, perhaps?"

"No ... no ... he doesn't like me having guests, but whether I do or not, he would have reacted the same way. I hate him feeding Cooper and he knows it, so he does it all the more."

"I should leave," offered Meg, but Joby was insistent that she stayed. Gully would not reappear tonight. They settled down to another bottle of wine in front of the open fire.

Mary Mackie thought she had hidden herself away, never to be found again. She thought wrong.

As darkness enveloped the old beaten remains of Mary Mackie's caravan, she crept through the shadows carefully. Mary's dogs roamed free, new additions to her security measures, muscular specimens of canine ferocity crouching among the mountain of discarded rubbish.

Using a high-frequency whistle that only the dogs could hear, she waited. Suddenly, out of the blackness, she heard them, rustling through the undergrowth and heading in her direction.

She hurled the first cut of steak and listened. The dogs found it, so she hurled a second and a third. In the stillness, she could hear the sounds of the cuts being devoured.

She checked her watch. Ten minutes should be all it takes to put these beasts to sleep. She had made sure the sedative was strong; she couldn't afford them waking and disturbing her plan.

Fifteen minutes later, all was silent.

Stealthily, she crept towards the caravan, kicking one of the sleeping dogs as she passed - no reaction. Peering into the sad and lonely world of Mary Mackie, she eyed the old crone, alone, watching tv.

Without a sound, she removed the cap from the propane bottle at the front of the caravan and quickly attached a hose to one end. She then threaded the other end through the nearest window close to where Mary was sitting. The gas had no odour, leaving Mary unaware of its presence. She did the same with the second bottle and when she thought enough gas had escaped into the caravan, she struck a match and lit the edge of Mary's curtain that was flapping through a break in the window.

She sprinted at speed from the vicinity of the tin box and kept on running until the sound of the explosion stopped her in her tracks. Catching her breath, she could see flames leaping above the treeline, the darkness glowing as the fire burnt through it.

A smile began to form, then it grew wider and wider until she was laughing hysterically.

Blue lights and sirens flashed across the night sky. It was time to disappear. Only the sound of laughter could be heard in the distance as she raced into the void of night.

CHAPTER 33
Victim Number 8

Meg received a call from Thackeray just as she was leaving Molecatcher Farm. "I'm on my way, Will. I'll meet you there."

The route to Mary Mackie's home had been difficult enough during daylight - the woman had done a pretty good job of turning her back on society and disappearing for a reason that only she knew the answer to.

A couple of wrong turns later, Meg arrived at the scene where Thackeray was deep in conversation with the Fire Chief. Castleton pulled up minutes later.

"It appears that the explosion was caused by LPG gas," explained Thackeray.

"How?" Castleton enquired. "LPG gas is very difficult to ignite; there would need to be a lot of it in a small area to have lit up like this."

"Exactly," the Fire Chief interrupted. "I can't say for definite until we have the forensic reports, but the canisters both had their caps removed and were empty, and hosing was discovered attached to the canisters, tracking the gas through an open window. At a guess, I'd say this was intentional. The remains of a body were found inside, identity currently unknown."

Meg glanced from Castleton to Thackeray and back

again. "Is this another murder or just an unfortunate accident?"

"I'd love to say the latter," replied Castleton, "but I fear we could be looking at our eighth victim." There was nothing they could do now so they headed away from the wreckage of what had once acted as Mary Mackie's home.

Thackeray suddenly found himself hitting the ground with a thud, and Meg and Castleton turned to investigate. A startled constable rose from the undergrowth, pointing to the obstacle responsible for his tumble. "There are three dogs here, all out for the count."

Sure enough, three scary-looking hounds lay at Thackeray's feet, their black coats making them invisible against the darkness.

"Think we might need to involve the RSPCA, Thackeray, and quickly too before these things wake up," joked Castleton.

The following morning, forensics confirmed that the fire had indeed been deliberate and that the victim was in fact Mary Mackie, the midwife who had secretly delivered the Cross's second child, Ayda.

"That's another link," said Thackeray excitedly.

"It is," admitted Castleton, "but does that help us any?"

"Only that the common denominator in this case is still Ayda Cosward," added Meg.

Thackeray recounted the information that Ernie, the security guard, had reluctantly provided him with at the

Good Samaritan Asylum.

Castleton seemed inspired and began barking out his orders. There was no CCTV to trawl through as Ernie had turned them off to aid Ayda's escape, but surely there would be phone records.

This was a job for Alex Chaplin at The Yard; if anyone could trace Ayda's calls, he could.

Meg grabbed the phone and dialled Alex for a chat. Alex was not particularly hopeful that he would get a hit on the phone, being as it was so many years since it had been used, but he promised he would give it his best shot and Meg was happy with that.

Castleton felt that though the cameras at the asylum were useless, cameras elsewhere in the vicinity could possibly have picked up an image of Ayda Cosward as she made her escape. There were hours of footage to investigate, a long and tedious assignment, so, as the videos arrived via courier, the three settled in for another long night.

By the early hours, it seemed like their quest would be fruitless until Castleton spied a young girl crossing a road about five miles from the docklands area. She climbed into the fuzzy outline of a vehicle, possibly a truck, but the image was extremely pixelated.

"We'll need that tidying up if we have any chance of getting a make, or dare I say, a reg number," said Castleton.

They were just about to call it a night when Meg

chanced upon a girl entering the dock via gate number 6. The footage traced her disappearing into the distance and she was gone. She appeared to be alone at that point with no sign of the vehicle or anyone else.

"I know where I'm going in the morning," mused Meg. Castleton nodded his agreement and they all retreated home for some much-needed sleep.

Castleton did not look back as they jumped into their cars. Meg felt slightly disappointed. Since their tumultuous night of passion, he had hardly passed a glance her way. She feared he was regretting it or had he just used her body for his own satisfaction? However, as she neared the cottage gate, her worries melted away.

Castleton was standing on the gravel path waiting for her. Trying not to appear too excited, Meg made her way casually towards him. Castleton grinned as she sauntered past.

Meg awoke feeling on top of the world once again. All signs of tiredness had melted away at Castleton's orgasmic touch and their second night together had been as pleasurable as the first.

CHAPTER 34

Meg set off to the docklands in search of answers.

She met the manager, a small, stocky chap with oversized glasses, a fake aristocratic accent, dishevelled clothes and cheap cologne.

Meg followed the manager to gate number 6.

It was something of a disappointment - instead of a huge yacht-shaped vessel, there were only a couple of dinghies and a dilapidated fishing boat. From the manager's description of the marina, she had been expecting hundred-foot yachts.

Back in the office, the manager took to his PC for information on gate number 6.

"We have a log of every vessel that docks here," he explained. He huffed and puffed from behind his screen, just the top of his balding head visible.

"Everything ok?" enquired Meg.

"Yes, yes, fine, just give me a minute," growled the man. Eventually, he rose from behind his desk and scurried towards a set of filing cabinets on the wall opposite.

Drawers opened and closed spontaneously and then, triumphant with file in hand, he returned to his desk and adjusted his glasses.

Meg, whose patience was about to wear out, slid beside him as he searched the file for the date in question.

"Here it is, January 14th, 2007," muttered the man, adding, "it's too old to be on the system, you see. It would be paper files before 2010."

Meg wasn't interested in the history lesson; she pulled the file into view.

"What does this mean?" she asked. The manager, adjusting his glasses again, shifted his chair to review the file.

"Let me see, well, the date is self-explanatory, and the gate number, and this is the name of the vessel and this is who chartered it."

"I need a copy, please." The man scuttled off into the next room where Meg could hear the workings of a photocopier groan to life.

'New Beginnings' was the name of the boat, which had been chartered in the name of Henry Attwood.

Henry had helped the girl to escape by chartering the boat, but had he also picked her up in the van, or was someone else involved?

Meg could only think of one person loyal enough to help Henry and keep his secret safely - Lester Darrow.

When Meg arrived back at the station, Lester was already sitting in an interview room.

Castleton had worked quickly on the information Meg supplied and sent a car to pick up Darrow for questioning.

"I'd prefer not to sit in on this. Darrow is far more likely to converse with you freely if I'm not there," said Meg as

Castleton handed her the preprepared file.

"Fair enough. Thackeray, follow me; this will be good experience for you."

Meg found it hard to believe that Sir Henry and Lester Darrow were mixed up in all of this. Sir Henry was Ayda's biological father, but he had never shown any interest in the child, so why would he involve himself now? It just didn't make any sense.

A couple of hours later, Castleton and Thackeray returned to the office, but their expressions said nothing.

"Well," prompted Meg, "how did it go?"

"Darrow says he knew nothing about Ayda Cosward, the escape or the boat." "And you believe him?"

"Actually, I do," Castleton responded. "He really had no idea what we were talking about."

"Oh, thank God," sighed Meg, relief washing over her.

"So, if Darrow wasn't the mysterious driver, who was?" asked Thackeray.

"That's the big question, Will. Looks like we're back to square one again."

Without Sir Henry able to corroborate their information, they needed a lucky break to answer the question.

A sense of despondency filled the room; they were deflated yet again.

The silence in the office was deafening, with everyone deep in thought, desperately looking for a break in the case that had claimed the lives of eight people.

The quietude was suddenly shattered by the sound of a phone ringing. It was Meg's. Alex Chaplin was on the line with some important news. He had traced the calls that Ayda made and received to a cell tower just five miles from the village. Not only that, he had triangulated it to the grounds of the Manor House.

The news was welcomed. Alex had done well, but that still didn't give them an idea of who the phone belonged to. Meg knew the Attwood's social calendar was a myriad of engagements and, at any one time, there could be close to fifty people on and around the estate.

"Perhaps we should look closer to home," suggested Thackeray, "eliminate the staff, regular visitors to the estate and the family members first."

Meg and Castleton agreed, so they drew up a list of possibilities.

Darrow was first on the list, simply because the man would do anything for Henry Attwood, hence making him a strong suspect. Granted, he appeared to know nothing about Sir Henry's activities on the night that Ayda Cosward escaped from the asylum, but that was only if he was telling the truth.

Abby and Theo were deemed too young, so the final list comprised of: Darrow; Mrs Hobson, the main cook; Ruby Grimshaw, the second cook; Austin O'Leary, Darrow's assistant; Jenny and Grace Massey, the cleaners; Riley Silk,

Ben Hobson and Theodore Gimp, the groundsmen.

Almost immediately, the list depleted - Ruby, Austin and the Massey twins were too young. Geraldine Hobson was a no-nonsense, forthright woman who would readily speak her mind. Meg could not see her getting embroiled in a scheme to save Sir Henry's illegitimate child. She would most certainly not have approved of the whole situation.

Ben Hobson was the cook's son and just as outspoken as his mother, so that left Riley Silk and Teddy Gimp.

Lilia had not yet met Sir Henry and therefore she had not been added to the list.

"Time to bring in Riley Silk, I think. Let's have a chat, get a feel for the guy, then we'll call on Theodore Gimp," stated Castleton.

Riley, a thin weasel of a man with bright red hair and a disjointed nose, was more than happy to spend a couple of hours in the interview room. The monotony of his voice was enough to send Meg and Castleton to sleep. He digressed at every question. His Irish brogue was difficult to understand and he was forced to repeat most sentences, much to the despair of his interviewers. When Castleton called time and switched off the recording equipment, Meg wanted to kiss him; the relief was overwhelming.

Back in the office, Thackeray found the situation amusing. He poured extra strong coffees and suggested they all visit the Snooty Fox pub on the way home for something a little stronger.

Everyone agreed.

The Snooty Fox, Brightmarsh's only public house, was as old as the village itself. Damien and Rachel Kemp had worked behind its antique bar for the last twenty years. They were a cheery, welcoming couple with a thirst for conversation, especially when their customers' inhibitions had been freed by great quantities of ale.

The place was all but empty save for a couple of regulars hugging the bar. In a quiet corner sat the three detectives, work still foremost on their minds.

"Perhaps this will give us some much-needed inspiration," Thackeray suggested, as he lifted the liquid trophy to his lips.

"I don't think Riley's our man," said Meg, sipping happily on a thirst-quenching mojito.

"Me either," added Castleton. "He would have only been 16 himself and has only recently been employed at the Manor House."

"That leaves Mr Gimp and Mr Darrow," proffered Thackeray.

Meg could not accept that Darrow was involved, though she had to admit his loyalty to Sir Henry was unfaltering.

"Don't forget about the numerous services that visit the estate, some on a daily basis, and the hundreds of guests that frequent galas and dinner parties there."

"Noted." Castleton drained his glass and suggested a refill, which was happily accepted. "I understand why the family mean so much to you, Meg, honestly, I do, but someone in that household, or very close to it, helped Ayda Cosward escape and disappear. We already know Henry was involved. I'm sorry, but my money's on Darrow." Castleton peered over the top of his pint glass and waited for a reaction.

"Let's see what you think of Teddy Gimp tomorrow before you stamp guilty on Darrow," pleaded Meg. "This morning, you said you believed him, so what's changed?"

Castleton grinned. He loved her optimism, but all the signs were pointing in Darrow's direction. "It's just the connection he had with Sir Henry - a bond that strong can be unbreakable. Darrow must remain on the suspect list until we're sure he wasn't involved."

"What do you think, Will?" asked Meg, bringing him into the conversation.

Will Thackeray looked nervously from one colleague to the other. He had been happily enjoying his pint until Meg threw the spotlight on him. He had seen the way they looked at each other, the electric vibe in the office when they were together and the tender way their fingers touched over a coffee mug exchange. It was one thing to take sides with a colleague, but a whole different ball game to become embroiled with a pair who were romantically involved.

Will considered his answer very carefully. "Well, I think we should wait until we have met Mr Gimp before putting a label on anyone."

"Very diplomatic, Will," joked Castleton. "If you ever leave the force, there could be a place for you in Westminster."

They laughed and drank together until last orders were called.

CHAPTER 35
Theodore Gimp

Meg was the first to arrive in the office the following morning. She wanted to make sure that everything was ready for Teddy Gimp's interview. The clock was only just touching 9 when Will arrived. He was humming and whistling as he set up the coffee machine, excited at the prospect of partnering Meg and questioning Mr Gimp.

Meg had never really taken the time to get to know Thackeray. She had presumed that her involvement with the case would be short-lived, affording no time to establish friendships, but the three of them had been working closely now for several weeks.

Will stood around six feet tall, a slim but sporty build, with twinkly brown eyes that matched his hair colour. He was a handsome specimen, to be fair, though Meg had only just realised, with a devilish sense of humour and a cheeky smile.

Will had been born in the neighbouring village of Ambleton. His parents were divorced and he had two younger sisters. He supported his family financially, including his elderly grandmother who had moved in with them three years earlier. She had a diagnosis of Alzheimer's and Will's mother had given up work to look after her. Will was a fastidious colleague and cared as much about his work as his family and always gave one hundred percent to both. Someday, he would make someone a lovely husband.

As Will handed out the first coffee hit of the day, Castleton arrived, looking a little flustered as his alarm clock had not woken him. He hadn't spent the night with Meg as it was late when they left the Snooty Fox and both yearned for sleep, which wouldn't have happened had they shared a bed.

Meg checked the clock impatiently; it was nearing 10. Teddy Gimp should have arrived half an hour ago.

"Relax, he's only half an hour late," said Castleton. "Give him another 30 minutes; you know what these country folk are like - time means nothing."

Meg wanted to feel reassured by the statement, but she had an uneasy nagging in the pit of her stomach. She tried to busy herself, but her eyes were constantly drawn to the clock. She paced a little to ease the tension, visited the ladies' room, drank another coffee and answered her emails, but Teddy Gimp still hadn't arrived.

She dialled reception; he wasn't there. She called the Manor House, but no one answered, so, as a last resort, she rang Abby. It would be unusual for Abby Attwood to have dragged herself out of bed at this time in the morning, but Meg needed to try her. Just as she thought, Abby's voicemail answered.

"I think I should take a drive to the Manor House. See

what's keeping Mr Gimp. I've got this uneasy feeling."

Castleton nodded his agreement. He had to admit to feeling the same, though he was sure there would be a good reason for the groundsman's absence.

"Perhaps he's just forgotten," proffered Thackeray.

Meg smiled, though she didn't really believe that was the case. The feeling of unease was growing. She grabbed her keys and headed for the door. Castleton was right behind her, so without saying a word, they jumped into the car and sped off down the lane.

The Manor House was unusually quiet. Castleton headed off to the gardening sheds in search of Teddy Gimp, while Meg found Darrow in the conservatory. He was setting up a breakfast table and hadn't noticed as she entered through the open French doors.

Darrow let out a startled cry as his eye caught sight of something moving towards him. "Miss Meg!" he exclaimed.

"Sorry, Darrow, the door was open. I'm looking for Mr Gimp."

Darrow consulted his wristwatch. "He will be in the sheds; he's a very early riser, even by my standards."

"Well, my colleague should have found him then." Darrow didn't notice as Meg left the room and continued with his duties.

Mrs Hobson came scuttling out of the kitchen with a basket of fresh pastries and jams. "The place seems very quiet today; where is everyone?" queried Meg.

"Oh, this is how it is most days now, dear," answered Mrs Hobson. "Mr Theo has practically moved to Ireland, and Lady Attwood comes and goes .... it's just not the same." She cast a glance towards Darrow and shook her head. "Poor dear, he's a shadow of himself; missing Sir Henry, I shouldn't wonder."

Meg ventured upstairs to Abby's bedroom. She knocked quietly knowing that Abby would probably still be wrapped in her duvet. There was no answer. Meg tiptoed away, descending the grand staircase she had raced up and down as a child. She remembered the first time she had visited the Manor House all those years ago. It was like entering Cinderella's castle, so grand and beautiful, filled with so many wonderful treasures. Sir Henry and Lady Isobel were the king and queen in her eyes. She envied Abby so much.

Nowadays, the castle was an empty shell of memories, lifeless and ageing, the treasures tarnished, the king and queen gone. She passed the family portrait that she had so often stopped to admire. The family had disintegrated but the picture still hung in a prominent position at the very top of the carved oak staircase.

It was in that moment of reflection that Meg realised she knew the identity of Sir Henry's accomplice.

She met Castleton hurrying towards the Manor House.

"Gimp hasn't turned up for work," he gasped, catching

his breath. "I've got his address." They were back on the road and heading for Teddy's abode. Meg knew her feelings hadn't been unfounded. Teddy Gimp was a relentless employee, and missing work was not in his nature.

23 Woodpecker Grove was a tiny weaver's cottage on the edge of Appleton Village. It's drab, neglected facade was exactly what Meg had imagined. Gimp himself was a drab, neglected individual and his personal life was a mystery - in fact, what was known about the man wouldn't have filled a postage stamp.

They approached a rotten, faded, wooden door, a splinter of colour here and there hinting at its original patina. There was no bell or knocker, not even a letterbox. The windows were overgrown with roses, wisteria and dirt; any daylight would have been a triumph. Castleton moved from door to windows, knocking impulsively, but there was no reply.

He signalled that he would check the back of the property and disappeared down a side alley. Meg waited.

A couple of minutes later, the door opened and Castleton was standing there. "Back door was open."

Meg followed him into the house. It was just as dark and dingy on the inside with an overwhelming smell of faeces. Teddy Gimp lived in squalor; there was no working electricity or running water, as both had presumably been cut off for failure to pay. There was little in the way of furniture, or anything else, and the source of the unrelenting stench was the animal excrement that covered the entirety of the ground floor.

Castleton climbed the stairs, picking his way carefully through the piles of faecal matter. Meg declined the invitation allowing Castleton to investigate alone. It wasn't long before he appeared at the top of the stairs, his handkerchief covering his mouth and nose. "Call forensics and animal rescue."

Outside, where the air was less pungent, they waited for the teams to arrive. Castleton had found Gimp hanging from the ceiling in his bedroom. He'd been there for quite a few hours and the rats had already got a taste.

"Suicide?" questioned Meg.

"Not sure," was the response. "Certainly made to look that way, but, as we know with Sir Henry, looks can be deceiving."

Theodore Gimp, encased in a black body bag, was stretchered past. Castleton stopped the gurney and unzipped the plastic shroud to reveal Teddy Gimp's decaying torso. Chunks of flesh had been devoured, his tongue was bulging from his mouth and his eyes were milky white. There was a ligature mark around his neck where the rope had sealed his fate. He was not a pretty sight. Meg caught sight of something emerging from his shirt pocket. She pulled at the object to reveal a feather, a black shiny feather.

Castleton searched the sky for signs of ravens, then he

faltered backwards as his eyes rested on Teddy Gimp's roof - there sat a row of imposing black birds, avian magistrates waiting to impose sentence.

Animal rescue rounded up a host of neglected breeds and pest control had been informed about the infestation of unsavoury squatters that had taken up residence in Teddy's home.

Castleton asked about the posse of birds that had invaded Teddy Gimp's roof.

"I imagine they come from Weaver's Wood," informed the animal rescue officer. "They like that kind of area. They're given a bad representation, being associated with witches, evil and such, but they're harmless and have an incredible repertoire of vocalisations. They can mimic human speech and other bird sounds with their deep voice, and they can sing."

Castleton felt less comfortable at the rescue officer's words. Birds with intelligence and the ability to talk were unsettling; perhaps Hitchcock had felt it too.

The ravens on Teddy Gimp's rooftop did not explain how one feather had ended up in his shirt pocket.

"You saw the house - every manner of scavenger had been through that place. What's to say a raven hadn't been in, dropped a feather and Teddy had picked it up and placed it there himself?" Meg tried to calm Castleton with her explanation, but it was futile; the raven certainly had Castleton rattled.

Meg felt itchy and desperate to shower after leaving

Mr Gimp's unenviable abode, but that would have to wait. She needed to expose to the team Sir Henry's accomplice, someone she hadn't thought of until today.

Watching from afar, she knew they had discovered Gimp's body. Hopefully, she had succeeded in staging a convincing suicide.

The detectives were an annoyance, a thorn she could easily remove, if necessary. They were sluggish and ill-prepared for the task she had set. They were no threat to her - she would be long gone before the blood dried on her last murder. She must remain focused; the list was coming to an end and she wanted to finish with a grand finale.

She hadn't felt the rush of exhilaration this time though, as the knife could not be used in 'suicide'. It was always by her side, a back-up in case of emergency or change of plan. The satisfaction she felt from the execution of the blade had been absent in the last three victims, but number 9 would be different. She would bathe in sanguine glory, worship the blade once more, and wallow in euphoric intoxication.

"Isobel Attwood?" Castleton scoffed, "What makes you think it was her?"

Meg explained, "I'm sure it's not Darrow, and judging by today I don't think it was Teddy Gimp, though his sudden suicide certainly leaves more questions than answers. The only other person that close to Henry at that time was Isobel."

"I think you're wrong, Meg," Castleton boasted. "Gimp knew we were onto him and killed himself, the reason being that he assisted Sir Henry in Ayda Cosward's escape."

"We'll have to beg to differ for now, then," and Meg dropped the subject.

A couple of days later, the autopsy report revealed that Theodore Gimp had been injected with a high dose of animal tranquillizer, strangled to death and hung to mimic suicide.

The dosage was the same as that used on Inge Stoltz, which probably meant it was the same killer.

Meg thought it the perfect time to bring up Lady Isobel again and this time, Castleton accepted that she may be worth looking into if they could find her.

Teddy Gimp was somehow connected to the other murders, though it wasn't obvious how or why.

Lady Isobel had last been seen strolling into the sunset on the arm of her new love. She had never looked back at her heartbroken children as they sobbed uncontrollably on the steps of the Manor House. Her actions were called callous, though Meg's memory of Lady Isobel was of a warm and caring mother who loved her children very much.

Local gossips declared that Sir Henry had only agreed to divorce on the stipulation that the children remain with him, but no one really knew if that were true. Lady Isobel must have been truly unhappy to have agreed those terms, thought Meg, or was public opinion right, that she was just a cold and heartless bitch who cared more about her own happiness than her offspring?

Abby and Theo never heard from their mother again, or did they?

Finding Lady Isobel was a mammoth task. She could be anywhere in the world... she could even be dead.

Meg dared not broach the subject with Abby or Theo, afraid of stirring up painful memories.

Sir Henry had never spoken of her again and it was unlikely that Darrow or the Manor House staff would have kept in touch. Sometimes, though, a sudden change of fortune can make all the difference, and that day, Meg was about to be touched by it.

In the secure knowledge that Teddy Gimp's house had been fumigated and the resident rodent population dispersed, Meg and Thackeray arrived to search through his meagre belongings.

There was very little of interest in Teddy Gimp's home; in fact, there was very little of anything, but in the main bedroom, Meg happened upon a shoe box, hidden beneath a chest of drawers. Inside lay a mountain of letters and postcards, all addressed to Teddy. At the very bottom of the box lay a couple of photographs showing a handsome man, who Meg assumed to be Teddy, with a very beautiful and young Isobel Attwood. Meg was intrigued as she called Thackeray over to take a look.

"Wow, who knew Teddy Gimp once looked like this!" exclaimed Thackeray, recalling the crime scene photographs of the bloated, discoloured body.

"Who's the lady... his wife?"

Meg turned the image over revealing the words, 'Izzy and I in Torquay'. Thackeray's eyes grew wider. "You mean Teddy Gimp and Isobel Attwood had a thing?!"

"It would appear so, but there's a lot of letters to get through and I'm eager to find out," answered Meg.

In the comfort of her jeep, she opened the letters and began to read.

A heart-warming love story unfolded before her eyes. It was the clichéd boy meets girl and they fall in love - Teddy, a weaver's son, and Isobel, the aristocrats' enchanting daughter. Love blossomed between them, but it was not to be. Prejudice against class, a divide so great, not even love could bridge the gap.

Isobel, however, as intelligent as she was pretty, found a way to keep the love alive by securing a job for Teddy as a groundsman at the Manor House, where she lived with her husband, Sir Henry. Their love affair was carried out in secret. Henry knew that Isobel was unfaithful, but he never knew who with.

Then, around ten years ago, the letters stopped and their love was silenced. Isobel and Henry divorced and she chose to leave her home, her children and Teddy behind.

The very last letter contained a photograph of Teddy holding a baby. It had been taken at the arboretum in the grounds of the Manor House and on the back were written the words 'Father and Daughter'.

The letter simply read: 'I leave you this parting gift, though I trust you will never betray my honesty. She is, and always will be, your daughter, a symbol of the love we shared, but no one can ever know. Goodbye, my darling, your Isobel.'

Meg was rocked to her core. It took her a moment to compose herself. She had just discovered that Abby Attwood was Teddy Gimp's daughter. What was she to do now? If the contents of the letters were to become known, then Abby would most certainly find out. Meg couldn't risk it. She knew Abby wasn't strong enough for such a revelation. She stuffed the letters and photo into her bag.

"All finished?" Thackeray tapped on the car window. Meg nodded. Thackeray had finished his sweep of the house and jumped in beside her. He talked the whole way back to the station but Meg was deaf to his conversation, still trying to come to terms with the information she had just discovered.

Eventually, Meg briefed him on the love story between Isobel and Teddy, leaving out the part about Abby being his daughter.

"Poor man," Thackeray exclaimed, "no wonder he let himself go. A girl like Isobel Attwood won't come along every day. I bet he never met anyone else."

Meg agreed. She now understood why Teddy Gimp always looked so downtrodden and depressed. He had obviously remained at the Manor House to stay close to Abby, who, sadly, was unaware of his existence.

Meg dropped Thackeray at home and made her way back to the cottage. She threw Isobel's final letter to Teddy and the photograph onto the open fire and watched as the evidence burned away. She would reveal the contents of the other letters to Castleton, but she would keep Teddy and Isobel's secret, just that; a secret.

By the time Castleton arrived, the fire had reduced them to ash.

The following morning over breakfast, Meg pulled the letters from her bag and gave Castleton the lowdown on Isobel and Teddy's clandestine relationship. Castleton listened intently with the same wide-eyed reaction that Thackeray had displayed.

"Well, I never," he exclaimed, "I wasn't expecting that."

He chomped on a slice of toast and took the envelopes from her. He wasn't interested in the letters themselves, just the postmarks. The majority had been posted in London, a place that Isobel and Henry visited frequently, sometimes together and sometimes alone. The last letter had been sent from Monaco.

"Nice place," said Castleton, "pricey, but nice. A tax haven for the rich and famous. She could still be there; it's worth a try. How's your French?"

Meg rolled her eyes. "I did German," she joked, "how's yours?"

Castleton spent a frustrating half hour struggling to communicate with the French Sûreté Publique. An amusing conversation of broken French and English words ensued until he made contact with an English speaker, Cherifa Kherzane. She directed him to their electoral role, where eligible voters were listed. Castleton managed to charm Cherifa into conducting the search for him, though he was no longer certain of Isobel's surname.

"Try Attwood... try Alexander (Isobel's maiden name)". He glanced towards Meg for inspiration. "Ask her if she can search by first name; it might be easier to eliminate Isobels from a list, and hopefully, there aren't too many with that spelling."

Castleton asked and by mid-afternoon, Cherifa had faxed across a list of known Isobels residing in Monaco. For such a small country, the list was surprisingly longer than expected, but when Thackeray, with his extensive knowledge of technology, highlighted the birth year and month for Isobel Attwood, only thirty names appeared on the list.

"That's 10 each," he said, splitting the names between them.

Ordinarily, a task of that size was accomplished within a few hours, but the language barrier proved to be time-consuming. There were a couple of calls where an English voice answered and they all held their breath, but Isobel Attwood wasn't one of them.

Castleton dialled Cherifa, his new French contact, and asked if she could provide a list of Isobels who had left the country and not returned. This was a big ask and Cherifa needed a few days to carry out the task.

The connection between the victims was no clearer. Interpol and associated organisations had nothing to report on the elusive Ayda Cosward; she remained a statistic in an ever-growing world of missing persons.

CHAPTER 36

Meg had neglected her friends over the past couple of weeks and the guilt was palpable. She decided to ditch work early and invited Abby and Joby to the cottage for a sleepover and much-needed catch-up.

Joby arrived armed with ingredients to prepare his signature gourmet dish and Abby provided a magnum of pink champagne. The three of them sat down to dinner and the bubbles flowed. Joby, eager to address his newfound skills as an interior designer, talked Abby step by step through the ground floor rooms of Molecatcher Farm.

Three glasses of the pink fizz later, he was slurring his words, and before 9 pm, he was snoring into the cushions of Meg's old sofa. That gave Abby and Meg the chance to chat freely.

Abby, still reeling from her father's sudden passing, admitted that she had taken to her bed for a couple of weeks extorting comfort from Xanax and vodka.

Meg felt disgusted that she had allowed her friend to suffer alone, but Abby was adamant that company was the last thing she wanted, even from her best friend.

"I'm feeling much better now though," Abby reported. "I think the dreadful news about Teddy grabbed me from the abyss and made me realise just how short life is."

"I'm so glad," replied Meg, gently stroking her arm.

"Why would Teddy kill himself?" she asked. "I don't understand."

Meg suddenly realised that the truth of Teddy's death had not been reported to the Manor House. She didn't feel the time was right to avail Abby of the news, especially when she was just getting her life back on track.

"Who knows why people do these things," shrugged Meg. "I suppose only they know. Do you speak to Theo?" asked Meg changing the subject quickly.

"Perhaps once a week. He's loved up with Verity," she sighed. "Shouldn't wonder if he pops the question. I think she might be 'the one'."

"Wow, I never thought I'd see the day that Theo Attwood would settle down," joked Meg.

"I know, me too. I'm happy for him, but it's lonely at the Manor House nowadays and I miss him so much."

"What about Lilia, isn't she there?"

"Not much, I don't think. She has a very engaging calendar and she never tells anyone where she's going or when she will be back. Let's be honest, Meg, she's our age, so who can blame her for living life? I think I would."

Meg agreed. Two more flutes of champagne and Abby was beginning to relax. Meg thought she would slip a couple of questions into the conversation, just as a fishing exercise.

"Let's raise a glass to Teddy Gimp." Meg held the

crystal high and Abby followed, giving a chink of glass and a 'cheers' to Teddy.

"How long had he worked for your family?" Meg enquired.

"Oh, let me think ... he's been there since I was born. There's a tree in the arboretum he planted in honour of my birth - wasn't that nice?!"

"He seemed a nice man, though I didn't really know him," admitted Meg.

"He was; he always made time to stop and talk to me. It was usually about boring stuff like gardening and fishing, but still, he made the effort."

"Fishing?" Meg's ears pricked.

"Oh yes, he loved fishing. He used to take Theo on his boat." Meg's ears pricked up again. "He had a boat?"

"Yes, he always promised to take me, but Mother wouldn't let him. I was too young she said."

"I wonder what it was called... can you remember?" questioned Meg.

"The boat's name, do you mean?" giggled Abby, rolling around the floor.

"Yes, the boat. They usually have a name," explained Meg.

"I bet it did, but I have no idea." Abby paused for a moment, then reached for her mobile. "I'm texting Theo; he will know."

Another chink of glass and they started laughing

again. Joby was still comatose on the couch.

Theo responded quickly. Abby, in a state of intoxication, desperately tried to focus on his reply. "Uhm.... Theo says it was called ... err... new ... new beginnings."

Meg choked on a large gulp of champagne. Abby howled with laughter as a huge spray of pink fizz hit her directly in the face. Meg, wiping away remnants of the liquid, tried to compose herself. Her mind was racing.

That was the name of the boat that had been chartered by Sir Henry to aid in Ayda Cosward's escape. Teddy Gimp owned that boat. Everyone who had died was connected with Ayda Cosward in one way or another.

Meg, feeling more than a little tipsy herself, took her friend by the hand and directed her upstairs to bed. Abby was asleep in no time.

Meg messaged Castleton and Thackeray but neither replied - perhaps the fact that it was 2 am was the reason.

At breakfast, Joby and Abby were nursing hangovers. Meg, on the other hand, was fine. The revelation of the previous night seemed to be the sobering factor.

Joby could not muster the enthusiasm to cook pancakes, so they walked to the Snooty Fox for breakfast and a 'hair of the dog'.

Joby, still worried about Gully, ate a piece of toast and left.

Abby, despite her post-alcoholic state, managed to annihilate a full English, four rounds of toast and a pot of

Earl Grey.

Meg picked her way through muesli and fresh fruit. She could never stomach a large meal at the start of the day, even though she had to admit it looked and smelled divine.

"I've never asked you this before," Meg began, "but have you ever heard from your mother?" Abby stopped in her tracks, two pieces of bacon and a slice of sausage hanging in mid-air. "Sorry," apologised Meg, "I shouldn't have asked."

"No, it's ok," replied Abby, "you just took me by surprise, that's all. It's the first time anyone has mentioned her to me for years. I started to forget I ever had a mother. Whatever made you think of her?"

Meg paused for a moment. Her answer had to be credible without alerting Abby to the fact that Isobel was a person of interest; "I suppose I was just thinking about your father being gone, and it made me think of Isobel, that and the beautiful portrait that still hangs prominently at the top of the staircase".

Abby's mood became pensive after that and Meg didn't want to push any further. Isobel was obviously still a sensitive subject, and Abby's reaction had more than answered the question. Abby finished her feast, pushing the plate sideways and releasing a trickle of tea leaves into her teacup.

"Theo has," she stated suddenly.

Meg remained silent. Perhaps Theo was the person to contact. She smiled gratefully and they never spoke of Isobel again.

CHAPTER 37
Isobel

When Isobel was sixteen, her father, Earl Sinclair Alexander, introduced Sir Henry Attwood.

At the time, she hadn't realised the importance of that meeting. It was a couple of years later that the reason became clear when the Earl informed her that Sir Henry was to become her future husband.

At sixteen, marriage was the furthest thing from Isobel's mind, and yet, if Teddy Gimp had asked her, she would have accepted without a second thought.

Isobel and Teddy conducted a secret love affair under the veil of friendship.

Teddy was a private in the Army. He was often seconded to serve dinner at the officers' mess, where Isobel and her mother would dine amongst the elite of the British armed forces. It was love at first sight when her eyes met Teddy's, but she knew that her father would never accept Private Gimp as marriage material.

Their backgrounds and upbringing were polar opposites, but class and wealth did not deter them and their love blossomed.

At eighteen, Isobel's father announced her engagement to Sir Henry, and her betrothed, who was twenty years her senior, proposed with a ten-carat diamond ring. Isobel, despite her love for Teddy, knew that the time had come to honour her family and marry the man her father had chosen.

The wedding was a lavish affair held in the grounds of Dunstable House, the family home. Teddy, though not invited, watched from afar as Isobel danced the night away with her new husband.

Isobel, though fond of Henry, never found love with anyone other than Teddy.

She found salvation in his arms, and Teddy resigned himself to his fate, safe in the knowledge that he could continue to see and love Isobel.

He joined the Manor House ground staff to be close to her and rented a home in the village where they could be together.

Isobel bore two children for Henry, but the marriage soon became intolerable. Henry, a self-confessed adulterer, could not keep his hands off the young and pretty female inhabitants of Soho. He was constantly away from the family travelling around Europe and Asia in the pursuit of business.

When Theo was 10 and Abby 6, Isobel filed for divorce citing irreconcilable differences. Henry, powerful and stubborn, agreed to the terms, providing Isobel allowed the children to remain with him. It was the hardest decision she had ever faced, but she knew that even if she disagreed, Sir Henry would win in the end.

On that fateful morning, she left the house and never

looked back, hanging on the arm of a handsome stranger as she battled to save her dignity. No one knew that the stranger was, in fact, her brother-in-law, sent to play a deceptive role in her departure.

She could hear the children sobbing and calling for her, and the tears flowed over her cheeks and pooled on the crisp white collar of her linen blouse. She wanted to turn around, run to her children, hug them and whisk them away, but she couldn't. Her heart was breaking. Henry had ripped away the very core of her existence and, by doing so, he had destroyed her.

She dared not glance towards Teddy, though his silhouette haunted her vision. On hearing the commotion, he had joined other members of the household to watch the scene unfold. Teddy would never forgive her.

She could feel his disbelief emanating from the spot where he stood, silent and statuesque. Teddy had devoted the best years of his life to her and she had destroyed every fibre of his soul in an instant.

She had left him a note, pinned to the greenhouse door, in which she had tried to explain. She hoped that time would heal his pain and the knowledge she had imparted in her note would give him the strength to move forward with life after her departure.

She stayed at the family home for a while, gathering her thoughts, then began an addictive relationship with painkillers and an unhealthy liking for cannabis. She clawed her way through life, a faded portrait of her former self. She would not afford herself a speck of forgiveness for what she had done and the lives she had ruined, and she had no preference for whether she lived or died.

Several years later, in a rehabilitation clinic, she befriended a man with a similar story to hers. They could relate to each other and found the pathway to a cure, and beyond that, a semblance of love and happiness. They flew to Monaco where the man had once lived and made it their home. A new life, a new start, finally casting off the shadows of the old one. Perhaps there was a happy ending for Isobel after all.

It happened unexpectedly, that call from France.

It didn't come from Interpol or Castleton's helpful French counterpart, or any other organisation, but from a man called Max Keller.

Keller had specifically asked to speak with Meg. He wouldn't give a reason but said that it was urgent.

Max Keller identified himself as the husband of Isobel Attwood, as she was last known. Meg almost fell out of the car. She had been poised to ring Theo in Ireland and, at that very moment, her phone had buzzed and the call from Keller had been transferred through.

"My name is Max Keller, and I am the husband of the lady you knew as Isobel Attwood," said the voice. "I understand you are looking for her."

"That's right," replied Meg. "I've been trying to find her. Is she alright?"

"Yes, she's fine. She doesn't know that I am contacting

you, but I saw in the English newspaper that Teddy Gimp had died. Isobel and I are very honest with each other and I know that Teddy once meant a lot to her. I wanted to know what had happened before I broke the news. She is still fragile where Teddy is concerned, and she has spoken of you in the past. She knew you were back in the village and working for the Police Department."

"How did she know that?" pondered Meg.

"Her son, Theo, he has kept in touch with her and keeps her up to date."

"Well, thank you for ringing, Mr Keller. I am relieved to know that Isobel is okay. I cannot give you any details on the death of Mr Gimp, as our investigations are ongoing. Would it be possible to speak with Isobel herself?"

The voice went quiet, then the sound of agitated breathing could be heard in the microphone. "Mr Keller, are you still there?" enquired Meg.

"Yes, I'm still here," came the reply. "I think it best that I break the news to her first, and then, if she is happy to speak with you, I will ask her to call."

Before Meg could answer, the line went dead and Keller had gone.

She watched pensively as Isobel crossed the street in front of her, having no idea about the woman who stalked her or why. To Isobel, she was just a face in the crowd.

She followed as Isobel passed through the casino square, watched as she lunched at the Café de Paris with girlfriends and waited patiently for her to leave.

Isobel was a shadow of her former self, skinny, touching anorexic. The beauty was there but masked beneath years of self-abuse and unhappiness. No amount of makeup could conceal the sadness that still lived in her eyes. She was, in essence, a broken object, held together by self-will and determination.

Isobel waved as a small convertible Jaguar pulled up beside her. She hopped in and kissed the driver. They sped off in the direction of Port de la Voilier.

Leather-clad, astride a Honda Gold Wing she followed, along the scenic coast road turning into Monte Carlo's most upmarket area. They turned right towards Larvotto beach until they reached Avenue Princesse Grace. The car disappeared beneath the Roccabella high-rise.

She would return later - now she knew where to find them, they wouldn't see her coming.

CHAPTER 38
Victim Number 10

Meg had spoken with Theo and, for once, he had been pretty open. Perhaps Verity's influence was reinventing the former playboy and, for the first time, Meg actually had an adult conversation with him that didn't leave her exasperated or angry.

Theo, being the older brother of her best friend, had never been easy to get along with. The spoiled heir to the Attwood fortune was a brat, self-absorbed and egotistical.

As a brother, he was brutish and conceited, the living description of a narcissist. Abby and Meg hated when he was home from school, hanging around for the holidays. He was bossy and loud, he sulked, and always wanted his own way.

Nowadays, the loss of his father, combined with his love for Verity, seemed to have mellowed the altruistic Theo into the shape of an almost recognisable decent human being. Perhaps Verity was 'the one'.

Theo confirmed that he had stayed in contact with his mother and that Max Keller was indeed her husband.

He had tracked her down with the aid of a Private Investigator, knowing she was undergoing rehab somewhere in the south of England.

He had briefly spoken with Max and was happy to

know that his mother had found love and security with a decent man.

He knew the true story of her departure from the Manor House that fateful day and the hatred he had held onto for years melted into insignificance at the sound of his mother's voice and the guilt that had plagued her for so many years. It was easy to forgive her knowing the agony she herself had suffered and that she was truly repentant for her actions.

Theo was not confident that Isobel would contact Meg - it would stir up too many memories he thought, something she had tried for so many years to hide away.

Meg thanked him for his time and reminded him that her name should be on the guest list if he were ever to propose to Verity. Theo chuckled and the conservation ended.

Meg remained hopeful that Isobel would call her back, but as the hours ticked by, the reality looked decidedly different.

Castleton had a family meal to attend, leaving Meg home alone. He had practically moved into Pebble Cottage, with evidence of his presence scattered sporadically throughout the dwelling.

Meg soothed away the day with a flamboyant bubble bath. The tub foamed with scented delights while flickering candles and soft music created a spa atmosphere. Every aching muscle in her body enjoyed warmth and tranquillity and she wallowed there for hours until the aching was relieved and her eyelids were fighting to combat sleep.

She snuggled beneath a fluffy duvet and drifted into oblivion, calmly and deeply.

It was past 5 when she woke to the sound of buzzing. Damn, she hadn't silenced her phone. She wanted to ignore the persistent noise, but her mind wouldn't let her. She dragged the phone to her ear and waited.

At first, she thought her sleep had been disturbed by a crank call, and she was just about to give whoever it was an unpleasant mouthful, when suddenly, a desperate voice whispered, "Meg, its Max Keller. I think someone is trying to kill me."

Meg sat bolt upright; he had got her attention. "Where are you, Max? Who's trying to kill you?" Max was in mid-sentence when the line went dead, a distant groan being his final communication. The phone was then switched off and her call-backs went directly to voicemail.

Meg felt desperate and useless.

She rang Castleton who was sympathetic but did not see what could be done at this hour of the morning. He promised to contact his French counterpart first thing in the morning.

Isobel and Max regularly walked their poodles beside the ocean, laughing and hopping playfully as the waves lapped around their ankles. The sun waved goodbye in the distance and slowly disappeared from view.

She watched from the safety of the promenade. The beach was deserted now, but even in the shadow of dusk, it was too risky to commit cold-blooded murder. She had to be careful; public assassinations would attract too much attention.

She sipped on her cocktail and waited.

Finally, they headed for the promenade, kissed and parted company, Isobel heading in the direction of home and Max disappearing in the opposite direction with their dogs. This was perfect.

She followed Isobel back to her apartment and followed behind her as she held open the door. They exchanged niceties in the elevator as it rose to Isobel's floor. Stepping out, she pretended to have lost her bearings as she passed Isobel unlocking her front door. Then suddenly and violently, she pushed Isobel inside.

The apartment was just as she imagined; typically Isobel. Her name may have changed but her palette for distasteful decor had not. A little redecorating was needed and the knife would help her do it.

Blood sprayed across the room clinging to everything it touched. The knife was relentless, stabbing at the victim who was obviously already dead. She cleaned its blade, leaving a crimson smear across a nearby white velvet chaise. Isobel lay lifeless, her mutilated body viciously carved and cut at the hand of the bloody knife.

She hadn't given her a chance to retaliate. A sharp thrust through the ribs, targeting the heart with practised accuracy, rendered Isobel defenceless. She hit the marble floor with a thud, clinging to the last moments of her life, desperately trying to splutter forth her dying words. She was silenced instantly, struck by the blade incessantly until her life force was drowning in a river of her own blood.

She felt exhilarated, the rush of satisfaction coursing through every fibre of her being. She carefully removed her shoes, the soles discoloured red, and replaced them with a pair of Isobel's from the dressing room. There was an impressive collection of designer footwear mounted in regimented order on countless elevated racks, so the choice was difficult, but they fitted perfectly.

She opened her bag and removed a sleek black feather, then she tucked it inside her discarded shoe with a smile.

Pulling the high knot from her hair, she shook it free, allowing the soft curls of her coiffure to wrestle into place around her shoulders. She checked the room and headed towards the door, stopping to admire herself in the baroque-style mirror, and styling an abandoned fedora at an angle on her head.

The apartment looked far less boring now - a splash of colour was all that was needed.

As she reached the freedom of the hallway, Max passed close beside her. "Bonjour," he muttered as the dogs barked at his feet.

A moment later, she heard a male voice cry out in horror - he had clearly discovered the murdered body of Isobel, unrecognisable beneath her blood-soaked shroud.

She heard his shouts for help echoing in the distance as she exited the building and slipped deftly back into society. She bathed in a cocoon of bubbles, sipping expensive champagne. Tomorrow, she would fly home; her work here was done.

Max was inconsolable, scooping the remains of his beloved wife into his arms and rocking her gently. He wailed uncontrollably, refusing to release her body to the Police and paramedics. He was eventually dragged from the building and driven to the nearest station, where following examination by a doctor, he was questioned about Isobel's murder, but later released without charge.

The following morning, as she ate breakfast on the balcony of her hotel room, her attention was drawn to a folded newspaper placed beside her coffee cup. Staring up at her in black and white print was a crude drawing of a face.

She felt her heart rate quicken, a feeling she did not recognise.

Max Keller had given a detailed description of the woman he had passed in the hallway on the night of Isobel's murder.

She recognised it immediately; the face was hers.

All of a sudden, she felt gullible, exposed, panic quivering beneath her usually stoic demeanour. She hadn't factored Max into her carefully executed plans. His name was not part of the list but maybe it should have been.

Perhaps her stay in Monaco wasn't over, but she couldn't risk being recognised. She felt overwhelmed; she needed time to think.

Castleton spoke with Cherifa in France the next day.

She had limited information but confirmed that Isobel Keller was dead, brutally murdered in her home.

"What about Max?" Meg questioned.

"He was taken in for questioning but has since been released. You know the score, Meg, it's always the closest to the victim that is the first suspect."

"Yes, but he rang me last night, believing that someone was trying to kill him. I heard a groan, then the line went dead."

"Why don't you ring him back? I'm sure he's fine," encouraged Castleton.

Meg tried the number, but it went straight to voicemail. She tried a different number, but that was discontinued. Meg had that feeling again; something wasn't right...

Castleton declined to authorise a trip to Monaco, but he did arrange a Skype call with Cherifa and she kindly invited the pathologist to join them in the hopes that Meg would gain a morsel of satisfaction.

Isobel had died instantly, her last vision being the identity of her killer as death tugged violently at her soul. She would have known her fate, though, and judging by the gruesome crime scene, she had exhaled her last breath in the presence of evil.

Max Keller had been released from custody and as far as the French knew he had checked into the L'Hermitage Hotel for a couple of days until the police vacated his apartment and it was able to be cleaned.

Those words did not speak comfort to Meg, who imagined him lying dead in an unmarked grave, the finality of his demise unknown. She longed for him to get back in touch, but she knew it was futile - Max Keller would never contact anyone ever again.

Max had never been part of the plan, as he had not featured in any part of her life until now. His mistake had been describing her to the police, and, by doing so, he had unwittingly sealed his fate.

She needed to leave Monaco as soon as possible. Her face was on every news channel and in every newspaper headline and that disturbed her. She was angry with herself; how had she allowed this to happen?

Her window of opportunity was very small, so Max must be eliminated tonight. She dared not risk another day in the south of France.

That evening, as a sorrowful Max walked his dogs along the beach, she followed closely.

He stopped to make a call as she stooped in to admire his poodles, carefully covering her face beneath the generous brim of a straw hat.

She rose slowly as she heard the call connect, their eyes now aligned, and his expression changed instantly from a friendly smile to a sudden grimace of realisation.

He whispered desperately as the caller answered, but it was too late.

She jabbed the needle into the side of his neck and almost instantly, he was on his knees. His hand released the excitable hounds and they raced off into the distance, disappearing into the veil of darkness that was slowly dragging the cover of night across the deserted beach.

There was no one around to observe her hauling a heavily sedated Max to the water's edge. She waded just far enough to allow the waves to catch hold of him and she watched as he floated, unaware of his fate, into the watery abyss.

Max would drown long before the sedation wore off and he would wash up on a distant shore in a couple of days. It would be assumed that he had thrown himself into the water unable to bear the death of his murdered wife, and the case would be closed.

She checked her watch - her flight left in two hours and this time, she would be on it.

The Skype call was in full swing with the gruesome details of Isobel's murder laid bare.

She had received at least thirteen wounds, all inflicted

by the same weapon. A large dagger-style knife with a sharp, serrated edge had cut and thrust its way through Isobel's body; she hadn't stood a chance of survival.

There was no material evidence or DNA found at the scene.

Meg and Castleton agreed that the modus operandi of Isobel's killer was likely to have made her the latest victim in a string of connected murders.

There was no sign of the bereaved Max, but his dogs had been caught that morning weaving frantically among traffic in the town's centre. They wore identity tags and were recognised by the Keller's neighbours.

Meg knew then that her hunch had been right - the sight of the dogs wandering aimlessly without Max could only mean one thing.

Monsieur Aubert, who bore the rank of police chief, revealed the description of a woman Max Keller had passed in the hallway of the apartment building shortly before discovering his wife's body.

She was an immaculately dressed woman wearing a black designer suit, sunglasses and a matching fedora. She carried a cream leather handbag, a Birkin. Max knew it instantly as Isobel had once owned such a bag. She had brushed Max's arm as she passed and they had exchanged niceties.

"Was she not just another resident of the building?" Meg enquired, adding, "A beautifully dressed woman with a cream handbag is hardly likely to have committed murder just moments before.

Where was the blood? She should have been covered."

Meg had a point; the violence imparted on Isobel Keller would have left the murderer as bloody as the victim.

Monsieur Aubert agreed, but he promised to fax over a copy of the image drawn from Max's memory anyway. The woman was not known in the building and did not live there.

"I think we can rule her out," said Castleton quite definitely. "How so?" asked a pensive Meg.

"She was probably visiting someone. I don't think she's our murderer." "Women murder too," Meg snarled.

"Myra Hindley, Rose West..." Thackeray began to list historic names of female serial killers.

"I know that," scolded Castleton, "but think of the practicalities of murdering someone while dressed in designer gear; it just doesn't fit."

Meg decided to change the subject, sparing the French voyeurs the wrath of an irritated sergeant.

The following morning, it was there sitting on the fax machine, the face that Max had described.

Meg felt slightly disappointed when she saw it; perhaps Castleton was right. The woman staring up at her was the epitome of French chic, and women like her frequented the restaurants and designer shops of Monaco on a daily basis. Meg knew the designer suit hid a toned, bronzed figure and, beneath the sunglasses, a youthful complexion and immaculate makeup would adorn her face.

Her eyes were shaded behind large black sunglasses and her hair was masked by the hat she wore slightly tilted to one side. This woman represented half the population of Monaco; it was a melting pot of glamorous, wealthy women just like her.

"There's really not much to go on, is there?" said Castleton, handing the image over to Thackeray. "That's disappointing," added Thackeray. "Looks like we're back to square one... again."

The day passed slowly after that, a feeling of disappointment gripping the team, and they found it hard to motivate themselves.

Around 3 pm, Castleton suggested they call it a day and start early the next morning. He needed to make decisions on their next move and he couldn't think at the office, so he headed to Aunt Imelda's B&B to think alone.

Thackeray was eager to meet up with friends at the Snooty Fox and shoot some pool.

Meg dragged herself home to find solace in a bottle of wine. She texted Abby for company, but Abby didn't reply.

"Looks like it's just you and me again, Pepper," as the dachshund curled up beside her and they drifted into unconsciousness together.

A couple of hours later, Meg woke to a buzzing sound.

Her mobile phone was tucked down the side of the sofa and vibrating like an angry wasp. It was Abby. They chatted for a while. Abby sounded better, more positive, and much like her old self.

Meg didn't dare broach the subject of Isobel, fearing her friend may spiral back into depression. Theo was the best person to break it to her.

They arranged to meet up at the weekend and spend a day in London shopping and lunching, followed by a sleepover at the Manor House.

Meg thought it would be nice to catch up. Speaking with Abby had brought Joby to mind; she hadn't heard from or seen him for a while. She promised to make the effort to contact him the next day and organise a get-together.

When Castleton returned to the office bright and early the following morning, his mood had lifted. He suggested that they trawl through the information they already had just in case they had overlooked anything. It was a laborious job and the only conclusion they could draw was that the victims were still connected to Ayda Cosward.

Ayda had disappeared into Europe and there was no trace of her after that. They were desperate for a breakthrough.

An unexpected call from Cherifa in France gave them a ray of hope. On deeper investigation of Max and Isobel's apartment, a pair of shoes was discovered by a keen-eyed detective. He had noticed that the apartment was immaculate with not a thing out of place, but in Isobel's dressing room, one shoe was slightly askew to the others, and it caught his attention.

On further analysis, the shoe bore the tiniest trace of blood just inside the leather upper. It was immediately sent for testing, and, under ultraviolet light, both soles were found to be heavily bloodstained.

Finally, and somewhat strangely, they found a black feather tucked inside the shoe, which turned out to belong to a raven.

The three stared at each other and smiled.

This wasn't definitive evidence, but it sure as hell put them on the right track.

The black feather was a poignant discovery in the investigation and a very significant one too.

In the late afternoon, as Meg was ready to leave the office, she received a call from Theo. He had been informed that Max Keller's body had washed up on the shore of La Rochelle, a thousand kilometres from Monaco. It was currently awaiting post-mortem examination.

This wasn't entirely surprising to Meg, she knew Max Keller had not survived on the night he had made the panicked call, but the reality was sobering.

Theo was planning a trip back to England in the next few days. He had relayed the news to Abby who brushed it off with an 'I don't care' attitude. Theo knew his sister well enough to know that deep down, she would be wrestling with the demons of her mother's departure and now, her death. He felt he should be her shoulder to cry on and offer his support.

Meg was grateful for the information and the fact that Theo, the self-confessed narcissist, had thought about his sister's feelings and not just his own.

CHAPTER 39

Arriving at Molecatcher Farm, Joby was pleased to greet Meg. As usual, he had cooked and they dined together, whilst Gully remained in his room.

"I really don't know what's got into him," said Joby, "he hardly ever leaves his room these days. He sneaks around when I've gone to bed. It's as if he doesn't want to be around me, but I've no idea why."

"You need to try talking to him, Joby," advised Meg. "He's your brother and if there's something bothering him, you need to know."

"I don't think he would tell me. I've thought about reading his diary!"

Meg raised her eyebrows; "That would need to be a last resort. You can't go invading his privacy unless you have a really good reason."

Joby agreed.

Gully, though mute, was able to communicate by writing in a crude, infantile fashion. It had been his only real voice since childhood, as his parents had never taken the time to learn to sign. Gully communicated with them through pencil and paper, a laborious and time-consuming task, though it helped develop Gully's understanding of the English language and his writing skills.

Meg was intrigued to know what Gully wrote about

in his diary. The very fact that he kept a diary was an alien concept, but she could not condone Joby taking a peek.

"I'm seeing Abby at the weekend; we have a girlie trip to London planned," said Meg, changing the subject.

"Nice!" Joby replied, "I haven't seen Abby for ages, but I know she has been going through a lot." Meg updated Joby with the deaths of Isobel and her husband, Max Keller. He was horrified to learn of their fate. "I always liked Isobel - she was a kind lady," he stated.

"She was indeed," agreed Meg, "but keep this to yourself; I'm telling you in confidence."

She edged closer to Joby and confided, "We think she was killed by whoever committed the other murders, and at the moment, our prime suspect is a woman."

Joby listened intently but said nothing. A sudden creaking sound caught their attention; Gully was lurking in the shadows. How long he had been there and what he had heard was impossible to know.

The blood on the shoe in Isobel's dressing room was her own, but the shoes were not. Madame Giraud, the Keller's housekeeper, had confirmed that Isobel did not own black velvet Prada's with diamanté trim. The shoes taken from Isobel's closet were black crocodile skin by Christian Dior; they were a special edition and had been terribly expensive.

The search was now on for the first tangible piece of evidence.

The weekend arrived faster than Meg had anticipated. Abby was determined to take the London trip even after receiving the news from Theo.

Meg knew her friend would be struggling emotionally, and the weekend would be a good way to distract her.

They caught the 11 o'clock train to Euston and hit the shops immediately. By lunchtime, Abby was drowning beneath a sea of designer bags, whilst Meg sported Selfridges' smallest carrier which housed a pink lipstick.

Abby insisted on paying for lunch at Harrods. It was a grand affair with an afternoon tea fit for a queen. Prosecco flowed encouraging loquacious chatter and the hours ticked away.

Abby babbled on about everything and anything but avoided bringing up the subject of her mother. That evening, they found a champagne bar and continued their fizzy liquid marathon.

How they managed to arrive back at the correct hotel Meg was not sure, but a very helpful cabby had been their saviour.

It was early morning as they crashed into bed and slept until the maid woke them knocking at the door for room service. Both were feeling delicate, but a greasy breakfast was always the cure and Abby was adamant about returning to Harvey Nichols to buy the pair of shoes she had rejected the day before, but then dreamt about all night.

The sun was shining on the streets of London as they made their way through the crowds towards Harvey Nichols.

Abby, an avid if not compulsive shopper, tried almost every shoe in the store, again. Meg watched; the price tags made her eyes water and there was nothing she could afford.

One shelf was devoted to Christian Dior, so Meg studied them. There were no black crocodile skin ones. The sales assistant hovered close by, so Meg asked if that particular shoe was a recent design, but the assistant shook her head and smiled politely. "That shoe is a very exclusive vintage style; there are probably only a handful of people in the world who could afford to own them."

The train journey home was a sleepy one and before they knew it, they were en route to the Manor House, courtesy of Darrow.

Meg longed for her own fluffy duvet, but she had promised Abby a sleepover and she never broke her promises.

The house was quiet - Sir Henry's death still cast a sombre cloud over the whole estate. A chapter of its history had closed that day and the book would never read the same again.

Darrow went about his routine in hypnotic mode, but there was a sadness in every movement and an emptiness in his eyes.

Mrs Hobson was her usual, red-faced, jovial self. She hugged Abby as if she were her own child and made two mugs of hot chocolate, Abby's favourite.

Dinner was served in the dining room, the place where Sir Henry had met his fate.

The flashbacks were uncontrollable, the whole dreadful evening replaying constantly as Meg tried desperately to concentrate on Abby's conversation.

Lilia, as stunning as ever, was on her way to a charity event that Sir Henry had set up in her name when they first married. She wore a sequinned evening dress and cream stilettos, dazzling diamonds draped her neck and ears and she carried a crystal-studded purse.

Meg couldn't help but feel a hint of jealousy as she gazed upon Lilia's beauty. She was the woman every man desired.

She bade them goodnight and left with Darrow minutes later.

"Oh, Abby, how I wish I had her presence in a room." Meg's head sank onto her hands. "I know; sickening, isn't she?" joked Abby. "How's it going with your sergeant anyway?"

"Oh, I don't know, one minute I think he's really interested and then the next I'm not so sure. Am I just a sex toy when he's feeling horny, or am I in a relationship with him? Who knows."

Abby giggled, "Men! Can't live with them, can't live

without them, unfortunately."

They played old disco tunes and danced the night away aided by Abby's stash of alcohol. They were two young girls again reliving this childhood.

When morning broke, Meg left before Abby had opened her eyes. She had never been an early riser especially when alcohol had been involved. Downstairs in the hallway, she waited for Darrow to drive her to the station. She admired the ornate architecture of the Manor House; it was still as beautiful today as it had been back then, and she felt privileged to have spent so much time here.

Darrow had always been a prompt timekeeper, but today he was late. He bustled out of the drawing room, red-faced and agitated, apologising repeatedly for keeping Meg waiting.

He was carrying a woman's handbag, then he rushed past Meg and placed it on the console table. Its quality was undeniable, the stitching exquisite, and it sat like a piece of art where Darrow had placed it, waiting patiently.

"Darrow, what is this bag?" Meg asked curiously.

Darrow turned as if he had not realised what he had been carrying. He looked at the bag and then at Meg, then said, "It's a Birkin."

Meg felt a sudden rush of anxiety as Darrow was disappearing out of the door towards the car.

"Who does it belong to?" she called after him.

"Originally, it was Lady Isobel's, but I believe she left it behind for Miss Abby."

"I see, and what, if you don't mind me asking, are you doing with it?"

"It's going to be cleaned," Darrow grunted, as he jumped into the car and beckoned for Meg to join him.

On the way to the station, Meg's mind was in overdrive. As Darrow pulled the Rolls to a stop, she hopped out and turned to thank him. "Just one more thing, Darrow, where do you take a Birkin to be cleaned?"

"I believe there's a place called the Cleaning Clinic. Someone is picking it up so I must dash." Meg raced into the office and googled the information immediately. There were three in the area, but the closest was probably Oxford.

She called the on-line number and a well-spoken man answered. Meg described the bag and asked if it was scheduled to be picked up by them. The man disappeared to consult his diary and came back with a resounding 'Yes'. Meg asked him to keep the bag to one side as she would pick it up before lunchtime. The man reluctantly agreed.

Castleton hadn't arrived in the office by the time Meg was ready to leave, so she asked Thackeray to accompany her on the journey to Oxford.

She left a message on Castleton's desk and they set off in Thackeray's car, as Meg's was back at the cottage.

"You think this bag has something to do with the

case?" quizzed Thackeray, unsure as to why he was making the journey to Oxford for the sake of a designer handbag.

"I don't know, Will, it's just a hunch; could turn out to mean nothing."

Meg felt ashamed at the thoughts that were currently racing around inside her head. She tried reasoning with herself; 'The bag once belonged to Isobel, who left it for Abby. A cream Birkin was described by Max Keller in his description of the woman he had passed on the evening of Isobel's murder. Did two and two make five or was she on the right track?' Meg desperately wanted to be wrong; 'Surely Abby had nothing to do with the murders - she wasn't capable of such barbarity, was she?'

The journey was fraught with anxiety. An hour later, they parked outside the Cleaning Clinic. A well-maintained shop front with an eye-catching display of designer bags told them this was the right place. The well-spoken man handed over the Birkin shrouded in protective wrapping and asked Meg to sign a disclaimer.

With the bag on board, they headed straight for Scotland Yard's forensic department. Time was of the essence as the bag was scheduled to be returned to the Manor House the next day.

"I understand why you are interested in this bag, Meg," said Thackeray, "but surely you don't think Abby is involved in these murders, do you?"

"Of course not, Will, but it's a cream Birkin and

it's going for cleaning; don't you think that's worthy of investigation? I mean, why is it going for cleaning? I'm not saying it will tell us anything, but it's such a coincidence, don't you think?"

Thackeray looked confused.

"I'm clutching at straws here, I know that, but we are desperate for a breakthrough, so just bear with me, okay?"

Thackeray nodded.

The Yard provided endless mugs of coffee as they waited patiently for forensics to work their magic. Castleton finally touched base. He hadn't felt well, but was back in the office and feeling much better.

"Meg, there must be hundreds of Birkin bags around the world, maybe thousands; we can't go chasing around the country testing every bag we find."

Meg was not amused, but the results were in.

The bag was clean. Fingerprints had been lifted and kept on file, but otherwise, there was nothing notable to report.

Meg was disappointed and relieved at the same time. She scolded herself for allowing the thought to have crossed her mind, but these were desperate times and desperate measures were called for.

She returned the bag for cleaning and Thackeray drove her home.

Max Keller had undergone a post-mortem examination in France and the report had been emailed to Castleton.

Max had drowned and his death would have been ruled as accidental or suicide, save for the small puncture wound on his neck, consistent with a needle mark. There was no further evidence and whatever had been injected into Max's body was, by now, undetectable.

The French police allowed the Kellers to be buried and arrangements were made for the following week.

Theo had organised a small service in the local chapel at which he and Verity would be the only attendees.

Isobel had thankfully left a Will, which stated that, following the death of Max, her estate was to be divided between her two children with a donation of half a million pounds to Teddy Gimp. The later decision served as an unexpected surprise and left Theo with a lot of unanswered questions.

Meg, of course, knew the truth, but for Abby and Theo, it would remain a mystery.

Castleton arrived unexpectedly at Pebble Cottage with wine and roses. Meg was desperately sleep-deprived and wanted to send him away, but his winning smile and thoughtful gifts were enough to charm his way into her bed.

There was an animal passion between them, reaching sexual heights Meg had never experienced before. Michael had been a considerate lover, but sparks almost never flew in the bedroom department.

She hadn't chosen a corner of the English countryside

as her new home believing that love would find her again, and yet, here she was entwined in the arms of a man who had brought passion and happiness into her life once more.

She had resigned herself to a life alone with her dog, her friends and her Aunty June for company. Another man had never featured in her future after Michael's death, but here he was lying beside her breathing softly, slowly stealing her heart and soul.

Time was against her; Max Keller had seen to that. She needed to finish the list and disappear.

This would be her finale, her pièce de résistance - it would be memorable; it would be her defining moment.

She would be free from the chains of suppression, the debt would be paid and she could live life knowing she had eradicated those who sought to exploit and abuse her.

CHAPTER 40

Another week rolled by and no progress had been made in the search for Ayda Cosward, or the glamorous woman in Monaco.

Then, just when hopes were vanishing, Castleton received a message from Cherifa, his French connection.

The woman in the photo-fit had boarded a private plane the day after Max Keller's death. It had flown from Monaco to Heathrow carrying a small crew and one female passenger. The aircraft had been chartered under the name of Theo Attwood, and the woman on board was his sister Abby.

Meg felt a shockwave course through her body. She sank onto her desk. "I can't believe it," she said over and over again.

Castleton wanted to throw his arms around her and console her, but Thackeray's keen eyes were upon him.

"What does this mean?" asked Thackeray, breaking the deafening silence.

"I'm not sure yet, but it does mean that we need to speak with Abby and Theo Attwood immediately."

Castleton felt it was better that he visited the Manor House and bring Abby Attwood in for questioning.

"I've known Abby all my life, and Theo. She... they are not capable of murder," Meg muttered. "Let's get her down here and see what she has to say. At the moment, we just have her name and nothing else."

"That's right," added Thackeray, "someone could have used her identity. I'm sure there's an explanation for this."

With Castleton gone, Thackeray plied Meg with hot strong coffee and as many words of comfort as he could muster.

Meg, feeling bewildered, would not believe that Abby was in any way involved.

Abby was equally disturbed when Castleton arrived at the Manor House to take her in for questioning.

Darrow was instructed to contact Theo immediately.

A tearful Lilia wanted to accompany them to the station, but Castleton was adamant that he needed to speak with Abby alone. She watched from the steps of the Manor House as they drove away.

Meg was not allowed in the interview room, so Thackeray took her place. Her mobile buzzed and she recognised the number - it was Theo.

"What the hell is going on? Darrow informs me that Abby has been arrested."

Meg tried to explain but Theo constantly interrupted; "We often charter private planes... anyone could call pretending to be me... that doesn't mean anything," Theo ranted.

"I know, Theo ..."

"How could anyone think Abby could be involved in

all this? It's bloody ridiculous; you're pissing in the wind, Meg."

Theo finally calmed and Meg was able to explain that Abby was reportedly on the flight from Monaco the night after Max's death, and the plane had been chartered in his name. "Someone could be imitating us, using our names. Come on, Meg, you know Abby, she doesn't have it in her."

Meg had to agree with everything Theo Attwood said, but it didn't change the fact that intel had to be acted upon and the sooner Abby was interviewed, the sooner she could be eliminated from the investigation.

Theo promised to take the morning flight from Ireland and drive straight to the station.

An hour or so later, though it seemed nerve-rackingly longer, Castleton and Thackeray emerged from Interview Room 2, closely followed by Abby. She looked deflated and tired. Meg looked to Castleton; "She's free to go," he said.

Meg breathed a sigh of relief and Abby fell into her arms. "Let me take you home," she said. "Theo will be here in the morning."

Abby said very little on the journey home and Meg respected her silence. She helped Abby to her room and into bed, then said, "I'll send Mrs Hobson up with hot chocolate." She smiled, but Abby had already closed her eyes and sunk into sleep. Poor Abby - this year had taken a toll on her - she was fragile and vulnerable, and she needed Theo now more than ever.

Meg spent a little time in the kitchen with Darrow and Mrs Hobson, trying to explain the reason why Abby had been taken for questioning, but without giving away too much information.

"Poor love," exclaimed Mrs Hobson, "as if she hasn't been through enough without the accusation of murder being added to the list."

Darrow listened intently but said nothing. He knew the truth about Isobel and Teddy Gimp, he knew Abby was their love child and he knew that Sir Henry had played a key part in Ayda Cosward's escape from the asylum. Meg wondered what else Darrow knew.

"It's absurd, of course, but leads need to be followed up, Mrs Hobson," explained Meg.

Mrs Hobson promised to make a mug of her delicious hot chocolate and check on Abby later.

Darrow walked Meg to the door as usual, although she felt him hesitate momentarily as though there was something on his mind. She lingered for a while hoping he would find the words, but when he didn't, Meg drove away, his lone figure reflected in her rear-view mirror.

By noon the following day, Theo had arrived as promised. He couldn't prove that he hadn't chartered the plane nor could anyone prove it. The booking was made by telephone and there was no recording of the conversation to identify the caller's voice.

Theo was angry that Abby had been dragged to the

station without his support. Meg tried to comfort him, but Theo left under a cloud of discord and headed off to the Manor House.

That same afternoon, Meg rang to check on Abby and spoke at length with Theo.

"Someone is trying to ruin this family, Meg," said a concerned Theo, "not that it isn't already, but we seem to be the target of animosity; first Father, then Isobel and now us."

Meg had to agree the Attwoods had most definitely captured somebody's attention, but the question was whose?

"Have you ever heard of Ayda Cosward?" Meg asked suddenly.

"No, can't say that I have, why?"

"I think she may be at the centre of all of this and if we could find her, then we may be able to answer some questions."

"So, you're looking for a woman?" Theo was inquisitive.

"Yes, but not necessarily in connection with the murders. We just need to eliminate her from our enquiries, that's all," answered Meg.

"Perhaps Darrow has heard of the woman you're looking for?"

Perhaps Theo was right. Darrow knew more than he was willing to admit, and he certainly had something on his mind the last time Meg saw him. The problem was that Darrow's loyalty to Sir Henry was unwavering and any secrets he had would no doubt be taken to the grave.

CHAPTER 41
The Invitation

A knock at the cottage door saw the postman depositing a small package on Meg's doorstep. It was unusual to receive post, let alone a parcel, and Meg couldn't help feeling a little excited.

Inside the neatly wrapped brown paper sat a beautiful satin box. Meg's name was precisely embroidered on the lid in shiny gold thread. A professional job, thought Meg, whose needlework skills left a lot to be desired.

A beautiful invitation card sat within the decadent casing and the scripted gold-leaf calligraphy read: YOU ARE INVITED TO A FAREWELL PARTY AT THE MANOR HOUSE, Saturday 10th, drinks at 7 followed by dinner at 9. RSVP to Lady Lilia Attwood.

The fine print at the very bottom read: Please come dressed as your favourite villain or superhero.

Meg was intrigued; why was Lilia throwing a farewell party? Was she moving away? Was the Manor House to be sold, and if so, what would happen to Theo and Abby? So many questions she needed answers to - perhaps all would be revealed on the night.

CHAPTER 42

The French police had made contact again, this time with a colour photograph of the mysterious woman who had caught the flight from Monaco to Heathrow.

Initial excitement waned as the photo revealed nothing but a side view of the woman emerging from the plane wearing large, black-rimmed sunglasses and a black fedora.

Meg studied the image for ages.

"It's not going to change the more you look at it," joked Castleton.

"I know, but I don't want to miss anything. Do you have a magnifying glass?"

Castleton rummaged around in his desk and finally pulled out the antique object with an ivory handle.

"You've my grandfather to thank for that," he said, passing it to Meg.

Meg hovered over the photo like a bee on a flower, exploring every inch with care. "Who took this?" she asked.

Castleton read the email in which the photograph was attached. "A member of the airport staff; they thought the woman may be famous."

Meg continued hovering for a while longer. She moved the glass up and down, and side to side. "Is there any way we can enlarge this?"

Thackeray rose from his desk; this was his territory. Sitting at Castleton's computer, he edited the photograph and printed out a larger copy.

Meg began studying again.

"You've turned into a right Inspector Clouseau," laughed Thackeray.

"You won't be laughing when I find something," she replied, and in that moment, as she had spoken the words, she looked from Thackeray to Castleton and back again.

The laughing subsided - "What is it?" they asked simultaneously.

"Come and look at the shoes..." There was a hint of excitement in Meg's voice as the constable and sergeant gathered around her desk.

"Black shoes," noted Castleton.

"Black crocodile-skin shoes," corrected Meg.

"This has to be the woman who killed Isobel; it's no coincidence that she's wearing her shoes!" Castleton wasn't sure. "So, she's wearing the same shoes; that doesn't prove anything."

"Don't you think it's odd that a woman was seen in the hallway outside the penthouse where Isobel was murdered, a pair of Isobel's black exclusive Dior shoes are exchanged for a pair stained with blood and here she is getting off a flight from Monaco wearing them?"

"She has a point," added Thackeray.

"Well, let's say that you're right, this is the killer, but we still don't know who she is or where to find her."

Meg sat pensively for a moment; "... perhaps there is CCTV of her leaving the airport... a vehicle we could trace; it's worth a shot," she begged.

Castleton nodded. "Contact your friend at Scotland Yard; see if he can pull anything for us."

That evening, Joby called to say he had received an invitation to Lilia's party. The invite was for both brothers to attend, which struck Joby as rather odd. Lilia had only met Joby on one previous occasion, and, to his knowledge, she had never met Gully at all.

"Perhaps she's inviting the whole village," joked Meg, "either that or we are very privileged. I wouldn't think too deeply about it, Joby; accept it in the manner in which it has been sent and make sure you reply. It would be good to see familiar faces."

Joby seemed unsure but reluctantly agreed. "Have you mentioned it to Gully?"

"Yes, and his reaction was rather weird," answered Joby. "Weirder than normal?" laughed Meg.

"He ran off to the barn and didn't return for hours. It was his face that bothered me most; he looked like he had seen a ghost."

"That is weird, but then we are talking about Gully," mused Meg. "If he doesn't go, make sure you do, but reply for the both of you just in case."

Meg put in a call to Aunty June who she had not spoken to for several days. She felt slightly guilty and invited her round for dinner. Aunty June understood an increasing workload had kept Meg busy, and, within twenty minutes, was knocking at the cottage door.

Aunty June was always a good source of information as she played canasta and bridge with Bea Tilley, the postmistress, who knew everything about everybody.

During lunch, Meg showed off her invitation to Lilia Attwood's party. Aunty June was intrigued, but Bea Tilley had not mentioned anything about the Attwoods recently which probably meant she didn't know.

Aunty June promised to speak with the postmistress at their next meeting and report back. Meg was grateful and walked her to the gate of her nearby cottage.

"Don't work too hard," scolded Aunty June. "There's more to life, you know."

Aunty June was right - Meg had moved to the countryside to get over the loss of Michael and start afresh with people she knew and loved, but so far, nothing had gone to plan.

Life was funny that way; change was good.

She hadn't reckoned on being part of the murder investigation or meeting Castleton, but here she was, involved with both.

She had no choice - the time had come to remove the last two names from her list.

Then she could finally lay the blade to rest and start afresh. The raven could sing again, but she wouldn't listen. She had paid her debts; she would be free to spread her wings and fly away.

Meg had heard nothing from her contact at Scotland Yard and the wait was impossible. Her thoughts were continually consumed by the sadistic murders and a growing hunger to catch the killer.

The French police had no further leads and the investigation there was at a standstill. Castleton was becoming severely irritated by their lack of progress. The atmosphere was palpable, frustration stalked the office, and a beastly rage was growing, its jaws of disappointment ready to snap away the morsels of a possible lead.

Thackeray kept his head down, ferrying supplies of coffee as and when needed.

Meg hadn't seen Castleton away from work for the last week. She wondered whether his pent-up irritability was the result of sexual tension, though she certainly wasn't in the mood to relieve it.

Perhaps a day away from the office was needed, and she suggested Thackeray do the same. Castleton was unapproachable, so time alone with his thoughts would probably help.

She booked a spa day in Oxford and took Aunty June along for the experience. Meg needed a little fine grooming as Lilia's party was looming and she wanted to look her best.

The pamper sessions and the healthy lunch were refreshing.

Meg had noticed the dark circles beneath her eyes and the odd strand of wiry, silver hair when she looked in the mirror. Where had the fresh-faced optimist of yesteryear disappeared to? Much work was needed to bring her back, but today was just the beginning - Meg promised herself that once the case was solved, she would invest as much as was needed to find herself again.

Aunty June had thoroughly enjoyed the whole day and was extremely grateful to Meg for the chance to spend some quality time together.

"Any news from Miss Tilley?" enquired Meg as they journeyed back home.

"No," scoffed Aunty June, "she was extremely put out that she knew nothing about the Attwood party and even more so, that I knew about it first."

"I bet she was," laughed Meg.

CHAPTER 43

Two days before Lilia's party, Meg, Abby, Theo and Joby decided to meet up for lunch at the Nodding Donkey public house in the neighbouring village of Wickerbridge.

There was excited speculation as to why Lilia was holding the party, but Abby and Theo could shed little light on the subject, having only been told that all would be revealed on the night.

"What costumes are everyone wearing?" enquired Abby. Theo had opted for the easy James Bond, tuxedo look.

Abby was dressing as Coco Chanel, her favourite designer, and it helped that she owned many items from the chic collection.

Joby was still pondering on his hero look, though Hercule Poirot was a distinct possibility. The attic at Molecatcher Farm was awash with baskets of old-fashioned garments which Joby was sure would contain some looks indicative of the Belgian detective.

Gully was still an uncertainty as every time Joby broached the subject, he disappeared into his room and locked the door.

Meg had no idea what to wear, having been too busy at the station to give it any proper thought. Playful suggestions were banded around, from Mother Theresa to

Pocahontas.

"It is intriguing, the party, I mean," said Meg. "Aren't you the slightest bit curious to know what's going on?"

Abby and Theo looked at each other and shrugged. "Of course we are, Meg, but we know as much as you do and that's the truth," stated Theo.

"I suppose we'll find out soon enough," added Joby, "after all, we only have two more days to wait."

Lunch was interrupted by a voicemail message from Scotland Yard. Meg retrieved it in the quiet of the Nodding Donkey beer garden and rang straight back.

"I'm sorry, Meg, I've not got much to report, I'm afraid. Your woman was picked up on the airport runway by a black car, most likely a Range Rover from the shape. Couldn't get a license plate, and pretty much lost her from there. Black Range Rovers are rife around London, so any I picked up later could be her, but without a plate, there's no way to know for sure."

"What about coming in - did you pick up a black Range Rover arriving?" Meg queried.

"I'm not sure how far the tape goes back, but I can take a look. Just be aware that without a plate or definitive markings on the car, it could be more bad news."

Meg was grateful for his perseverance and hoped he would be able to offer her something more definite.

Perhaps the car had been hired - it was worth a shot and she enlisted Thackeray's help to contact local companies to track a black Range Rover that was available for airport pick-ups.

The afternoon faded away as their calls yielded nothing.

Meg was heading for her car when Castleton caught hold of her. "Are you avoiding me, Meg?" His tone was demanding.

"Of course not! You've hardly been receptive to communication recently, so Thackeray and I have tried to keep a low profile," she answered.

Castleton accepted her description of him as being relatively accurate.

"I have been a bit of a pig, haven't I?" He smiled apologetically. "These murders are all I can think about. The pressure to solve them... honestly, it's tearing me apart, Meg. Thank God for you and Thackeray. I wouldn't have managed without you."

Meg was sympathetic to Castleton's candour; she knew too well the toll a murder case had on a person's wellbeing. She'd seen many a detective leave the force with their spirit in tatters, ripped apart by the burden of an unsolved case.

Meg headed home leaving Castleton standing in the distance. She had a party to plan for, an outfit to find and less than twenty-four hours to do it.

Google wasn't particularly helpful in her plight to find a costume. Halloween had come and gone and the need for dressing-up outfits had diminished leaving Meg with a meagre option between Florence Nightingale and Princess Diana.

She opted for the Princess and placed her order with next-day delivery, adding a short-haired blond wig to perfect her outfit.

The day before Lilia's party, Meg ran into Mrs Hobson at the local supermarket. It was unusual to see Mrs Hobson anywhere but the Manor House kitchen and Meg hadn't recognised her at first. It was Mrs Hobson who had approached Meg as she rummaged through a cage of reduced products.

"Oh, Mrs Hobson, I didn't recognise you without your apron on," joked Meg. "Are you all ready for the party tomorrow?"

"I'm ready alright, though I haven't a clue what's going on, dear." "I suppose all will be revealed," suggested Meg.

"She's been very secretive about it all, even with the staff. She gave me the menu and the date of the dinner and that was it. Darrow is normally the first to know everything, but even he says he's in the dark, if you can believe that."

"Makes it more mysterious though, doesn't it, not knowing? Anyway, we only have a few hours left to wait, Mrs Hobson ...". Before Meg could continue, the cook interrupted.

"True, but I like to know where I'm up to, who I'm

catering for, what the occasion is... I'm old school you see. Lady Isobel was the same, God bless her, always kept me informed she did, but this Lady hardly passes the time of day with the staff, let alone tells us what's going on."

Mrs Hobson would have continued her ramblings if Meg hadn't politely excused herself.

"I'm sure everything will work out fine. I'll see you tomorrow, Mrs Hobson," shouted Meg as she raced through the checkout towards her car.

Mrs Hobson threw back a half-hearted wave of acknowledgement and disappeared down the freezer aisle.

The day before Lilia's party, Meg visited Joby to assess the outfit he had retrieved from the attic. He wanted her to give it the seal of approval and ensure it was suitable to wear at the party.

When Joby made his appearance, Meg was amazed how well he suited the role of the fictional Belgian detective; he had nailed the look perfectly. A tweed suit and coloured waistcoat, black shoes with spats, a cane, a black homburg and the finishing touch - a fake moustache.

"Joby, you look fabulous! I thought it was Poirot himself entering the room," joked Meg. Joby was ecstatic at her response and marched about the room proudly.

"What about Gully, is he going to the party or not?"

"I've given up on him," sighed Joby. "If he comes, he comes, if he doesn't, then I'm going without him."

Meg understood. Gully was the eldest brother and yet Joby had shouldered responsibility for both of them. He had tried hard to please Gully since his parents' deaths, making the farm into a home again and providing Gully with everything he needed. Gully, on the other hand, had not tried at all. Alienating Joby only served to make the void between them wider, but Gully didn't seem to care.

CHAPTER 44
The Party

The day of the party arrived at last.

Joby arrived at the cottage, as Meg had suggested they could share a taxi together.

From the moment he arrived, the wine was flowing and the music playing. They danced around like teenagers to old familiar childhood tunes and the memories came flooding back.

At 5 pm, there was an unexpected knock at the cottage door. Castleton was standing there armed with wine and fresh pizza.

Meg was quite taken aback; her contact with the sergeant had been minimal for the last week and he was the last person she expected to be standing there.

Castleton looked uncomfortable - he certainly didn't expect to find Joby Cross sipping wine and jumping around maniacally in Meg's front room. Meg tried her best to sober up, eating as much pizza as possible and switching the wine for water instead.

Castleton was unaware of Lilia's event, having not received an invitation himself, and aside from the delicious cream horns, he wasn't in a hurry to go back to the Manor House.

Castleton offered to drive Meg and Joby to the party and they disappeared upstairs to change into costume, eager to watch Castleton's reaction when he saw them. They had decided, in a fit of uncontrollable laughter whilst bopping feverishly to David Bowie earlier that afternoon, to swap outfits.

As they entered the room together, Castleton burst into uncontrollable laughter. He laughed so much that his eyes watered. Meg had never seen him laugh so hard or for so long.

She had to admit though, they did look fantastic.

Joby, in blonde wig and royal blue skirt suit, had already laddered his tights struggling to make them fit his hairy, muscular legs. He staggered to walk in three-inch heels, traversing the room with less ability than a store mannequin. A string of enormous pearls hung around his neck with clip-on earrings to match. Meg had painted his face with makeup and filled an old bra with socks allowing him a sizeable cleavage. By this point, Joby had drunk so much wine that he was past caring.

Castleton was still struggling to pull himself together as Joby strutted up and down trying to adapt to wearing women's shoes, which he had somehow managed to force his man-sized feet into.

Meg, in total contrast, was dressed as Hercule Poirot in a tweed suit, black shoes with spats and an oversized homburg. Joby had pushed a couple of pillows up her shirt, to establish the Belgian's rotund figure. She carried a cane and sported a stark black moustache on her upper lip. The result was a cross between Charlie Chaplin and Adolf Hitler.

"You both look fantastic," cried Castleton between fits of laughter. "I'm sorry I'm not going now." By 8 pm, they were arriving at the Manor House. Joby jumped excitedly out of the car and was gone.

Castleton grabbed Meg's hand. "Can I pick you up later?" "It could be after midnight," warned Meg.

"That's okay, just ring me when you're ready." Castleton kissed the back of her hand and drove away.

As Meg approached the Manor House, she could already hear screams of laughter coming from inside. Joby had obviously made a huge impression.

She made her way through the hallway and into the drawing room, where guests were gathering. She could hear Joby's voice bellowing from somewhere inside the room. He was having fun and he deserved it.

Abby, in pink Chanel suit and stilettos, was nursing a champagne flute in the far corner. She was thoroughly amused by Meg and Joby's outfits.

"That's hilarious and genius," she cried, handing Meg a crystal flute.

"I was slightly tipsy when I agreed to it," admitted Meg, "and now I've sobered up, I'm not so sure."

"Nonsense, I love it!" cried Abby.

Theo was standing beside the great open fireplace where his father had stood on many occasions. He was dressed as a cowboy. "John Wayne, I presume? Err, what happened to James Bond?" asked Meg with the hint of a French accent. "He was already spoken for," countered Theo with an outstretched hand. "Sherlock Holmes, I presume?"

Meg threw a friendly punch against his shoulder. "How dare you, Sir, you are standing in the presence of the great Hercule Poirot."

Theo sniggered as Meg pointed out Joby sporting his Princess Diana look in the opposite corner of the room.

"I see Darrow has come as a butler," mused Theo, and they all set off laughing again.

The room was awash with conversation, drinking and laughter. The evening was looking promising.

"I thought there would be more people here," said Joby who had now joined them. "He's just looking for a date," joked Meg.

"You were hoping to see Madison again, isn't that right, Joby?" Joby blushed innocently as though the name had no meaning to him.

"I must admit I'm not sure who most of these folk are," said Theo.

Meg looked intently around the room. She had to agree that the faces were all new to her - perhaps they were Lilia's friends.

"Any idea what this is all about yet?" asked Joby. "Not a clue, darling," was Abby's reply.

Around 9 pm, Darrow ushered the crowd from drawing room to dining room, where the table was laid in exquisite Manor House style with named place settings. Everyone found their seats and the drinking and conversations continued.

It was another hour before Lilia entered the room; she always did like to make an entrance.

Lilia, svelte in a classic cut figure-hugging black suit, entered the room to the usual audible gasps. Her hair was parted at the centre, and one side was jet black and the other snow white. Even a short-haired styleless wig made Lilia look amazing.

She floated towards the table ingesting the array of colourful characters that graced her dining room. "Wow, you all look incredible," she said clasping her hands together and smiling ecstatically. "Good evening, everyone, and welcome to my party. My name is Lilia DeVil." She welcomed the room and everyone applauded spontaneously and laughed at her joke.

She took her seat and almost immediately the doors opened and trays of delicious home-cooked foods were served. Mrs Hobson had surpassed herself.

For starters, smoked salmon and caviar, followed by melt-in-the-mouth boeuf en croute, and to finish, Manor House-style Eton Mess.

Each serving was accompanied by wine chosen from the Attwood family cellar. It was a magnificent feast for the eyes and the palate.

Coffee and liqueurs made their way around the table as the signs of the evening's feast were removed. Huge Cuban cigars were available for the men, who, in Manor House tradition, excused themselves to the drawing room, whilst the women were offered champagne and handmade truffle chocolates.

Joby and Theo disappeared and the ladies retreated to one end of the dining table to be closer to Lilia, who spoke of her inspiring charity work and held the ladies spellbound by her eloquence and poise.

In a sudden moment of silence, the woman sitting opposite Meg asked the ultimate question - "Why are you having a farewell party, Lilia? Are you going away?"

Lilia shot a glance her way. There was a hint of anger in the look between them, but Lilia calmly replied, "All will be revealed, ladies, in time. The night is still young, so come, let us join the men." Lilia rose from the table and everyone followed.

The drawing room hung heavy with the stench of cigars and brandy.

Lilia drew the ladies out onto the patio beyond, and moments later, the sky was ablaze with a burst of colour as fireworks shot in every direction, illuminating the sky with a sprinkling of coloured stars. A magnificent display lit the darkness momentarily; an unexpected but appreciated surprise.

Midnight was almost upon them and guests were beginning to leave, yet Lilia had not explained the reason behind her little soirée.

As Meg and Joby approached the door, Darrow stepped in front of them and closed it firmly. "What's going on, Darrow? Step aside!" demanded Joby, but Darrow stood firm.

Theo, on witnessing the situation, stepped forward. "What's got into you, man? Let them go." Darrow didn't falter from his position.

"I think that would be me," answered Lilia coolly, as she stepped towards Theo.

Meg turned around. Most of the guests had dissipated leaving only Abby, Theo, Joby and Meg standing in the hallway of the Manor House, somewhat bemused.

Meg looked at Abby and then at Theo. They looked back at her with puzzled faces. "Come," beckoned Lilia, "let me explain."

Castleton had been feeling on edge all night, ever since he'd dropped Meg at the Manor House. He had a feeling he couldn't explain, something was niggling deep down inside, but he didn't know what. He now knew the feeling Meg had so often described during the investigation - a gut feeling.

He knew his feelings for Meg were sincere and he liked

her more than he cared to admit, but that wasn't what was bothering him. He had a gut feeling, but about what, he needed to find out.

He pulled out his laptop and it opened on the image that Meg had spent so long inspecting. He smiled inside as he recalled her hunched over the desk for hours with his grandfather's old magnifying glass in hand.

His gut was telling him to look closer at the photograph. He enlarged it again and again until he would have lost it to pixelation had he tried a third time.

He positioned himself in such a way that the light source from a nearby table lamp brightened the image to give a much clearer view. Castleton pulled the laptop closer, straining to focus. The woman could be anyone, dressed all in black, with features shaded by a large hat and sunglasses. It would be impossible to identify someone from an image such as this.

His eyes scanned the woman from top to bottom and settled on the black designer shoes that Meg had been so obsessed with. He stared for a moment and there it was, a little hazy, but definite; he had just discovered the killer's identity.

Castleton felt the hand of fear caress his spine, his heartbeat gathered momentum and moist beads of sweat crowned his forehead. For a moment, he felt breathless; he dropped to his knees and slipped unconsciously into darkness as he passed out.

The image on the laptop blinked on its screen. The ankle of the woman in the photograph had been enlarged and it wasn't the shoes that had sent Castleton spiralling into shock, but the dark, black outline of a tattoo on the woman's ankle. It peered beneath the hem of her trousers as she stepped out of the chartered jet - an unmistakable flying bird; a raven.

Lilia locked the patio doors of the drawing room and invited her remaining guests to sit.

She paced the floor, and only the tapping of her pencil-thin heels on wood could be heard above the silence.

"You're pissing me off now, Lilia," scolded Theo. "What the hell is going on?"

Lilia jolted towards him, one heel gauging a furrow in the aged oak varnish. The sound attracted Meg's attention, and her eyes were drawn to Lilia's footwear. She hadn't given them much attention earlier, but Lilia was wearing black, crocodile-skin shoes.

As Meg's eyes rose upwards, they met Lilia's staring back at her. Lilia had noticed the sudden expression of realisation on Meg's face. "Exquisite, aren't they?" she purred. "Christian Dior." Meg rose to her feet, rage building inside her. "It's you! You're the woman we are looking for!" Lilia pushed Meg back into her seat with one hand. "Well done, Detective, you are correct."

Theo and Abby were vying to be heard as multiple questions spewed forth, but Lilia screamed for silence.

She pulled the wig aside and shook her head allowing recently dyed blonde locks to tumble free.

"There will be no more rude interruptions; you can all listen to me."

The four exchanged glances, Joby's confused, Theo and Abby's questioning, whilst Meg was desperately trying not to show the fear she felt inside.

Lilia Attwood was the woman in the photograph; Lilia Attwood was a killer.

Castleton woke suddenly, rolling across the floor seeking the answer to his current position. As his eyes regained focus, he recalled his last memory before the darkness hit, the image, the tattoo, the killer. He dragged himself up. It was well past midnight. Meg hadn't called. A feeling of dread shuddered through his body. He dialled Thackeray.

Thackeray listened intently. The call was brief, but Thackeray understood the significance of Castleton's instructions. Meg's life depended on it.

"Where to begin," Lilia said as she caressed her cheek and looked towards the uncertain faces of her sombre guests.

"Perhaps I should explain that the other guests were actors, hired by me for the evening. They were very good though, convincing, don't you think?" Lilia was now standing beside the fireplace. She poured herself a neat whiskey from the decanter that lived beside Sir Henry's leather armchair. She raised the glass up high; "Cheers," she said swigging back a mouthful.

She paced the floor, glass in hand.

"Maybe I should introduce myself to those of you who don't know me, eh, detective?" She giggled as she passed in front of Meg. "You know me as Lilia Czechova from Hungary," she stated in her sketchy European accent, "but, I'm actually Ayda Cosward of Brightmarsh; surprise!" The fake accent had disappeared and her British heritage was soberingly apparent.

Abby was tearing up at this point. Lilia threw her a disgusted look and snarled, "Poor little rich girl, can't you cope with step-mummy's revelations?"

Theo threw an arm around her and hugged her close.

Joby raised his hand in the air attracting Lilia's attention, so she moved towards him. "You have a question?"

"Yes, what do we call you, Lilia or Ayda?" Joby's question was perfectly valid, but Lilia was not amused. She knelt in front of Joby. "What do you want to call me?" she mocked.

Joby was actually mulling the question over in his head, but Meg had a feeling that this would not end well.

"You really don't know who I am, do you," Lilia grunted, growing impatient. Joby shook his head. Lilia grabbed her stiletto and struck Joby full in the face, the heel of the shoe embedding in his cheek.

Joby instinctively pulled it free and threw it across the floor. Blood flowed from the wound and within minutes, the crisp white blouse of his Princess Diana outfit was stained red.

Joby sat silent, shocked, unaware of the profuse river of blood spurting from his swollen cheek. "Look what you made me do, little brother," snarled Lilia, retrieving the shoe and placing it on her foot.

Joby didn't react; he stared into the distance, Lilia's last statement not registering. Meg wanted to go to him, but Lilia's body language told her it was not a good idea.

"Of course he doesn't know you. You had left home before he was born," stated Meg.

"Left home? I never left home! I was forced out by the sycophants who masqueraded as my parents."

Lilia's eyes were bulging, her temper rising. She swigged at the whiskey for comfort. She turned towards Abby; "And what kind of sister are you?" she snorted.

Abby looked puzzled as she clung to Theo's side.

"Leave her alone, Lilia, she's never done you any harm," replied Theo.

Lilia moved towards Theo. She ran her hand through his hair. "We could have been good together, you and me," she teased. Theo pulled himself out of reach.

"I don't think it matters that we're related, after all, I married your father."

Theo looked lost. "What the hell are you rambling

about? You're drunk and I'm leaving." Theo pulled Abby from the sofa, but before they could move away, Lilia was brandishing a monstrous dagger and waving it under Theo's nose.

"Sit back down, Theo; don't be a fool for the sake of Abby."

Theo, convinced by the sight of the knife, regained his seat, pulling Abby beside him. "Look, say, do whatever you want to me, just leave my sister out of it," begged Theo. Lilia pouted and mimicked Theo's words using a high-pitched, squeaky voice.

"Sister? Huh, don't make me laugh," scoffed Lilia. "How sure are you that this snivelling little wreck of a girl is your sister?"

At this point, Meg could not stay in her seat. "Leave Abby out of this," she demanded.

Lilia turned towards her. "Oh, but I can't. She is part of this whether she likes it or not, now sit down and shut up, or you will regret it."

Meg unwillingly took her seat. Abby grabbed her hand. "What does she mean, Meg?"

"Aren't you going to answer your friend's question, Meg?" Lilia paused for a moment as Abby looked from her to Meg and back again. She shrugged her shoulders and poured another whiskey. "Okay then, I'll answer for you."

Meg closed her eyes tightly, forcing back the sting of tears and gripped Abby's hand even tighter than before.

"You, Abby, are the result of your mother's affair with the gardener, Theodore Gimp." Abby and Theo looked at each other, the shock of Lilia's revelation visible on their faces. "Henry Attwood is not your father," continued Lilia.

"Not true!" snapped Theo.

"Oh, but it is true, isn't that right, Meg?"

Theo and Abby turned to Meg searching her eyes for confirmation that the words Lilia spoke were nothing but lies.

"Well?!" demanded Lilia.

Meg nodded her head slowly. "I've only just found out myself, Abby. I was going to tell you, but with everything you've been going through, I was waiting for the right time."

Abby turned away and buried her head in Theo's chest. Theo shot Meg a look of disapproval. "Don't feel left out though, Theo; you are named after him," Lilia laughed wickedly, "and if that isn't enough to get your juices flowing, I am your half-sister; Henry is my father."

Theo was dumbfounded. Lilia's revelations were a shock to the system. Meg knew that Theo would be questioning every moment of his life, which part had been lies and which truth.

Theo was getting angry and demanded, "Why are you doing this? What are you after, is it money?"

Lilia laughed again. "Money ... I have more than enough money, Theo. I'm simply getting my revenge on the people who turned their backs on me," she said staring straight into his eyes.

"Revenge for what?" Theo was even more confused.

"For all the people who used and abused me, for being the bastard child hidden away in a cupboard the size of a shoe box. For being forced into a convent in the middle of nowhere to save your father and my mother from disgrace."

Lilia was gathering momentum; her eyes were growing wider and wilder with every word. It was the wrong time for Joby to re-join the conversation, but he did it anyway. "Does that mean that you're my sister?"

Lilia stormed across the room, dagger in hand. She thrust it deep into Joby's abdomen, and this time he did react. Joby slumped to the floor, blood enveloping him, pooling around his dying body, soaking the blue suit and being absorbed by the rug beneath him.

Abby and Meg screamed, Theo was speechless, but Lilia was unphased.

"Now, where was I?" She sank into Sir Henry's winged-back chair and crossed her legs. "For years, you have lived here in this beautiful house with all the privileges money afforded you. I lived in squalor, like an animal, a forgotten shameful secret. Ben Cross loathed me; he locked me in that box for hours, fed me scraps, sometimes nothing at all. I sat in my own urine and faeces; the smell was appalling, but no one cared.

Alice, weak and feeble, didn't have the guts to overrule

him. She buried herself in her knitting and pretended I didn't exist." Lilia took a breath and another swig of whiskey. The glass was empty, so she filled it again and circled the rim with her finger.

"It must have been horrible," proffered Meg in a soft voice. Lilia glared at her. "Horrible?!" she raged. "Horrible isn't the half of it. Can you imagine being me?" The knife, still coloured by Joby's blood, was animated in Lilia's left hand.

"Of course I cannot," murmured Meg. "I can understand why you want revenge, but murder? Wasn't there another path you could have taken, legally, maybe?"

Lilia studied the whiskey for a moment. She began to laugh, slowly and quietly at first, then louder and hysterically. "I would have been taking on Sir Henry Attwood; how could I have beaten him legally?"

She was probably right; the Attwoods had every barrister in London on their payroll, so she would not have stood a chance.

"I'm so very sorry for everything that you've gone through, Lilia, I really am," Meg changed tack hoping that Lilia would calm down. "Let me help you."

Lilia leapt from her chair and smashed the whiskey glass into the open fireplace. She marched towards Meg, grabbing her by the hair and yanking her head upwards, their faces just inches away from each other.

"Everyone I met wanted to 'help me'!" she screamed.

"Father Maloney wanted to help me, but really, he wanted to help himself to an innocent, mistreated little girl. No one even blinked when he pulled me behind a curtain and forced me to perform oral sex." She slowly released her grip on Meg's hair and stepped backwards. "No one can help me; I had to help myself."

Thackeray had joined Castleton at the end of the Manor House driveway. There was no time to wait for backup. Meg and everyone else's lives were in danger, so they needed to diffuse the situation as quickly as possible. Castleton prayed that Meg was still alive.

They crept stealthily along the driveway, ducking behind greenery to disguise their presence. Castleton had no particular plan in mind as an operation like this was new to him, but he knew that he couldn't leave Meg to die at the hands of a psychopath. They edged closer and closer until the lights of the Manor House came into view.

Eventually, they were crouching beneath a window and listening for signs of life. Everything was silent, but the Manor House was substantial and there was a lot of area to cover. They moved in formation from one window to the next, stopping and listening beneath each one. As they rounded the back of the house, there was a large patio area where the windows became full length. Castleton cautiously peered into the first window, and there, the dining table bore the remnants of drinking glasses and discarded napkins. Where were Darrow and the kitchen staff?

Lilia was slowly diminishing the contents of the once-full decanter and Meg hoped that alcohol would make it easier to overpower her if the situation arose. Remembering that Castleton had offered to pick her up, she devised a plan to contact him. She had carefully concealed her mobile phone inside the tweed pants of Poirot's suit when Lilia had not been looking.

"I really need the loo," professed Meg, wiggling about on the sofa.

"Darrow! Darrow!" Lilia's voice pierced the air.

Darrow had kept a low profile and remained out of sight, but at the sound of his name, he appeared at the door.

"Take the detective to the toilet and keep your eye on her."

Darrow grasped hold of Meg's arm as she approached him and led her from the room.

"What's going on, Darrow?" she begged, but Darrow remained stern-faced and silent. He pointed her in the direction of the downstairs bathroom, as if Meg had never visited the Manor House before. He pulled the door shut and waited outside. There were no windows to the outside and no means of escape, but that wasn't Meg's plan. She pulled the phone from its hiding place and texted a message to Castleton and Thackeray, in the hope that one of them would receive it, but the message failed to send;

there was no signal.

Darrow escorted her back to the drawing room and pushed her inside, closing the door behind her. She took her seat beside Theo, all eyes fixed on Lilia. Meg realised that Lilia was now brandishing a handgun; the knife was nowhere in sight.

"Oh my God, Lilia, put that down," Meg begged. "No one else has to die." Lilia pointed the pistol straight at her. "Do you want to be second, detective?" Meg sank back in her seat desperate for the cushions to swallow her up.

"I say who dies," cried Lilia. "It's my decision, understand?"

Meg nodded then said, "But why does anyone have to die? Can't we work this out sensibly, like adults?"

"Sensibly," scoffed Lilia, "I'm done with sensibly. No one was sensible where I was concerned; no one gave a thought for little Ayda. I've waited my whole life for this moment, and I'm going to finish it my way."

Meg tried to plead, but Lilia was beyond moral rectitude. She dragged Abby screaming from the sofa, Theo desperately trying to pull her back to him. Lilia held the gun to Abby's temple and pulled the trigger. The noise reverberated around the room. Meg and Theo winced, eyes tightly closed, praying silently.

Theo lunged forward and fell at the feet of his trembling sister. Lilia howled with laughter; the gun had fired, but Abby was not dead. The bullet had lodged into the top panel of the oak door.

Lilia waved the firearm in the air and pointed it at Theo. He closed his eyes but nothing happened. Lilia cackled, "Oh, you should see your faces. I have to say you are not disappointing me; tonight is everything I hoped it would be. I just wish I had thought about filming it - imagine the audience it would pull."

Theo and Abby crawled back towards the sofa, but a flash of silver sliced across Abby's throat before she reached it and she sank to the ground as blood gurgled and poured from the gaping mouth, pouring across her neck. Theo and Meg were on their knees, but the blood was overwhelming. She was choking beneath the sanguine liquid and, within minutes, Abby was dead. Theo jumped to his feet and rushed towards Lilia, but Meg held him back, struggling and crying. "Why would you do that?" sobbed Meg. "What has she ever done to you?"

"She had the life I should have had, as did he," said Lilia, pointing the dagger towards Theo.

Theo was beside himself with grief. Meg could not console him. Lilia was becoming more dangerous; she had snuffed out Abby's life like blowing out a candle, showing no empathy or remorse. The situation was becoming volatile; Meg could only hope that Castleton and Thackeray had received her message and armed police would be surrounding the Manor House imminently, but if they were not, Meg feared she would die tonight.

Castleton and Thackeray were still skulking at the back of the house. Fearful that security lights may announce their presence, they edged along each window tucking themselves away from the infrareds. At last, they found an unlocked window and entered the Manor House via the formal lounge. The hallway was brightly lit in the distance, but there were no signs of life.

Thackeray checked the kitchen which was empty of staff, however, evening dishes and tableware cluttered the sink area, an unusual sight in the Manor House.

Castleton crept into the pantry and laundry rooms consecutively; they were empty.

As he met up with Thackeray, Darrow passed the doorway of the kitchen. He paused as he saw the two policemen standing there. He was carrying a beautifully crafted shotgun, cocked over one arm, as though he were ready to go hunting.

Castleton and Thackeray froze as they looked from Darrow to the gun and back again. Darrow, aware of the fear on their faces, said nothing and walked on by.

Thackeray was visibly trembling. "I thought we were goners," he gasped. "Me too," admitted Castleton.

They followed Darrow, keeping far enough behind that they could dive into an open doorway if the shotgun fired.

Darrow was heading down the hall to the drawing room. He stopped outside the door and loaded two cartridges into the gun, then he turned to look at Castleton and Thackeray as they hovered in the shelter of the lounge door. It was the last look Darrow would ever give to anyone; he opened the drawing-room door and fired.

Lilia was now barefoot, the shoes thrown to one side, the soles dripping with Abby's blood. Abby lay lifeless across the Persian rug, her blood becoming a part of the intricate woven scene. Theo was a gibbering wreck curled in one corner of the sofa, face-down in the nearest cushion.

Meg looked in disbelief from Joby to Abby, her best friends, murdered in succession.

Suddenly, the drawing room doors flew open and the piercing sound of shotgun fire echoed across the room.

At the very same time, the patio doors were ripped apart, glass scattering across the floor as more shots were fired.

Meg had dragged Theo behind the sofa, so she slowly raised herself upwards to survey the scene. Standing at one end of the drawing room had been Darrow, Sir Henry's hunting rifle in his hands. He had fired at Lilia but missed and shattered a pane of glass in the patio window. At the sound of breaking glass, Gully Cross burst through the window and fired back at Darrow, hitting him straight between the eyes. Darrow was lying face-down in the open doorway.

Gully spotted Joby's blood-soaked body; he paused momentarily before throwing Lilia over his shoulder and disappearing with her into the night.

At this point, Castleton and Thackeray raced across the drawing room in pursuit of Gully, but it was futile - Gully was a practised marksman carrying a heavy-duty shotgun, so what chance did they stand of arresting him? However, undeterred, Thackeray drew his baton and Castleton his taser.

Meg checked Theo was not hurt, then followed her colleagues into the darkness of the Manor House garden. She found Gully face-down on the lawn, incapacitated by the electrical current that was currently surging through his body. Castleton was securing his handcuffs and Thackeray was struggling with an exceptionally unhappy Lilia.

Within minutes, the landscaped garden of the Manor House was bathed in bright light as a helicopter hovered overhead like a giant mobile torch. A team of armed officers surrounded the area and both Gully and Lilia were wrestled into waiting police vans.

Castleton threw his arms around Meg and squeezed tightly. "I was afraid I'd lost you," he whispered, brushing her hair with his hand and kissing her forehead.

Theo emerged from the house wrapped in blankets. He was shaken and suffering from shock, but otherwise unharmed.

Paramedics rushed into the drawing room to find their patients' bodies cold and lifeless. Abby and Joby were removed to the hospital morgue and Theo was to spend the night under medical observation.

Meg needed to go home and absorb the events of the night. The deaths of her two best friends and of Darrow were not going to be easy to come to terms with. It was the stuff of nightmares that would haunt her memory forever.

Castleton helped her into bed and snuggled down beside her. It took a while to still the flash of images in her mind - Abby's blood-soaked body lying at her feet, and Joby murdered for his innocence. Eventually, sleep devoured her and the evening's events, at least for now vanished into the darkness.

CHAPTER 45
Ayda's Story

From the moment of conception, Ayda Rose Attwood was doomed. An unplanned pregnancy between two disparate people was to form the crumbling foundation of her unsettled, superfluous life.

Her birth was a nondescript moment in time.

Alice felt nothing but relief when she expelled the living being inside her, an unwelcome event and a time she was desperate to forget. A stolen moment of bliss in the arms of a charming philanderer forged her nine-month journey of regret and remorse.

Mary Mackie, the midwife hired to attend Ayda's birth, was sworn to secrecy about the child's existence. Well-known amongst medical professionals for her love of the demon drink, she was a virtual outcast in the nursing community. She had been known to arrive at imminent births unable to form a sentence, and her lack of professionalism saw her stripped of her license to practise.

Sir Henry paid the midwife handsomely for her services and advised her to leave the village and never return.

Ben Cross could not forgive his wife's indiscretion and the news that a child was to be born from the collaboration filled him with distaste. Long before Ayda made her appearance, anger swelled within him, growing steadily as each month passed, so that when Ayda finally made her appearance, Ben was ready to explode with indescribable rage.

What chance did the child have when her very existence was despised by the people who were supposed to love and care for her?

Sir Henry made sure that Ayda Attwood never existed, forging her birth certificate by changing her name to Cosward, a combination of letters from her biological parents' surnames.

I suppose from that moment, Ayda's fate was sealed; legally, she did not exist. She would grow to become a woman without an identity.

The only member of the Cross family that showed her a speck of decency was Gully.

Gully was enchanted by his new baby sister and was often the only person to answer her cries in the middle of the night.

When visitors arrived at the farm, which didn't happen often, Gully was charged with keeping his sister quiet, a task which eventually became impossible.

As Ayda grew, Gully began to distance himself from the child, tired of her constant thirst for attention, keeping her entertained and comforting her in the blackness of night.

As Ayda grew, she constantly disobeyed the parents, who, until now, had barely acknowledged her existence. She would throw tantrums and display aggressive behaviour. Ben's loathing of the girl drove him to devise a secret hiding place where Ayda could be locked away.

Ben despised everything about her, especially the fact that Henry Attwood was her real father. He could not find it in his heart to feel any emotion for the girl and found himself releasing his frustrations upon her.

Alice, whose adultery had brought shame and an unwanted child into the family, allowed her husband to vent his feelings in any way he pleased, not caring whether Ayda lived or died.

As the years passed, Ayda spent more and more time in Ben's homemade hiding place. To call it a room was an insult to even the tiniest of rooms, as it was nothing bigger than a cupboard; a standard kitchen cupboard to be precise. Fashioned from discarded off-cuts of hardboard, the cupboard measured no more than four feet square. It was cold and dark, the wood was scratchy against her skin and she could hear scary noises around it.

Ben had forged a series of six holes along the outermost wall, allowing air to flow freely, but sometimes, furry creatures managed to push themselves through the holes and scurry over Ayda, scratching and biting. Her screams could not be heard though, as she wrestled the unfriendly visitors in the dark.

Once, when Ayda was trying to fall asleep in the cupboard, she felt a soft object fall gently into her lap. She fumbled in the darkness to discover the fragility of a baby bird that had somehow managed to fall through one of the holes in her cupboard.

Ayda held the bird and stroked its silky feathers gently. She was smiling but the bird could not see; it was so young that its eyes had not yet opened.

The bird grew stronger. Ayda found insects and stockpiled crumbs from the scraps of meals she received, choosing to feed the bird before herself. She talked to the bird and the bird talked back. It was the beginning of a beautiful friendship.

Living in a box that she was rapidly outgrowing, Ayda's behaviour became more and more feral. An animal cannot spend its life in a cage and then, upon its release, be expected to display social awareness.

Ayda's life had been devoid of interaction, love, attention, learning, a comfortable bed, adequate nutrition and life skills; no wonder the child was wild and undisciplined.

The bird was her only means of communication. Sometimes it would fly away and Ayda would feel sad, but it always returned, bringing scraps for her to eat, just as she had done for it. The bird, which years later Ayda learned was a raven, plucked a beautiful black feather from its plumage on each return visit and laid it in Ayda's hand as a gift.

With the raven for company, Ayda forgot about her bone-aching hours of imprisonment in the box, or the rancid smell of urine and faeces that had been absorbed into the wood where she sat. The only thing that mattered to her was the raven.

When Ayda would no longer physically fit the dimensions of the box, Ben and Alice decided it was time to get rid of her. They couldn't set her free in the woods or she would be found, they couldn't risk her talking about her monstrous experience within the walls of Molecatcher Farm and they couldn't admit the truth.

They devised a plan involving Hegarty Baxter and Father Maloney, their local catholic priest.

They explained that they had found the girl living wild in Weaver's Wood, catching her as she stole apples from their tree.

Hegarty was full of praise for their kindness, but appalled at the state of the child and even shed a tear for the plight of the minor's predicament. She promised to hunt down the parents, who had heartlessly cast the girl aside, not caring for her well-being.

Father Maloney insisted that the Crosses would receive their godly reward, if not in this life, then in the next.

Ayda, who grunted and whistled rather than spoke, was tied to a rocking chair in the kitchen, unable to elaborate on the Crosses' distinct lie. She was dirty and dishevelled, thin and pale, her hair was matted in knots and the stench that emanated from her presence was sickening.

All of a sudden, Ayda disappeared from their lives, and finally, everything at Molecatcher Farm returned to normal.

Hegarty Baxter was instrumental in arranging a placement for Ayda at the Catholic Convent, mostly on the promise that Father Maloney would visit regularly to ensure the child was making progress. Of course, in reality, Father Maloney had an insatiable fondness for young children, a sordid secret he had so far kept hidden.

Within hours, Ayda was unrecognisable. The Nun's pampered and preened until her hair glistened and every inch of filth and grime had been washed away.

They discovered a child of beauty hidden beneath the layers of abuse and neglect - angelic features, dark soft curly hair and beguiling almond eyes.

It was easy to wash away the visible layers of dirt, but the scars of abandonment and ritual ill-treatment could not be erased simply with soap and water.

Ayda did not integrate into her life at the convent. She trusted no one. She fought and struggled through every moment, she ate like an animal and went to the bathroom wherever she pleased.

She disrupted every lesson and her classmates were afraid of her.

The only stable influence in her life was the raven she

had nursed to health. It visited her often, sitting on the ledge outside her bedroom window.

She talked to the bird, and, on occasion, it would sing.

It was the Mother Superior who came to realise the significance of the raven singing, as something bad always happened afterwards and it was always by Ayda's hand.

Before Ayda spoke, she was able to cause all manner of trouble without the need for speech, but as her language skills began to improve, she became more and more malevolent.

Late-night whisperings occurred regularly. She would leave her bedroom, target a child and leave them shivering with fear at her words.

It was decided amongst the sisters that Ayda had to go. She needed specialist help in a facility for the mentally insane.

It was a cold November morning when a white van arrived at St. Agatha's and two men clad in blue uniforms manhandled Ayda into the back and drove away.

The whole convent, stone walls and all, could be heard sighing with relief as the vehicle drove out of sight.

Ayda was taken to the Good Samaritan Asylum, under the care and supervision of Dr Darryl Frobisher, and head nurse, Bunny Maguire.

The asylum had a prison/hospital vibe, but Ayda was unperturbed. The building may have been different but her rules remained the same.

In the asylum, she was locked in her room. If she became disruptive, she was sedated, then she would wake strapped to her bed, but none of this deterred Ayda.

Professor Amelia Beddoe, a psychiatrist with a special interest in childhood trauma, was introduced to Ayda a couple of weeks after her arrival at the facility.

Amelia had worked intensively with neglected, disturbed, and even feral children and she was particularly interested in getting to know Ayda.

Of course, Ayda wasn't going to make it easy. Amelia would have to work hard to unravel her psyche.

Months turned into years of therapy, building a relationship, understanding the complex working of Ayda's mind and bonding sessions to establish a friendship and, ultimately, trust.

Time spent with Amelia was liberating, though Ayda was careful to keep that secret. When Amelia left the building each day, Ayda reverted back to her old self; it was a form of protection, Amelia explained to the staff.

Ayda grew strong in mind and body. She learnt to use her beautiful face and developing, shapely body to her advantage, ensuring she got exactly what she wanted.

She wanted to be free from the restraints of this cage. It was nothing more than a bigger, fancier cupboard, but still a cupboard nonetheless.

The raven still visited and sang for her, her faithful, feathered friend.

Ayda devised a plan to escape. She bribed a security guard, asking him to contact Sir Henry on her behalf. At first, the man refused, but when Ayda laid bare the truth of what would happen if he didn't help her, he reluctantly agreed.

Sir Henry, stunned by her sudden communication, promised her a new passport and a boat to carry her across the channel to France.

She was met by Isobel Attwood, Sir Henry's wife, who handed her an envelope of cash and a passport that read Ayda Watson. She drove Ayda to the docks where she boarded a vessel named 'New Beginnings'. A man named Theodore Gimp sailed her across the Channel and, hours later, she reached the shores of a French coastal town, where her new life would begin.

The town of Corbeau was where she spent her first night, tucked safely inside a small fishing boat on the beach.

Ayda searched for work, but her ignorance of the French language was unhelpful. The task seemed impossible, until she met a kindly French woman who invited her into her home. The language barrier did not seem to matter and Ayda, for the first time in her life, felt safe.

A warm bath and a good meal, a soft bed and a long sleep and Ayda, the homeless teen, was no more.

The woman, Delphine, was a cleaner in a nearby chateau

and she took Ayda along to help with the housework. They cycled each morning along country lanes, through woodland and down the expansive driveway that led to the French castle.

It was here that Ayda caught the eye of the handsome and charming Monsieur Garnier. He was a wealthy French businessman who had a penchant for young women. He bribed the pubescent Ayda with promises he never kept, but Ayda was no ordinary girl and the French aristocrat was soon to find out that he was no match for her.

Monsieur Garnier invited Ayda to visit the chateau after dark as he was throwing a party for his most influential friends and he thought Ayda would like to join them.

When Ayda arrived, it was immediately obvious that she was the party. The room was filled with a variety of different-aged men, some lurking stealthily in the shadows, eyes undressing her nubile body as they enjoyed an endless supply of expensive champagne.

Garnier pulled her to the centre of the room, but she struggled and ran towards the door, pulling frantically at the handle. However, the great oak doors were locked. Ayda had no idea how to handle the situation, but it didn't feel right. Garnier tried to calm her with the offer of alcohol and drugs, but Ayda, not used to either, refused.

Garnier began a bidding war amongst the gathering, in French, of course.

Ayda felt the surge of panic coursing through her body,

her heart rapidly beating inside her chest, her breaths growing quicker with every moment she remained in that room.

She watched as hands shot upwards sporadically, and finally, a cheer echoed around the room and Garnier, grabbing Ayda by the wrist, pushed her forward into the waiting arms of an elderly, white-haired gentleman. Ayda struggled and clawed at his face, but he laughed sadistically as he pulled her from the room in the direction of a huge staircase. She fumbled and fought at every step, but the man, unhindered by age, was strong. He struck her hard; she felt a slight trickle of blood leave her mouth. Weakened by the blow, her body was now floating through the open doorway of a chateau bedroom.

The man dropped her onto the waiting bed.

Ayda struggled to focus; the blurred image of a naked chest was visible - the man was undressing. Folds of aged skin sagged loosely over his trousers, and pendulous breasts dangled as he bent forward removing his underwear.

Ayda had no idea what was about to happen, but she feared it would not be good.

She was too weak to move, as the naked form of the white-haired man strode towards her. He stopped beside the bed and ripped at her top; his eyes rolled and his face reddened as he caressed himself vigorously. Ayda watched as the lifeless appendage swinging limply between his legs slowly gained form. As it stood erect, the man launched himself on top of her, pinning her in position. She wriggled with discomfort as the thing he had coaxed to life was thrust inside her, painful and stinging between her legs.

It wasn't long before she heard the mournful groan of climax, then he rolled away from her, breathless and damp with sweat.

For a moment, she lay motionless, not daring to move. The obese rapist beside her lay with the blissful look of satisfaction on his face.

Ayda jumped from the bed, grabbed the remains of her clothing and ran for the door. She raced down the stairs, passing Monsieur Garnier going in the opposite direction. He raised his glass in the air and shouted, "S'amuser, Ayda". Loosely translated, Ayda knew it meant 'have a good time'; she had heard it repeatedly before.

There was a tone in the Frenchman's voice that Ayda would never forget, a tone she used many years later when she ended his life with a large serrated kitchen knife, and whispered, "batard" as she left him to die.

In the safety of darkness, she didn't stop running until she reached Delphine's.

Delphine was waiting for Ayda to return. She hoped the girl had brought a reasonable price, after all, the higher the price, the more commission she received.

Ayda burst through the door and slumped onto the

hallway floor. Delphine could see her clothes were torn and dried bloodstains painted her inner thighs.

Ayda was a virgin, so the price would have been considerably higher.

That night, Ayda relived her nightmare awake and in sleep. Garnier's smile, the room full of men, the old man who had blown his load and the subdued greeting she had received from Delphine. She was smart enough to know that she had been set up by the very people she had grown to trust.

Ayda refused to accompany Delphine to the chateau the next day. As she heard the squeaky wheels of Delphine's bicycle pull away, she packed a bag, retrieving items from Delphine's wardrobe. She searched the house for the money - Delphine's stash was easy to find, and the considerable wad of savings would ease the pain of her betrayal.

She left Corbeau, a beautiful place soured by the memories of deceit, and headed to Paris. This time, she was ready; no one would ever get the chance to take advantage of her again.

Ayda travelled back to England, hitchhiking her way to London. There, she would become invisible, amongst the city's over-population.

She sourced a bed in a hostel and a job at a local bar.

The raven, which had not crossed the Channel with her, suddenly re-appeared, as though news of her return had travelled to Brightmarsh. Ayda was overjoyed.

She threw herself into everyday life, but the memories that haunted her past life would not release her from the nightmare she had endured, no matter where she settled in the world.

Ayda responded to an advert; a flat-share close to her place of work. The dwelling was dingy, but Lilia Czechova, the Hungarian student who already lived there, was wise and knowledgeable.

Ayda enrolled with a modelling agency for day work and took dance classes by night. Lilia made extra money at a sassy strip joint called Blue. She said the job was easy and the pay worthwhile. Blue was located down a back street in Soho, ravaged by drug addicts and prostitutes. Ayda took one look at the fat, bloated customers, who drooled and leered at the young girls draped across the stage, and left.

Flashes of her night in the chateau at the hands of the white-haired rapist flooded before her; she was not looking for more of the same - she was aiming much higher.

The Buccaneer's Club was a classy gentleman's retreat in a smart part of town. The manager took one look at Ayda and hired her. She adopted a sketchy accent and told him her name was Lilia Czechova. That night, the real Lilia Czechova met her fate. It wasn't murder, it was necessity, Lilia told herself.

As money flowed at the Buccaneer's Club, the woman now known as Lilia, booked a flight to France.

She had two things on her mind, Monsieur Garnier and Delphine.

They hadn't seen her coming, hadn't expected their fate, but Lilia didn't forgive or forget; she got revenge.

They died simple, yet painful deaths at the hands of a very sharp knife and Lilia returned to London revelling in the knowledge that the scales of justice had swung in her favour.

It was quite by chance that Lilia discovered that none other than Sir Henry Attwood frequented the Buccaneer's Club when visiting London.

It was the perfect opportunity for Lilia to acquaint herself with the father who had abandoned her to the abusive Ben Cross.

Lilia set her plan in motion to woo the wealthy lord and infiltrate the Attwood family.

It took no time at all for Sir Henry to succumb to the salacious charms of Lilia Czechova. He became spellbound, hypnotised by her outstanding beauty.

Sir Henry wasted no time in securing his bride's hand with a ten-carat Tiffany diamond, and they were married a month later.

When Lilia Attwood entered the Manor House for the first time, she couldn't help but smile.

The sickly-sweet family that fluttered around her had

no idea of the life-changing events that Lilia had planned for them.

The following morning, Meg knew the unenviable task of interviewing Ayda and Gully lay ahead of them.

She stalled with a third mug of coffee, pacing the cottage in banana-coloured pyjamas.

Castleton would not allow her to spend a moment in the interview room with Ayda, fearful, not that Ayda would harm Meg, but more likely, Meg wouldn't be able to stop herself from harming Ayda.

Castleton and Thackeray were to take the lead and Meg was banished to watch via CCTV link.

Ayda had spent the night in the belly of the station, where Gully had deprived her of sleep by snoring like a grizzly bear with sinus problems.

The pains of the sleepless night hung heavy beneath her eyes, the dark circular shadows being payment for an uncomfortable mattress and a noisy neighbour.

A sumptuous memory foam mattress and feather menu were not so readily available in the police cells.

Castleton offered her coffee and the interview began. There were so many questions it was hard to know where to start, but he began with the murders of Ben and Alice Cross.

"Okay, Ayda... may I call you that?" enquired Castleton. Ayda moved her head slightly in acknowledgement.

"Please, can you answer out loud, for the tape?"

"You can call me whatever you want, Sergeant," came the reply.

"Were you responsible for the murders of Ben and Alice Cross, the residents of Molecatcher Farm and a hitchhiker by the name of Dalton Emery ...?" Before he had finished his sentence, Ayda interrupted; "Yes!"

"Why did you kill them?" asked Thackeray. Ayda turned her head towards him. "Why do you think?" Thackeray was at a loss for words. Ayda was quick; she answered a question with a question, so he wasn't sure how to handle her.

"We have no idea," growled Castleton. "You tell us."

Ayda sipped her coffee. Even a night in the cells had not tarnished her beauty, and the dark circles were nothing that a little concealer couldn't fix. Castleton wondered how someone so beautiful on the outside could be so ugly inside.

Still waiting for a reply, Castleton continued, "Alice was your mother..."

Ayda scoffed, "Mother in name only. A mother doesn't lock you away; a mother doesn't neglect you; a mother doesn't allow her husband to abuse you."

Castleton and Thackeray looked at each other. "When you say abuse, do you mean sexually?"

"Absolutely not, I wouldn't have let that old bastard near me. He beat me, starved me, deprived me of everything. He hated me with a passion. He never got over the fact that Alice betrayed him, so he needed someone to take out his frustrations on. He was a coward; a weak, pathetic excuse for a man. No wonder Alice cheated on him; it was the only decent thing that woman has ever done."

Ayda drained her coffee and handed the empty container to Thackeray. "More," she demanded. Castleton nodded and Thackeray left the room.

"You had a brother though... Gully?" Castleton prompted.

"And?" She threw both hands into the air. "He was seven; what could he do to defend me?" Ayda paused for a thoughtful moment. "Gully is simple, a child locked in a man's body, but I couldn't hold that against him. He showed me kindness in his own way; he was the closest thing I had to a family."

For the first time, the glint in Ayda's eyes dulled. Was it a display of emotion, was she capable of such a feeling, did the mention of Gully stir something inside her?

Thackeray reappeared with fresh coffee and Ayda watched as he took his seat. All emotion had vanished and the eyes of a cold-blooded killer stared back at them again.

"I understand why you feel animosity towards your parents, Ayda, but the killings were brutal," began Castleton.

Ayda didn't flinch. "They got what they deserved," she

stated.

"Really?!" Castleton scowled, "They deserved mutilation, beheading..." he thrust the crime scene photos of her parents in front of her, "and what does this mean, the knitting needles?"

Ayda remained calm. "You have no idea of the world I lived in at the hands of these two. Can you imagine being invisible to your own parents? Being locked out of sight because your presence offended them? They had every opportunity to get rid of me in the womb, and that would have been the kindest thing to do, so yes, they did deserve it; they brought it on themselves."

"And the needles?"

"Alice was a meek, weak-willed woman, who pretended I didn't exist; she knitted to forget about me. Do you understand the significance of them now?!"

There was nothing Castleton could say to her, after all, she was right - Alice could have aborted the child before anyone knew of her existence.

"What about Dalton Emery, what did he do to upset you?" Castleton's tone was sarcastic.

"He was in the wrong place at the wrong time, that's all. He saw my face, so I couldn't let him live." Ayda's explanation was nonchalant, as if the murder of Dalton Emery was a normal solution to her problem.

Castleton turned the pages of his report. "What about Hegarty Baxter, did she deserve it?"

"She was an interfering busybody, and she placed me in the Convent and the Sanitarium. Both hell holes!"

"Wasn't she trying to help you?"

"Help who?" exclaimed Ayda tossing her hair. "She didn't help me; I was just a number to her. She wanted me off her desk and out of her hair as quickly as possible. She made all kinds of promises, made all the right noises, but did she ever actually do anything?" Ayda answered her own question, "No, she did not."

Meg watched intently from the room next door. She wanted to feel a hint of sympathy for Ayda, for the tragic life she had lived, afford her the revenge she had bestowed on those who wronged her, and yet, try as she might, Meg could not feel anything but anger towards the woman who, hours before, had murdered her best friend.

Castleton continued; "Let's move on to Father Maloney; he was your fifth victim, am I right?" Ayda sat back in her chair and traced the outline of the coffee cup with her thumb. "Father Maloney," she sniggered, "ah yes, the clergyman, the man of God. He was nothing but a disgusting predator, a paedophile. He preyed on the children at the convent. Many suffered at the hands of Father Maloney."

"What about you?"

"Well, he was more of a taker than a giver, if you know what I mean." "I do," agreed Castleton, "but can you say it for the tape, please."

Ayda sat forward. "Father Maloney wanted hand jobs and oral sex. He thought that made him exempt from sin. He never laid a hand on us, you see. He would damn us to hell if we told anyone, and of course, I did, but no one believed it, after all, he was a Catholic Priest."

"Is that the reason you cut off his penis and stuffed it into his mouth?" "Oh yes," smiled Ayda, "karma is a bitch!"

The hours were ticking by and Castleton was tiring. He decided to take a break.

Ayda was returned to the cell, while Meg began her interview with Gully Cross. A local social worker, adept at sign language, had been asked to accompany Gully, as his brother was dead and there was no one else to take his place.

CHAPTER 46
Gully's Story

Gulliver Cross was the first-born child of Ben and Alice.

On a bright sunny day in August, he weighed in at just over a stone and only clothes designed for a six-month-old would fit him.

Gully continued to regularly outgrow his clothes and his peers. By the time he was seven, he stood at nearly five feet tall and shared his father's clothing.

Despite his massive physique, he was a placid child with curly brown hair and pale blue eyes. He had a liking for tractors and dinosaurs.

His physical growth was not replicated mentally - he lacked intelligence, was unable to read and had the educational ability of a four-year-old. He was an easy target of manipulation, which his parents practised in abundance.

There was nothing remarkable about his childhood, until the day he heard a baby cry, and from that day forward, his whole world changed.

Baby Ayda, a sister, had joined the family and Gully was excited to no longer be the only child. From the moment he set eyes on the tiny bundle, his heart grew larger.

He couldn't understand why his parents weren't

interested in her, and he readily accepted the duties they gave him to care for the new arrival.

Gully attended the local school until Ayda was born, then, after that, he was home-schooled, though his lessons were rare and most of his time was spent tending to the needs of his baby sister.

Whenever a visitor arrived at the farm, unexpected or otherwise, Gully was ushered out of sight with baby Ayda and told to keep her quiet, but as she grew, so did her voice and it became obvious that new measures were needed.

Gully watched his father create a wooden box where Ayda would be deposited when visitors arrived. The project was secured with a padlock and soundproofed by an army of hats, coats and scarves.

At first, Gully would hide in the secret room with Ayda, but as his sister grew, the space became too small for the both of them.

As Ayda was locked in the room alone, Gully started to forget about her.

On the odd occasion when Ayda was allowed in the kitchen, she would sit just feet away from Alice, who, ignoring the child's presence, continued her knitting.

Ayda became more and more agitated, and she screamed and kicked each time Ben forced her into the cold, dark space. Each time, he lengthened the time she was locked away until she spent more time in the box than anywhere else.

She was fed scraps when Ben remembered, and sat for hours in her own excrement. He would beat her for the foul smell she created and refused to change her soiled clothes.

Ayda grew more and more disturbed. She talked to herself, she tore at her skin, and she feasted on insects and rat droppings to lessen her hunger. She became unrecognisable as a child displaying feral, animal-like behaviour.

Gully grew afraid of her.

One day, Ayda was banging on the wall of the wooden box so violently that the coats and outer garments were falling from the hooks where they lived. Gully shouted to make her stop, but the banging continued.

Gully, fearing his father would find the heap of garments and fly into a rage, unlocked the door of Ayda's cupboard. As he peered inside, the head of a black bird lurched towards him, piercing his skin and throwing him off balance.

The bird flew at him and landed on his chest, pecking at his flesh and drawing blood. Gully knocked it to one side but the bird was back again, this time lunging towards his eyes. Gully shielded his face in his hands, while the bird continued to peck at his skin. Ayda laughed maniacally from her cupboard.

When Gully was certain the bird had retreated, he climbed to his feet, rushing forward to lock the cupboard door, but the bird was waiting. Gully watched, frozen, as glowing red eyes raced towards him from the depth of the dark cupboard. He wrestled with the door, but it was too late, the bird appeared in front of him, beak wide, rows of serrated teeth heading straight for him. An unearthly scream bellowed from its open beak and Gully hit the floor.

Ben found him moments later in a corner of the hall, shivering and crying, shaking profusely and covered in streaks of blood.

Gully was never able to tell his parents what had happened that day, but he never spoke another word.

When Ayda left Molecatcher Farm, Gully could not hide his pleasure at her departure, and a couple of months later, he was blessed with the arrival of Joby. Gully was delighted with his new baby brother and Ayda never crossed his mind again.

When Meg entered Interview Room 2, Gully was already seated. He didn't lift his head as she entered but stared firmly at the floor.

"Good afternoon, Gully," said Meg, breaking the silence. "You have nothing to be afraid of. You know me and this lady is here to support you and answer your questions."

Gully remained still but managed a sideways glance with his eyes to view the woman sitting beside him.

"We are going to play a game. I know you like games.

I'm going to ask you a question and all you have to do is answer it." Meg pulled a bag of Jelly Babies from under the desk. She pushed it towards Gully, knowing they were his favourite. "Every time you answer, you win a Jelly Baby."

Gully eyed the bag of sweets before him, eager to taste a green one in his mouth. "We will start with something very simple," began Meg. "Are you Gulliver Cross?" Slowly, with his eyes fixed on the prize, Gully nodded his head.

"Well done," praised Meg, "now, you go ahead and choose one." She pushed the treats closer to Gully, whose giant-sized fingers gently plucked a green one from the bag. He chewed and sucked the little sweet until it had disappeared, savouring every moment of its pleasurable taste.

The game was working, so Meg continued; "Okay, so, the next question is a little bit harder." Meg opened a pocket file and placed a photograph on the table. "Do you know who this lady is?"

Meg watched and waited. Gully's eyes flicked from the bag of sweets to the picture and back again several times.

Meg waited patiently, hoping that Gully hadn't already tired of the game, but then, just as she was about to repeat the question, Gully lifted an object from his pocket and placed it on the table.

Meg waited but there was no explanation; Gully simply slid the book towards her and helped himself to another Jelly Baby.

The book was Gully's diary. Joby had spoken of it and hinted at taking a peek. "Perhaps the answers to your questions are in here," he suggested.

Meg, stunned at hearing Gully's voice for the very first time, sat rooted to the spot. Gully smiled. She flicked through the pages briefly; the whole journal was Gully's life story from as far back as he could remember to the present day.

"Thank you, Gully, I think we're done here, for now anyway." Gully nodded.

"It's so nice to hear you speak; it would have made Joby extremely happy."

Gully lowered his eyes at the mention of Joby's name. "I wish he was here," he replied. "Me too," sighed Meg.

Meg took the diary to bed like a new novel she was excited to read. Written by the infantile hand of Gully Cross, devoid of punctuation and with words that were almost indecipherable, Meg was able to glean the early years of Gully and Ayda's existence.

For Gully, time spent with Ayda was, for the most part, happy, apart from the raven incident that was depicted in his diary as a series of disturbing drawings. Ayda, on the other hand, had suffered a deplorable depiction of hatred, cruelty and abuse.

She was a victim of circumstance, a monster created at the hands of her own parents, who, unknowingly, had sealed their own fate and that of many others.

It was late when Meg turned out the bedside lamp. In the darkness, she begged for sleep to find her, but she tossed uneasily, sporadic bursts of slumber interrupted by the harrowing words of Gully Cross replaying in her mind. Daylight was a welcome intrusion.

Ayda sat, as before, relaxed and unemotional. Another night in the cell and the woman still managed to remain attractive, and even the faded grey jogging suit she wore managed to exude a designer presence, fitting her body in a made-to-measure design.

Castleton admired her stoicism. Thackeray plied her with hot strong coffee and the interview resumed.

"Okay, Ayda, we've talked about five victims so far; were there more?" asked Castleton. "Sergeant, darling," mused Ayda, "you know very well there were."

Castleton coughed uneasily. Ayda's presence made him uncomfortable. "How did you pick your victims?"

Ayda leaned back, sipping at her coffee, eyes peering across the table from the sergeant to the constable and back again.

"I didn't pick them, they picked themselves."

"Perhaps you could elaborate on what you mean by that?" Castleton proffered.

"Surely, you have heard of the saying 'an eye for an eye', Sergeant. It's written in the Bible, I believe, not that I've read it myself." Ayda held Castleton's gaze.

"So, what you're saying, and correct me if I'm wrong, is

that you murdered these people because you had a score to settle with them?"

"Of course."

"Turn the other cheek is also in the Bible," added Thackeray, "surely there was an option that didn't involve murder?"

"Oh, Constable, don't be so naive. I wouldn't suit a halo, and I'll never earn my wings; my heart is black and I was raised by the devils." Ayda drained her coffee.

Thackeray took the initiative and disappeared to replenish the mug.

"Let's move on to Sir Henry Attwood. You knew he was your real father?"

"Of course I did. I planned this whole debacle, including my marriage to him," she boasted. "How could you be sure that he would marry you?" Castleton quizzed.

"Look at me, Sergeant; you would marry me if that's what I decided," she scoffed. "I knew Henry couldn't resist the charms of a young, beautiful woman; he was putty in my hands."

"So, you married him and then you killed him?" questioned Thackeray.

"I had to get close to the family, and the best way to do that was to marry Henry. He had no idea who I really was. I certainly looked nothing like the sweet innocent degenerate he had helped to rescue from the asylum. I used him to escape, but I always knew I would be back to settle old debts." Castleton was trawling through the mound of photographs in his file, the gruesome depictions of Ayda's murderous artistry.

He pulled out the photos of Mary Mackie and Inge Stoltz and placed them in Ayda's sight.

She looked from one to the other - "Beauty and the beast," she mocked, "the alcoholic midwife and the bitch who had her eyes on my prize."

"Mary Mackie delivered you?"

"She was there," snapped Ayda, "but as for delivering me, I pretty much did that bit myself!" She began to snigger. "They could have got rid of me then, a pillow over the face would have done the trick, or they could have left me on the steps of the Convent, but no... they didn't have the brains between them to think of that." She was laughing now - "Instead, they kept the baby they loathed intensely and made her life a living hell!"

Ayda's eyes grew wild, the beguiling beauty slipping into maniacal hysteria.

Thackeray and Castleton felt uneasy. They left the room as Ayda's chilling laughter echoed behind them.

Meg, who had witnessed the whole conversation from the safety of the CCTV room, decided to take Thackeray's place. The constable looked visibly disturbed by Ayda's behaviour, and a ghostly white pallor had stripped away his usual olive complexion.

As Meg entered the room, Ayda stopped laughing. She

eyed Meg intensely as she took her seat beside Castleton. Meg's sudden presence made him nervous. He would not have given his blessing to the suggestion, and, knowing that, she didn't give him the chance to object.

"Here comes the cavalry," Ayda joked.

"Not at all, just thought you might prefer a change of scenery," replied Meg. "The scenery was just fine," snarled Ayda.

Meg ignored her and placed the photograph of Teddy Gimp on the desk. "What did this man ever do to you?" she demanded.

Ayda, unperturbed by the female display of authority, took a fleeting glance at the image.

"He was a very good gardener, I believe," she began, grinning at Meg and waiting for a reaction. "He also had a boat, the one Henry chartered to take me across the Channel."

"So, he was helping you?" Meg questioned.

"He knew too much. I couldn't risk him talking. He was a big drinker, and drinkers don't keep secrets. I couldn't afford to leave any loose ends."

Meg sat quietly as Ayda continued, "I did the poor man a favour. It was only a matter of time before he did it to himself. Isobel Attwood broke his heart, so he had nothing to live for."

Meg felt rage simmering inside. "What gives you the right to decide who lives and who dies? What kind of person are you?"

Ayda sat complacent, emotionless, revelling in her ability to ruffle Meg's feathers. Castleton placed a calming hand on her knee. Her anger quelled, and the touch of his warmth against her skin restored her to a tranquil state.

"I know you're taking the credit for Mr Gimp's death," began Castleton, "but I'm finding it difficult to understand though. How could a woman no more than 55 kg have managed to hang a man the size of Teddy Gimp from his bedroom ceiling without help?" he asked.

Ayda remained stoic; "I drugged him and then strangled him." "Yes, but what I'm asking is how did you manage to hang him?"

For a moment, there was a slight hint of hesitation on Ayda's face. She pointed her nose into the air and keeping her gaze fixed on the ceiling she muttered, "I had a little help with that part."

Meg and Castleton looked at each other. "Help... from who?" they stuttered simultaneously.

Ayda checked her coffee mug; it was empty. She held it in Meg's direction, but Meg ignored her and carried on. "Well? Help from who?"

Ayda shifted uncomfortably in her seat, then muttered, "... Gully". The word stuck in her throat as if she were regurgitating a profanity.

Perhaps Ayda wasn't impenetrable after all; Gully was her Achilles heel.

Meg knew to press on while Ayda was at her most vulnerable. She placed an airline ticket on the desk and pushed it towards her, tapping it with her nail to emphasise the date. Ayda glanced down; "My spa holiday," she said grinning.

Meg tapped the ticket harder and growled, "If you were in Austria as the ticket suggests, who killed Inge Stoltz?"

Ayda held her gaze and calmly replied, "I did, of course." She waited for the exchange of questioning glances between the two detectives, "I flew to Austria and hired a car, I drove back to London, killed Inge and drove back to Austria the same day. I was back in time to enjoy a couple of days' relaxation. I then extended my stay and that was the reason why."

If this were true then Gully hadn't been involved in the model's murder. He was already an accessory to one murder, two and he could be looking at a life sentence even with a plea of diminished responsibility.

"Do you have any evidence to prove that what you're saying is true?" Castleton enquired. Ayda paused before answering, "I picked up a car from Hertz in Vienna. It was a black Range Rover sport. I flew in as Lilia Attwood, but I drove away as Bianca Romanoff."

Her analysis sounded convincing, but they would need to verify her story.

Thackeray entered the room with a tray of refreshments, as the interview was now entering its fifth hour. China mugs had replaced disposable containers, a lack of these having forced the change.

Ayda had requested iced water with lemon, but the best Thackeray could do was a jug of tap water. Castleton rearranged his papers and began, "I want to now draw your attention to these." He pulled out crime scene photos of Isobel and Max Keller.

Ayda glanced casually whilst sipping the tepid water.

"Isobel Keller, Sir Henry Attwood's first wife, was butchered in her penthouse at your hands, I presume?"

Ayda grabbed the images and held them close. "Some of my best work, wouldn't you say?" She grinned; "Such a beautiful home."

Meg began to realise the depth of depravity Ayda was capable of, the darkness within her soul and the evil that raged inside her. Ayda would remain a curse on humanity and a danger to society, so she could never be allowed to walk freely again.

Meg withdrew another photo from the stack, depicting a pair of black Christian Dior crocodile-skin shoes. "Recognise these?" she demanded.

"Of course! Beautiful, aren't they? She did have great taste in shoes." Ayda paused for a moment and then, with a hint of amusement in her voice, added, "Oh wait, is this how you found out it was me?"

"Not exactly," replied Castleton, "it was the tattoo on your ankle."

Ayda looked down and laughed. "My raven," she stroked the black ink symbol with a finger, "how remiss of me."

"Why a raven?" Meg enquired.

"It was a raven who saved me, fed me, comforted me, when no one else would. They are beautiful, intelligent birds, and they represent the courage to change.

I nursed the little chick when it accidentally fell into my cupboard. In return, it became my friend. It talked to me, kept me company through the long dark hours of entrapment, and followed me from home to home; we were inseparable."

Meg and Castleton listened as Ayda enlightened them on the powers of the raven. They tried to change the subject, but Ayda was intent on paying homage to the bird that had taken her under its wing, literally.

She paused briefly, but she wasn't finished. "The most intriguing fact about a raven is its song." Ayda's face glowed with admiration. "When the raven sings, it has a beautiful voice, mesmerising and hypnotic. It told me what to do and how to do it." Ayda's face looked serene as she gushed over her favourite bird.

"The raven told you what to do?" quizzed Castleton.

Ayda's dark eyes pierced Castleton as he waited for her answer.

"You wouldn't understand if I told you, Sergeant. The raven and I have a very spiritual connection, something that cannot be explained in words."

And that was all that Ayda would say on the subject no matter how hard Castleton pursued it.

"What about Max Keller then," asked Meg, "why did you kill him?"

"He saw me; gave my description to the police. He could have jeopardised my plans and ruined everything."

"So, you did kill Max?"

"I gave him a merciful end; I watched him slowly drift away upon the waves, calmly and quietly." Ayda took a moment of reflection as if she were suddenly standing beside the sea in Monte Carlo releasing Max Keller's lifeless body to the waves like an angel of mercy.

"How did you kill him?" Castleton continued.

"A lethal dose of sedative. He died almost instantly. As I said before, it was a merciful end." Ayda did not recognise the severity of her addiction - she talked as if her actions towards Max Keller had been committed with the best intention. She portrayed all the traits of a sociopath and psychopath, and adding to that a deeply narcissistic personality, she truly was a dangerous person.

"You feel no remorse for what you have done?" asked Meg.

Ayda held Meg's stare. "Remorse for what? I did that man a favour. He was mourning the death of his wife. He would have ended it all eventually; I just helped him along."

Meg was speechless. She had never dealt with a person whose mentality was as warped as Ayda Attwood's.

Castleton, sensing a disturbing cloud of tension, pushed on with the interview.

Ayda groaned with contempt, saying, "Sergeant, I'm tired, the coffee is like sludge and you can't even provide a decent glass of water. I'm afraid I have nothing further to say until I have been permitted to take a break and offered some decent nourishment."

Castleton broke with protocol and, placing Ayda in handcuffs, marched her upstairs to the communal dining area.

He gave her the pick of the menu. She grimaced at the choice but eventually chose a chicken salad and a slice of lemon cake.

They sat in one corner of the room and ate together. Ayda even received her iced water with a slice of lemon.

"I thought a change of scenery would be good for all of us," Castleton explained. "Perhaps for you, but I feel like a fish in a glass bowl," Ayda protested.

Meg scanned the room. Ayda was the focus of the entire dining area. "You're a celebrity," mused Meg.

"I always have been," snarled Ayda.

When the low-calorie feast was finished and the empty plates had been removed, the dining room was devoid of hungry police personnel, so Castleton continued with the interview.

"Okay, Ayda, you've eaten, you've had your iced water

and slightly better coffee, now it's payback." Ayda didn't comment.

"Let's go back to Isobel Keller. What reason did you have to kill her?" "She helped Henry with my escape," came the simple reply.

Castleton and Meg looked confused.

"Why the puzzled faces?" questioned Ayda, "I've told you before, there could be no loose ends. The more people who knew of my existence, the more fragile my position became, so anyone with the slightest jot of knowledge about me had to be eradicated."

Ayda was escorted to her cell to rest, but it was Meg and Castleton who craved time away from her malevolent aura.

"She really is a despicable human being," stated Meg. "I was actually feeling sympathetic towards her earlier after reading Gully's diary, but to be perfectly honest, I feel we should build a bonfire in the car park and put her on it."

Castleton grinned. "I get it, Meg, but it's not our job to judge. We just need to find out the truth. There's no way on earth Ayda Attwood will see the outside world again because, when she goes to trial, they will lock her up and throw away the key."

"I hope you're right, but that doesn't bring back the lives she took. Bring back the death penalty." Castleton sniggered. "Come on, let's get something a bit stronger and you can tell me all about Gully's diary."

CHAPTER 47

Half an hour later, Meg, Castleton and Thackeray were tucked away in a corner of the Snooty Fox with three rounds of drinks already lined up on the table. A much-needed alcoholic remedy was the only way to deal with the aftermath of Ayda Attwood.

Meg revealed that Gully's diary documented everything from his childhood to the present day. He wrote about hanging Theodore Gimp from his bedroom ceiling, about meeting Ayda in Weaver's Wood on previous occasions, and about her desire to kill a lot of people.

Ayda used Gully for his strength, his shooting skills and to assist her in accomplishing her murderous spree. Gully, a keen hunter, had never missed a shot. It was his bullet that claimed the life of Darrow. "Do you think a jury will go easy on him?" asked Thackeray.

"Absolutely not," stated Castleton.

"At the end of the day," started Meg, "Gully has killed one person and helped with another. He's looking at a life sentence; probably not in an open prison, but maybe somewhere like Broadmoor."

Ayda Attwood had sealed Gully's fate the day she involved him. She had condemned her giant of a brother to live his life as a caged animal. Perhaps subconsciously, Ayda was placing Gully in the same situation she had experienced as a child.

"Perhaps Ayda wanted Gully to know how it feels to be locked away and forgotten; perhaps this is her way of punishing him."

"You have a point, Will, but no jury is going to take that into account. Whatever Gully Cross has done, willingly or otherwise, he is an accessory to murder," added Meg.

Of course, it really wasn't that simple, and the justice system had its flaws.

Ayda Attwood had left a mark on many lives, including her own, Meg had lost her best friend, Abby, and the lives of those who had survived an encounter with Ayda would never be quite the same again.

It was time to leave as a third glass of red wine was turning Meg philosophical. They bade goodnight to Thackeray and headed back to Pebble Cottage where thoughts of Ayda Attwood could be put on hold until morning.

As the sun rose over the village green, Meg and Castleton headed back to the station for what was, hopefully, the last day of interviews with Ayda.

Ayda's last victim, Abby Attwood, was going to be the hardest for Meg to bear. She opted to watch proceedings from the privacy of the CCTV room and Thackeray took her place beside Castleton. Ayda sat, transfixed on her coffee mug, looking slightly more dishevelled than on previous mornings. "Bad night?" Castleton enquired.

Ayda didn't answer; she threw him a sarcastic look.

Castleton removed the bloody picture of Abby Attwood from the file and placed it before her. Ayda glanced at it briefly.

"What do you want me to say? Yes, I killed her," proffered Ayda. "I killed them all and I would have killed Theo, and possibly your detective lover, if she had got in my way."

Castleton closed the folder and tucked it under his arm as he stood to leave the room. "Is that it?" Ayda demanded.

Castleton turned to her, saying, "Unless you have anything else to say, yes, that's it. You're a murderer, you will go to trial and hopefully prison for the rest of your life." He looked back at Thackeray. "You can formally charge her," and with that, he left the room.

Meg was confused. Why had Castleton cut the interview short? But Castleton had done it for her, to save her from reliving the gruesome details of her friend's cold-blooded murder.

He wouldn't allow Ayda to wallow in another death; he was done with her - she was a disease that would never be cured. The sooner she left the station the better.

His thoughts were swiftly interrupted by the shrieking of a distant alarm. Castleton spun on his heels and raced down the hallway, recognising the noise as a panic alarm, an added security measure mounted on the inside of each interview room.

As he approached the only room in use, shouts of despair were echoing towards him and colleagues were gathered around the doorway.

Meg was at his shoulder as he entered the room.

Thackeray was slumped in a chair, limp and lifeless. His eyes fixed, pupils dilated, blood-loss fatal. A deep wound severed his neck. Meg was desperate to revive him, dragging him to the ground, but Castleton's hand squeezing her shoulder gave her the answer she already knew - Thackeray was dead. His carotid had been severed, the culprit, a broken china mug, the handle of which was still held in Ayda Attwood's grasp.

Ayda Attwood had taken her last victim, her final act of malevolence, before thrusting the jagged remains of the teacup into her own neck. She was failing fast, blood encircling her at an alarming rate. A knowing smile crossed her lips as she gasped her final breath.

CHAPTER 48

Six months had passed since Ayda Attwood's suicide and Will Thackeray's murder. After the funerals, Theo returned to Ireland where he intended to remain.

The Manor House stood empty, only the shadows of those who had once frequented its hallways living there now.

Gully had, as Meg suspected, been sent to Broadmoor, a prison for the criminally insane. He was to undergo evaluation, and his trial was pending.

Memories were amongst Meg's most prized possessions now. She had lost valuable, irreplaceable friends and life in Brightmarsh was going to be undeniably different.

Castleton proposed and moved into Pebble Cottage permanently. He continued to police the area requiring Meg's assistance from time to time, but Meg had ended that chapter of her life and was happy to dedicate herself to domestic bliss and the needs of Castleton and Pepper.

On the day that they married, church bells resonated around the little village. Brightmarsh was filled with happy expectations for the new couple.

They posed for photographs, locked in each other's arms, beneath an aged blossom tree. Sitting just above them in the branches of the tree, a lone bird was singing sweetly. Meg gazed upwards to find a raven, black as night, with eyes the colour of rubies, staring down at her.

An icy shiver coasted down her spine and the hairs on the back of her neck stood to attention. For a fleeting moment, Ayda Attwood filled her thoughts, a cold breath caressed her cheek and from beyond the grave, she heard a whisper... "When the raven sings..."

Printed in Great Britain
by Amazon

23202265R00212